Course Correction

2nd Edition
Written by Richard Cutler

Briley & Baxter Publications | Plymouth, Massachusetts

ISBN: 978-1-954819-43-6

Book Design: Stacy Padula
Cover Art: Maddy Moore

A story of families and friends separated by time, circumstances, and distance brought together to try to change a dangerous course of human history.

Contents

Introduction

During the course of human history, individuals and entire cultures have had to make changes in the way they thought and acted in order to prosper or even survive. These corrective actions may have been required as a result of wars, ecological changes, politics, technology, disease, population growth, or limited resources. All of these factors could come into play simultaneously in the not too distant future. If this happened, could mankind adapt to avoid being the next worldwide species extinction?

Assuming mankind did adapt in the past, did mankind possibly adapt with help from outside sources? If so than perhaps not the way history has been recorded. When people encounter something they don't understand they will naturally try to reason through the experience to develop an explanation. If in the distant past, before any thought of aliens from another world might be using incomprehensible technology to float through the air, what might be the explanation for such a vision? It would likely be something different than what the modern, cynical, human might conjure up. We like to think we are enlightened, but are we really? If we are, then why does mankind continue to face so many self-inflicted problems expecting "someone else" to solve the problem?

When I wrote this story originally, it was well before the COVID-19 pandemic. My thinking at the time was that 100 years previously there was the Spanish Flu pandemic that killed fifty million people worldwide. In my mind there seemed to be no reason why something like that couldn't happen again. Unfortunately I was frightfully close to being right. With travel worldwide so much easier now than in 1919, and a little tweaking of COVID, the number of people that have died so far could be a lot different. Let us hope and pray that will not be the case.

Course Correction is a story of hope. It is a story of families and friends separated by time, circumstances, and distance; brought together by strangers to hopefully change a dangerous course of human history. Parts of this story are true, some could be true, some might be true in the future, and some is purely whimsical; or not. The reader is left to decide. In any case, I hope it makes the reader consider possibilities and perhaps cause the reader to make their own course correction.

Disclaimer

I have used names of real places in this story. There was no particular reason for this except to make the reader run to the atlas to see where these places and celestial bodies might be. Any description by the author of these places is pure whimsy.

The people named and described in this story are pure fantasy. Any similarity to any person living, deceased, or yet to be born is purely coincidental. They are just names!

Important Names

Epsilon Eridani (EE): A star 10.5 light years from Earth
Epsilon Eridani b (EE b): The second planet in orbit around EE

Augustine Island: A volcanic Island In Cooks Sound, Alaska

CASO: Chief Academic and Science Officer (one per ship)
VAAS: Vice Admiral of Academics and Science
VAO: Vice Admiral of Operations

The team from Augustine Island:
Gabe-Re-El (Gabe): (Team leader) 7'-2", 300 pounds, blond
Kem-U-El (Kem): 6'-11', 280 pounds, blond
Ere-Mi-El (Ere): 6'-8", 250 pounds, blond
Na-ki-Ir (Naki): 6'-10" 275 pounds, dark complexion, black hair
Ara-Ri-El (Ara): 6'-7", 240 pounds, blond
Schem-Hampha-Rae (Schem): 6'-8" 250 pounds, blond.
(The El's are cousins)

United Nations Stellar Commission (UNSC) space fleet:
Starship British Commonwealth
Starship United States
Starship China
Starship India (Lost in 2075)
Starship Russia
Starship South America

Key UNSC Shipboard personnel:
Admiral Nimitz: First Admiral of the space fleet
Ada (Bickmeier) Sylva, First VAAS; became Admiral in 2075
Richard Sylva: Star Ship United States CASO, Became VAAS in 2075
Dawn (Sylva) Cohen: Star Ship United States Captain, Became VAO in 2075
Jesus Sylva MD: Medical Officer and Ada Sylva's husband

Earth Bound Bickmeiers:
Karl Bickmeier: Family Patriarch

Kim Sue Bickmeier: Karl's wife
Donald Bickmeier: Karl and Kim Sue's son
Maria Bickmeier: Don's wife
Leonard Bickmeier: Donald and Maria's son

Isolated Teckies:
Abel Fisher
Megan Benoit

Other Key Players:
Summer Snow: Earth's Wormhole Gate Keeper
John Carpenter: Houston Control Facilities Manager
Falkner & Roberts: Procurement Sergeants
Colonel Linda Sheffield: Military Governor of Alaska
General Grainger: Military President of the United States
Spoosh: Ambassador for the Second People

Prologue

The marine captain had been in charge of human resources for the United Nations Stellar Commission (UNSC) from the beginning. He had thought his job was done. He was not happy that he now had to find a qualified head bartender only a couple of weeks prior to the interstellar space-fleet launch. For years now, he and his international staff had interviewed and selected the ninety thousand people who would be on board the six ships bound for Epsilon Eridani (EE) 10.5 light-years away. Because the trip was so long and because there was so much that needed to be done at the end of the voyage, many people with a wide range of skills were deemed necessary.

To attract the best people for this mission, it was imperative that as many comforts of home as possible be included for the adventurers. The ships were large, with many amenities designed into the program. This included lounges where people could take a break from the trials and tribulations bound to occur. Lounges meant adult beverages but without an emphasis on truly hard liquors. As fresh beer and wine to last the trip was impossible, bartenders were not only required to serve beer and wine (and occasionally, something stronger), they were also required to brew beer and make a tolerable wine from the crops that would be grown on board the ships. So, while bartenders were not considered to be of the same status as the officers, engineers, and scientists, they were considered critical to overall crew morale. Each ship had one head bartender, and the human-resources officer was suddenly down one.

Finding qualified engineers, scientists, and officers wasn't easy, but the captain believed he had done a good job, even if he'd had to badger a few to get them to sign up. The crews had been set for months and were all on board their ships, familiarizing themselves with their duties. The captain had thought he was done when, for some inexplicable reason, one of the ships' head bartenders was given permission to resign. With all the people on board, finding someone to fill the role within the ranks seemed to be the obvious answer at this late date, but no, he had to find a replacement. *This is ridiculous on so many levels*, he thought. *But orders are orders!*

His staff had been asked to find candidates, so he had expected to see a number of applications, but as he opened his computer, he found only one, making him very cranky. "What? Are you kidding me!" he said to no one in particular. "Well, maybe, just maybe, I'll get lucky."

The captain asked his assistant to find this Sherman Hamer and set up an interview. He was then surprised when his assistant told him that the applicant had been in the waiting room for hours. The captain's assistant added, "This guy told me you'd be looking for him, so he just came in."

Very slowly, the captain looked up and wove his fingers together. After several seconds, he finally managed to draw out, "Oooo-kaaay. Show Mr. Hamer in."

When Mr. Hamer entered the room, the captain looked up and was surprised yet again when a man about six feet eight inches tall and of 250 pounds of muscle entered the room. The man had a pale, flawless, almost-white face that was framed with long, straight, shoulder-length blond hair. His blue eyes were penetrating. He was dressed in a white, baggy, long-sleeved shirt buttoned to the top and khaki slacks cinched with a blue sash. He wore sandals with no socks.

Regaining some lost composure, the captain said, "Mr. Hamer, please sit down." As he did, Sherman Hamer placed a large tote bag on the floor and smiled. At this, the captain's internal annoyances suddenly eased, though he didn't know why. The captain took a few minutes to read Hamer's application and asked, "It says here that you speak fluent Russian. Did you know you would be on the Russian ship if you were accepted?"

Avoiding a direct answer, Hamer said, "I guess that might be helpful."

"Yessss," said the captain. "It certainly would, though everyone in the fleet is expected to be able to speak English. Do you speak other languages?"

"I have had an opportunity to live in a number of places and am able to pick up on languages rather quickly," said Hamer. He actually didn't know how many languages he knew.

"Well, now, Mr. Hamer, excuse me for being a little blunt, but I'm in a bit of a bind trying to fill this one spot on the Starship *Russia*. I'm not even sure why this has become such a big deal, but it is. This is a head bartender position, and that means you are a counselor of sorts looking for telltale signs of people problems. You know, like someone about to go over the edge, for example. Do you have experience with this?"

"Sure," said Hamer. "I know how to read people and have great success in keeping them from boiling over at critical moments." The captain didn't pursue this line of questioning, because somehow, he simply "felt" that this was true, even though he couldn't explain that feeling to himself.

The captain went on, "Unlike earthbound bartenders who simply serve spirits, the fleet bartenders will also have to brew beer for the crew and help with the wine making. Do you know how to make a passable beer?"

In perfectly fluent Russian, Hamer said, "I have a sample here with me." He bent over and opened the tote bag, revealing a reasonably sized cooler. He opened it and removed a large brown bottle from its ice. Hamer continued, "This is one brew I'm rather partial to that was developed by Trappist monks."

While Hamer extolled the finer points of the brew in Russian, he pulled a pint glass from his bag of tricks. Then, not bothering with an opener, he flicked the cap off the bottle with his fingers and then poured the brew down the inside edge of the glass, producing a perfect head. He placed the glass on the captain's desk and sat back.

The captain hadn't expected this, especially since he did not speak Russian and so had no idea what Hamer was saying. He did, however, get the hint and sampled the beer, saying, "You provide one surprise after another. This is great stuff. Do you have any more surprises I should know about?"

Sherman Hamer thought, *You mean, like my name isn't Sherman Hamer? Or that I just woke up a few days ago? Or how about the fact that I'm not sure why I'm here at all, seeking a position that will likely leave me isolated from my own kind?* Instead, Hamer said, "No, I can't think of anything that is pertinent."

Still sampling the brew, the captain asked, "Do you have any family or friends on board any of the ships?"

"No."

"Your application says you're not married. Will you be leaving any other family members behind?"

Truthfully, Hamer said, "Yes, some cousins. But it's not an issue."

"Everyone who has signed on to this mission has had a reason. Some don't like the living conditions they've been forced into. Some want the adventure. Some see this as a huge scientific laboratory for them to play in. What's your reason?" asked the captain.

With an impish smile, Hamer answered truthfully once again when he said, "For as long as I can remember, I have been lured to serve a greater cause. This endeavor offers a challenge that I simply cannot ignore." While this was true, he didn't say that he actually hadn't been given a choice or that it hadn't been made clear to him what the challenge might be. It would take more time than the couple of days he'd been awake to figure that out. He had accepted that it was his turn to be first, and maybe the only one in this case, but the answer would be revealed in due time.

The captain knew he should be asking a lot more questions to get into this guy's head, but he was feeling so comfortable about this Mr. Hamer that he simply confessed, "You happen to be the only applicant, so even if this hadn't been some of the best beer I ever tasted and you didn't have the language skills I was hoping for, I'd probably sign you up anyway. I don't have the time to screw around trying to find someone else. Assuming you pass the physical, welcome aboard. Please don't let me find out later that I made a mistake. Do you have any questions?"

Hamer said, "I assure you, sir, you have nothing to worry about as far as I'm concerned. I do have one question. Will you be part of the mission?"

"No," said the captain quietly. "I was wounded in the last war and have a metal plate in my head. The plate didn't disqualify me, but the resulting occasional debilitating headaches did me in. I can handle this job, but the powers above me think I could be a liability to the mission if I went, so, no, I won't be going. What about you, Mr. Hamer? You certainly look healthy. Does your size run in the family?"

Hamer didn't want to outright lie, but he also couldn't provide complete disclosure. Truthfully, he said, "Yes, everyone in my family is large. I don't really think about it." Still truthful, though not relevant to him exactly, Hamer added, "Hamer is a Finnish name, and many Finns are large people."

The captain thought, *And Finns often have fair skins and blond hair. It all fits.* But, not ignoring Hamer's rather muscular body, the captain noted, "You must work out."

"Maybe," said Hamer with a laugh.

"My assistant will take you downstairs for your physical right now. We need to get you on board as soon as possible. You need to get familiar with the routine before the ships launch." Standing up, both men shook hands. The captain couldn't know it then, but in the months and years to follow, his headaches would never return.

Towering over the captain's assistant, Sherman Hamer was escorted down two floors for his physical. The doctor completed all the forms recording Hamer's perfect health. If the doctor had actually examined him closely, he would have found some anomalies, but nothing to keep him from his mission. But when Hamer entered the exam room and shook the doctor's hand, the doctor uncharacteristically decided that a full exam wasn't really required. Instead, they spent the next hour and half discussing some of the high-ranking people on the mission. Hamer learned a lot.

When Hamer left the exam room, the doctor reviewed his notes but somehow blanked as he tried to remember the exam he hadn't actually performed. He must have done one; his paperwork was in front of him, fully completed. He finally concluded by saying, "This is weird. I really need a vacation!"

The next day, Sherman and his very large duffel bag were shuttled up to the Starship *Russia* along with a large number of cases of adult beverages to be opened on special occasions. On June 29, 2067, at 12:01 a.m., Greenwich Mean Time, the UNSC officially launched the six starships with Sherman Hamer on board, all the time wondering how long it would take before he knew his true mission and if he would ever be with his family and friends again.

Chapter 1

Fog

Today was different. Instead of their almost-daily fishing trip, they were going to explore this mysterious fog that had surrounded one of their favorite fishing spots. It was July 14, 2085, and Don Bickmeier; his son, Leonard; and father, Karl, were in the Cook Inlet off the coast of Homer, Alaska. The sky was clear blue with only a hint of clouds. With a comfortable twelve-knot breeze, there was little stress for the crew or boat. Their boat, an ancient Canadian thirty-six-foot C&C sailboat built in 1976, was perhaps not the best they could have salvaged, but Don liked it. It felt comfortable even when the seas weren't as kind as they were today. He had renamed it *Elusive* to honor the fish he didn't catch, but he carried the optimism of all fishermen when they leave the dock visualizing fish boxes full upon return.

No new boats using fiberglass technology had been built in years—hard to say how many, but probably not in the last decade. With so many boats available to be salvaged, there was no market for new ones. Repairs, when needed, could still be made to the hulls with West System when the epoxy could be found, and it was certainly dear to anyone who had it. There were better designs for fishing, but boats of an earlier time designed for efficient fishing required significant fuel to drag nets and bottom trawls. So, for the most part, fishing had returned to modified techniques used before the advent of diesel fuel. Sometimes, the three men set longlines, and sometimes they fished with rod and reel, especially when they were close to shore.

But on this day, they had decided to circumnavigate Augustine Island to try to get a handle on this fog that had suddenly taken up residence two weeks ago. It was thick as soup and as far as they could tell from Homer, was nearly perfectly dome shaped. Their trip around the island was to see if it extended all the way around. If it didn't, they might be able get in to fish close to shore.

The day started out enjoyable enough. The trio left the dock at about 4:00 a.m., and with a favorable wind, they didn't have much to do except enjoy the cruise. It would be a long day, but with nearly twenty-four hours of daylight this time of year, they didn't need to worry about navigating in the dark. A couple of humpback whales were in the area, and one of them surfaced nearby, blowing out as it did. The fish-scented whale breath was a bit overpowering, but it soon passed. Large sea otters floating on their backs with their young watched the boat go by with little sign of any curiosity. They were mostly interested in the tasty morsels that lurked inside the shellfish they were trying to open. The usual sea birds came by looking for a handout and then left when they didn't get a treat.

Don had inherited much of his looks from his father, Karl, if not his size. Don was a rugged man of five feet eleven inches and 210 pounds of nearly all muscle, sporting shoulder-length brown hair, sparkling brown eyes, and fair skin set off with a mismatched red beard. He was usually in good spirits, with a long fuse that was known to sometimes end with a sudden explosive anger. When the fog had first settled in while the men fished near the island, the fuse burned fast, and he looked like he would blow at any minute, muttering, "Damn it."

Len had been surprised at his dad's use of even a single cuss word, mild as it was, and decided to keep out of Don's way that day. Today was different, as they weren't expecting any more surprises and were only "fact-finding," as his grandfather would say.

Karl had observed the fog with apparent detached interest. He had never seen one appear so suddenly, remain for so long, and stay in one place. His only verbalization about the situation, however, had been "Interesting!"

Just as puzzling as the fog itself was the smoky, acrid feel to it. It wasn't smoke exactly, but it was certainly more than a typical fog. "You don't suppose Augustine is getting ready to erupt, do you?" asked Len. Except for the same soft-spoken voice, it might be hard to see his relationship to his dad. Len was taller at six feet even and wiry at 180 pounds. The height had come from his dad's side of the family. But he had inherited his mother's Hispanic complexion with a hint of the Asian heritage in his dark eyes that his grandmother, Kim Sue, had provided.

Karl Bickmeier just stared at the fog, took in a nose-full of air as if he were sniffing a glass of wine, and then slowly looked around and said, "Interesting. But I don't think so."

The trio liked to fish for striped bass. The fish had been an east coast game fish during the early part of the century, but with climate change, they had migrated farther north every year until they finally found their way up through the Arctic Ocean to Alaska. They thrived on the fast currents the tides created. The stripers didn't seem to compete with halibut or the salmon. Certainly, the few salmon that were left weren't affected. The men liked fishing for the stripers because they could use relatively light fishing gear in shallow waters. It was a lot more enjoyable than deep-sea fishing with gear stout enough to pull up a ship.

Don, speaking to Len with a great deal of annoyance in his voice, said, "I know there are some huge stripers near the island if we could get there, but I don't dare bring the boat in any closer to the rocks, sailing blind. If there is an opening on the back of the island through the fog, we could get in and fish. If the fog comes in while we're there, we can sail away with little danger of grounding. Getting in through any fog, though, is a whole different ball game. Tomorrow, we'll actually have to fish, if not here, then in deep water and see if we can salvage the day with a halibut or two. I don't want to go two days in a row with no fish, leaving you to tell everyone they're going to go vegetarian."

"Me! Why me? You're the captain," said Len.

"Exactly," said Don, now mellowing and smiling broadly. "I'm the captain. So you do the dirty work."

"Oh, goodie. Humiliation followed by lonely veggies," said Len. "But I suppose it could be worse. Fresh veggies aren't all that bad once in a while."

"That is a great attitude, son. Soon, August will be here, turning to winter, and you can savor those nice greenhouse cardboard tomatoes you so enjoy. And if you get tired of those yummy veggies, maybe add a squirrel for protein," chided Don.

"Very funny," mumbled Len. "Do you have any more words of wisdom, or are you going to spare me?"

"What? You don't like my concern for your diet?" chuckled Don as they left that topic and approached the fogbank. "Turn fifteen degrees to starboard, and we'll go counterclockwise around the island."

Len turned the wheel, Don adjusted the sails, and Karl wrote something down in a notebook.

Moving around from the island, the fogbank remained a thick, gray wall on the portside of the boat. As they sailed, Len adjusted the heading a few degrees every fifteen minutes or so. He would tell Karl the new heading, and Karl would make a note. Karl, who had just been taking notes and not saying much, spoke up. "Let's just poke into the fogbank a few yards and head back out."

"Are you kidding? Why?" Don asked, not liking the change in plans.

"No, I'm not kidding. Pretend I'm your father and you want to humor me," said Karl with only a slight smile.

"OK, Dad. Whatever you say. Hard to port," said Don, and *Elusive* entered the fog wall, providing a nearly overwhelming thick acrid air to the boat's cockpit. After a few yards into the fog, Don yelled, "Get us out of here. Come about!"

The air was so thick, Don couldn't see Len only a few feet away from him, but he heard his son yell "Ready!" The boat did a 180-degree turn and emerged into clean air.

"Ah, that was awful," gagged Don.

"Yes, but what is interesting is that we're less than fifty feet away from the fog, and there is no hint of foul air here. Even with this breeze. It's like a wall that doesn't move, yet we can sail in and we can sail out. Interesting!" As he had stated what was now obvious, his son and grandson looked at him, waiting for more. Nothing came except his repeated, "Interesting."

It took *Elusive* about four hours of sailing around the island before they reached their starting point. No openings had been found in the fogbank. Referring to his notes, Karl said, "It looks like the fogbank, or whatever it is, is about four miles in diameter. It seems to be nearly perfectly round, and what we've seen from just about anywhere is that the top is somewhat dome shaped. I have never seen or heard of anything like this before. Even if the volcano was doing this, I can't imagine it would be this perfectly shaped and consistent. I wonder if this is some leftover military thing. It certainly is interesting."

As the boat headed back to Homer, Don took over the helm. They didn't really need a compass heading as the weather was as clear as it could be, but still Don asked for one just in case some other rude fogbank should appear.

Len was always asking questions about things that no one seemed to use anymore, and today was no exception. He wasn't sure why he had waited so long to ask about this one, but he decided today was the day. "Hey, Dad, how come you don't want to use that GPS thing?" using the initials for *global positioning system*.

Don sighed but answered, "The GPS used to be the greatest thing. I'm told when they were first invented, they were for military use only, but they quickly became the thing for every boater to have in order to pinpoint where you were and what was under the boat. They even had versions for road travel. I used to use it a lot in my early years, but it requires multiple satellites to work well, and satellites aren't being replaced as they fail. Just like everything else, I suppose. Anyway, I simply don't trust it anymore. And to make matters worse, they stopped making paper charts in 2014, so that poor excuse for a chart we have down below is the best I could find. We might get lucky someday and find a better one. In the meantime, we have the trusty compass, and as long as we stay in familiar waters, we'll be fine."

As *Elusive* sailed away from the island, Karl continued staring off the stern at the fog and repeated, "Interesting."

Don said to his dad, "Are you happy now? You got to play scientist for a day."

Still staring astern, Karl only said, "Yup."

Karl had been born in 2013, back in Massachusetts. His mother had been a research engineer at Lincoln Labs, a branch of the Massachusetts Institute of Technology. His dad had been a biochemist. They met when both were studying for their master's degrees at the University of Alaska in Fairbanks. Mom stood at five feet one inch and was very much a northern Yankee with an ancestry that dated back to the earliest settlers of New England. Dad was a foot taller than his wife but never tried to use his size to rule the roost. It wouldn't have worked anyway. There was no question of who was in charge, and it wasn't dad.

Karl had an older sister, Ada. With so many schools of higher education in Massachusetts and with everyone they knew having some kind of advanced education; it wasn't surprising that both Karl and Ada had followed along. As a child, Karl had always taken things apart and put them back together. Karl's granddad had been an engineer who used to let Karl drive his 1914 Model T Ford when Karl was a kid, and eventually the car became his. That influence likely moved him into the study of engineering, eventually earning him master-of-science degrees in both mechanical and electrical engineering. Physically, he took after his mother more than his dad. He was five feet nine inches tall and of average build with inquisitive brown eyes and graying brown hair. What he lacked in stature, he more than compensated for with stamina and efficiency in every move he made. He saw everything. Nothing got past him. This was a lesson that his son, Don, unfortunately, had needed to be taught repeatedly while growing up.

Karl, now seventy-two years old, was still sharp of mind, inquisitive, and could more than handle a full day's work. He felt lucky to have lived the life he had, with perhaps one major regret. He had moved his family to Alaska in 2050 for a better quality of life. The congestion and environmental damage from global warming that he had seen around him was more than he could take. So, at the age of thirty-seven, he had moved to start all over. It might have been a midlife crisis that was the real cause, but it didn't matter. He had done it. He'd learned to fish during the summers, and he taught college courses in the off seasons. The big regret was that he had gradually lost regular contact with his big sister. Because of that, he had been shocked to learn that she had been selected to be the vice admiral of academics and science for the Interstellar Space Fleet. Ada and her family were all going to go, and it left Karl with a big hole in his heart.

It wasn't that his sister and family shouldn't go; just the opposite. Ada had a PhD in astrophysics, having pursued what their mother had once wanted. Ada's husband, Jesus Sylva, was a medical doctor, and their twins were both well educated and respected in their fields as well. As a family, they absolutely fit the profile the United Nations Stellar Commission (UNSC) was looking for. Karl thought about them every day and simply missed them. He never spoke of it but hoped that one day, he would see them again.

Don had been thirteen when they'd moved to Alaska. He had gone to school like everyone else his age, but he had never really liked it. He learned by doing, and he did a lot. Young Don was ambitious and worked hard. He took vocational classes throughout high school and learned as much as he could from the many people he worked for. Karl had suggested many times that more schooling might be good for him, but as Don had been happy and seemed to be doing well, the subject was never really pushed.

Len had pretty much been home schooled, though everyone in Homer pitched in with lessons. He had received a high level of technical education from his grandfather and with that, combined with hands-on fabrication of everything they needed, he was extremely capable of building almost anything. However, he fancied himself as a student of history, and the little taste of history he would get from his parents and grandparent had just made him want to know more. There wasn't much recent history recorded so the last fifteen years or so seemed to be a mystery that he needed to solve.

Following the GPS discussion, Karl went below for a little nap, leaving Don and Len alone in the cockpit. This usually meant that Don would be subjected to more questioning, and today would not be an exception. Len got to thinking about what his dad had said about the GPS and said, "It seems to me, no one makes anything anymore. All we do is make do with what we can scavenge, and we never seem to go very far to look for anything either. How come?"

Don considered the best way to answer without getting into too much of the detail as that usually caused him to get overly cynical. He thought for a minute and finally said, "You need to ask your grandmother and grandfather to get a better understanding of how things got this way, but I will tell you that when the family moved here from what was then the lower forty-eight states, it was very fortuitous. We had lived outside of Boston, Massachusetts, and while we seemed to have enough space around us compared to many places, your grandfather thought it was simply too crowded. Your granddad's parents had met when they were in school at the university that had been in Fairbanks and always had a fondness for the state. Your granddad remembered coming up here as a kid to visit his grandparents on his father's side and how few people lived here, probably because the winters were really long and cold. Now, of course, the winters are still long, but not as cold.

"They used to say Alaska had four seasons: fall-winter, winter-winter, spring-winter, and the Fourth of July. I think that might have been an exaggeration because it sure doesn't feel that bad to me, though I must admit, the next-to-zero daylight in the winter is tough. Some smarter than me claim rapid global climate change really mixed things up.

"Anyway, things seemed to be fine for a while after the move. Others moved north, but there was still plenty of elbow room. With a lot of sweat equity, life was pretty good. There were lots of social gatherings, especially during the winter, but too much booze. I guess things weren't that great in the south as the world's population kept getting bigger and bigger, and only a few of the very rich had enough of anything. Something had to give, and it did. That's where you need to grill your grandparents, but be prepared. You're going to have to pry the full story from them, and you'll probably find it disturbing. Oh, and don't do it here on the boat. Bring them a bottle of wine and a couple of glasses to get them to loosen up."

"OK, I get that 'grilling' part, and I will. But why don't we venture very far? And, for that matter, why does no one else in town go very far?" asked Len. Then, slowly raising his voice and getting much more animated than usual, he started spouting. "It's almost as if everyone in town wants to stay hidden. And now that I'm thinking about that, I can't remember the last time anyone from outside our town ever visited. I know we're not alone in the world, so what's the scoop? And don't give me that crap about 'when you get older.' I'm twenty-five, and I really want to know! You guys owe me that. And while I'm on the subject, how come there is no one around younger than me, and no one close to my age?"

"Hey, buckaroo, you need to chill!" sputtered Don.

"I'm sorry," said Len, contritely. "But what's the big secret?"

"It's not really a secret," said Don. "It's just a bit hard. For now, I'll give you the short form. We think the world's population is around eight hundred million people, based on the radio news reports we get. That you knew. So we're not exactly alone. But when you were born, the population was around ten billion, probably more. It might have gone higher, but there simply weren't enough resources to go around, and when a worldwide pandemic hit, over sixty percent of the population died in a year from the sickness. Another thirty percent died from fighting and general starvation as the world's political and technical infrastructure started to fall apart. It was terrible in the most congested locations, but pockets of people, like here in Homer, were isolated from the initial waves of death. When the health authorities told people to stay put and not travel, our town closed its borders. Even today, enough paranoia remains that few ever want to go far and risk bringing something back."

"But Dad," said a somewhat stunned Len, "there can't be any further risk, can there?"

"Maybe not. But why take the chance?" Don answered.

Chapter 2

Homer, Alaska

Not everyone in town knew that *Elusive* was on a mission that had nothing to do with bringing in a fresh catch for the day. Normally, when back on shore, Karl would watch Don and Len hoist their catch onto the dock. The halibut, usually ranging in size from thirty to seventy-five pounds, was welcome in town. Even though the men were used to it, catching these fish was a lot of work. Tides had to be just right to avoid sinkers of three pounds or more in two hundred feet of water. When the anchor was set, the boat seldom was moved until the tide went slack. Many times in the past when winds kicked up and the tide was running, they would put a float on the anchor line and let it loose to be picked up at some later date. Freeing the anchor under those conditions wasn't worth the effort and was simply not safe. They had plenty of anchors and lines they had salvaged from other boats, so that was never an issue.

Today had been another long day. But the few people who ventured down to the dock to meet *Elusive* and bring home some fish soon learned it had not been a fishing day. They just shrugged it off. With the Bickmeiers few things were ever consistent.

Originally, there had been a spit of land that jutted out into the bay, but rising seas and an earthquake had forced the town to retreat up the banks. There was a road from Homer into the interior, but it had degraded to such an extent by 2085, it was rough going, leaving the two hundred or so Homer residents somewhat isolated from the rest of the world. Each family specialized in a trade to support the town, though everyone seemed to be able to do everything. The Bickmeier family specialized in fishing, and when they returned from a successful run, which was on most days six months of the year when the weather let them go out, the townspeople would head over to the dock or the Bickmeier house for their shares. Occasionally, old-fashioned money would exchange hands just to help keep shares straight, but for the most part, it was a communal system where everyone knew they had to pitch in.

While Len tied up the boat, Don's wife, Maria, had come down to the dock to greet them. They had married in 2060 in an old-fashioned ceremony even though most people didn't bother with the formality of marriage anymore. Leonard, their only child, had been born that year. They had never told him that he was an accident but were still very happy when he was born. Since few people wanted to bring any children into the world anymore, Leonard, given an old family name, had essentially been adopted by everyone in Homer. There was no one in town, other than Len, younger than thirty-five years old.

"Hi, hon!" said Maria. "Had a good day?"

Maria was 100 percent Hispanic, with both parents born in Mexico. Her family had been desperate in 2058 when they'd set out with another Mexican family to sail north. They had no particular destination. The plan, if one could call it that, was to sail until they saw forests. Preparing to escape from the parched earth and drug lords who had taken over the country, they had disguised the boat as a derelict. One member of the group was on board at all times with a crossbow to ward off anyone who might become curious. Desperate measures actually resulted in more than one curious person disappearing. The families had saved up food and supplies for nearly a year before setting out. In May, they sailed up along California, Oregon, and Washington, looking for their forest. When they were off the coast of British Columbia, they were hit by a typhoon. Their forty-one-foot sloop with nine people on board was disabled and eventually broke up as it washed onto the rocks of a small island just south of Alaska. The family members were in tough shape and, combined with little understanding of their completely foreign environment, became sick, were attacked by wolves, bears, and what turned out to be even worse: mosquitos. Maria, the lone survivor, had been able to keep a fire going after everyone else had died and were buried. Eventually, a pair of trappers had spotted the fire.

The trappers then brought Maria to the mainland and nursed her back to health. As she started to improve, the attention of the trappers towards her became something more than just health, and conversations between the trappers became more graphic. Maria didn't wait for the "something more" as she had seen what that could mean back in Mexico. She knew English from her bilingual education but didn't let on until one day when the trappers were both gone. Maria wrote a letter in clear English thanking them for their kindness and said, in part, "I will repay you one day for your kindness, but for now, I must continue my journey." She took a compass, a .22-caliber rifle, a box of long-rifle shells, a hunting knife, enough food for a few days, and some warm clothes, much like the furs fashioned by the Athabasca Indians.

In early September, the temperatures had started to fall as Maria headed due north and managed to find her way to a couple of small villages. Especially with the fur clothing, she appeared Athabascan to them, but any utterance of words soon made that thought disappear. She became a curiosity and, as such, was given provisions when she insisted that she must move on. She had no idea of where she would go. She only had a sense that she would know her destination when she got there.

By the middle of October, she had made it to Anchorage. Climate change had kept temperatures tolerable for her trek, but even so, it was exhausting for someone not used to hiking. When she reached Anchorage, she was already a celebrity. Word of this young woman moving north on her own had preceded her. Always wanting to beat out the competition, taverns and bars looked for celebrities to bring in customers. So eventually she found herself with a barmaid gig at the Glacier Brewhouse. While she knew nothing of the business at first, she learned quickly. Her celebrity status along with her radiant beauty increased business substantially.

Anchorage's population in 2058 was just shy of six hundred thousand but was quickly increasing. As the largest city in Alaska, that's where people went when they couldn't find whatever they were looking for somewhere else. So it was in May 2059 that Karl Bickmeier and his son Don, then twenty-two years of age, had traveled the roads from Homer over the Kenai Peninsula into Anchorage. They were after seeds, tools, canned goods, and other supplies that weren't available in Homer. One of their usual stops when in Anchorage was the Glacier Brewhouse. They found a table on a relatively quiet Wednesday afternoon and settled in to enjoy a couple of beers. Don liked girls and had had a few flings, but the thought of tying himself down with one woman had never entered his mind. That was until he saw the barmaid, Maria. *My God, she is beyond beautiful*, he'd thought. She was five feet five inches tall, dark complexioned, with large, nearly black eyes and black hair that flowed gracefully down her back. She had a figure that actually could stop a clock!

When Maria came to take their order, Don stammered as he ordered the beers. "Uh! Hi-eee. Um I…I…we'd like an IPA, and ah…ah…milk st-st-stout."

Maria wondered if this guy was OK but smiled a big, broad smile and asked, "Sixteen or twenty-two ounce?" He was kind of cute after all and close to her age.

"Ah, OK," was all Don could get out. He wasn't hearing a word.

With no hesitation, Maria laughed and brought over twenty-two-ounce glasses of beer saying, "You running a tab?"

"Ah, OK," was again all Don could say.

Karl watched all this as his son picked up his glass, turned, and with his hands shaking, spilled some of the beer. Maria noticed Karl chuckle, and that made her smile both with her mouth and inside her head while wondering to herself, *Why does that goofball make me feel like I've found my final destination?*

Karl said to Don, "You'd better stop staring, or they are going to throw us out. I'm willing to bet you'd like a piece of that pretty barmaid, eh?"

"What?" said Don as he came out of his stupor.

"Nothing," said Karl. "Drink your beer."

And Don did. Then another and still another. And over the next three months, Karl noticed that Don kept finding reasons to head for Anchorage. Then, on February 12, 2060, Lincoln's Birthday, Maria Santos became Don Bickmeier's wife. She moved to Homer with her new husband, and, nine months later, they had a son.

Having a kid hadn't been part of their plan. Most couples elected to avoid bringing children into an overcrowded world that was beyond stressed already. While Don and Maria wondered out loud how she could have gotten pregnant, Karl had asked seemingly innocently, "Gee, do you think it might be something you ate?" Maria, not amused, threw a frying pan at him.

After twenty-five years, Don's heart still skipped a beat when he saw Maria, even after being away for only a day. Today, her hair was in a long ponytail, but almost nothing else about her had changed in all that time. Taking a minute to enjoy the vision, he smiled and said, "It was a great day to be on the water. We did sail around Augustine Island, and the fog is all around it. It is nasty stuff, whatever it is. Beyond that, we certainly don't know any more than we did before. It's kinda scary, like maybe something left over from some military experiment or something. Of course, Dad thinks it's 'interesting.' Oh! Len was asking more questions about the old days while Dad was napping. I probably shouldn't have done it, but I told him to ask my parents about the pandemic, so I guess I better warn my folks that he's going to be bugging them."

Maria frowned. "Probably not your finest moment. That won't be easy for your mother." With the boat secured, they held hands and walked to their home.

The Bickmeier home was home to all the Bickmeiers: Karl, his wife Kim Sue, Don, Maria, and Len. Like most of the homes in Homer, it was a combination of elements that when put together provided an interesting domain. Very cozy, but also very substantial at its core to withstand the drastic weather that climate change had created. Beautiful weather for months at a time, often with no precipitation at all, then interrupted by fierce storms with winds exceeding two hundred miles per hour that might continue for days. When it snowed, as much as a foot an hour could fall. Weather extremes had become the norm.

As a result, the Bickmeier home was a combination aboveground house, belowground house, greenhouse, and yacht. Motor yachts had stopped being used for that purpose when fuel essentially became unavailable for such extravagances. And with the loss of owners because of the pandemic, these floating palaces had simply been abandoned. The family, with many helping hands and horses, had eventually dragged the ninety-eight-foot yacht *Change Order* up the shore and positioned it next to a gravel bank. This became their luxurious summer house. Between the boat and the gravel bank, a seemingly much smaller but more traditional structure was built with a south-facing greenhouse. A hole punched through the boat's hull butting up to the house allowed for easy access. Into the gravel bank the house extended to where the family resided during the worst of the winter months and most severe storms. It was very compressed living quarters, but it was always warm and cozy, no matter the weather out of doors. Connected and partially buried in the hill was a garage and workshop wherein rested Karl's treasured 1914 Model T Ford that his Grandfather Fisher had given him before the move to Alaska.

The family loved the yacht and sometimes fantasized what it would be like on the water, going from port to port. They even left one of the yacht's skiffs hanging from the davits to maintain the fantasy. They smiled when they thought of the original owner's sense of humor, as the skiff was called *Original Contract*.

The bridge of *Change Order* was where Kim Sue spent much of her leisure time these days. At seventy-two, she was still very active but liked to read and meditate. The boat's bridge provided a wonderfully bright but isolated location to fulfill this purpose during the warm-weather months. There were so many books to read! Kim Sue was half Chinese on her mother's side. The other half was never determined, as her mother died in childbirth and her father never came forward. She had met Karl in 2032 as he was finishing his master's degrees in engineering at the Massachusetts Institute of Technology (MIT). Kim Sue had been a meter maid in Boston, and when Karl had caught her giving him a ticket, he begged that she rip it up. She didn't, but she did turn on her best diplomatic charm, essentially telling Karl to go to hell. But she did it in such a way that it made him look forward to the trip, leaving him speechless.

When they'd happened to run into each other at a local watering hole, Karl struck up a conversation, telling Kim Sue how he had admired how she'd conducted herself on the job. She was beautiful, witty, and though not college educated, obviously very bright. He'd made up his mind that Kim Sue would add Bickmeier to her name no matter what. What Karl hadn't known was that Kim Sue was letting Karl pursue her until she finally snared him! Even though only 20 percent of couples were getting married in 2033, Kim Sue wanted a traditional family. They were married in a traditional Congregational Church ceremony followed by a traditional wedding bash and then a honeymoon, on which the couple didn't leave their room for three days.

Presently, Kim Sue's primary job in Homer was as a counselor and occasional religious leader. There was no church in Homer, but there was a meetinghouse where community decisions were made and potluck suppers were held, as well as the occasional dance. The meetinghouse was essentially one large room with big, wood-burning cast-iron stoves at each end. Being near the stoves on a cold winter day or night was to be envied. Those who held any religious beliefs were mostly of one Christian denomination or another, so the meetinghouse was the center for long Christmas and Easter celebrations. Kim Sue presided over these holidays, and if anyone had emotional difficulties, she provided an understanding ear and occasional advice. Most of her advice came from the many books she read, including the Bible. She wasn't sure about this guy Jesus Christ being who he said he was, but his teachings made a lot of sense to her, so she followed the Christian doctrine rigidly, seeing no contradictions in her approach. With her calm demeanor, she was held with a great deal of respect in Homer. When she spoke, people listened.

Homes and shops in Homer were arranged haphazardly. People had set up their domiciles wherever it suited them, always keeping severe weather conditions in mind. Before the town had moved up the slopes surrounding the lower part of Homer, there had been designated streets. But now, with little need for wheeled vehicles, horse drawn or otherwise, streets and roads were now mostly paths that connected doors. The exception was the one miserable road to Anchorage. Almost every home had a south-facing wall, and most of these had something like a greenhouse attached. Residents pursued the usual trades to contribute to the greater community such as plumbing, carpentry, machining, trapping, fishing, sewing and tailoring, and so on. One small group of three was made up of electricians who also maintained the community wind turbine and aging engine-driven generator used when the turbine was down for repairs, which was most of the time. Electric power was used sparingly. On most days, it was turned on from 9:00 a.m. to 6:00 p.m. Power for special occasions had to be planned well in advance, as fuel was an issue.

The engine for the generator that they were using now had originally been fueled with gasoline when it was first built some sixty years earlier. It was now fueled with hydrogen gas that the electricians produced by electrolysis powered by photovoltaic solar arrays: electricity from the solar arrays would break water down to oxygen and hydrogen, and hydrogen was stored until it was needed, mostly during the dark winter months. Making hydrogen is a slow and dangerous process, so only the electricians handled it.

Another limited source of energy used in the community was ethyl alcohol, or ethanol. The brewer in Homer made the beer that everyone liked but also brewed ethanol. A hundred-plus years earlier, it might have been called moonshine, but the alcohol proof of the stuff Homer's brewer made would put moonshiners to shame. No one would drink it, but it made a more-than-adequate fuel for internal-combustion engines. Functioning cars were scarce everywhere in Alaska, but there were a few. These were of very old vintage, from before cars became little more than rolling computers. The relatively crude engines were very forgiving, so fuel sources could be flexible. If it burned, it worked.

Karl had always understood that Henry Ford had first built engines to run on ethanol. Before 1900 a by-product of kerosene production was gasoline. It was considered too volatile for much of anything, except cleaning, so it was routinely dumped into pits and burned to get rid of it. Gasoline turned out to be great source of energy for the "horseless carriages" of his day, so Ford gave up on ethanol. But it wasn't hard for Karl to modify the carburetor of his Model T Ford to run on ethanol, so he did. He also used ethanol as a fuel for the ancient engine that was sometimes used in the family fishing boat, *Elusive*. After all, even in 2085, people needed hobbies!

From a distance, Homer appeared to be a perfect place to live. Everyone worked for the common good. Everyone had enough of what they needed. And if they weren't happy all the time, at least they were satisfied. A closer look over a period of years showed people getting older and eventually dying in the normal order of things. What wasn't the natural order of things was the lack of children. No one had any. No one talked about children. No one seemed to care except Len Bickmeier, but he was now determined to find out why. He had a mission. Talking to his grandparents was next on his list of things to do.

Chapter 3
Death

It took Len more than one attempt to get the Earth's population story from his grandparents. When it was finally told, it was very unsettling. Len had been eleven years old at the time of the pandemic. Being isolated in Homer and no one wanting to talk about what was happening, it meant little to him at the time. It was different now.

Leading up to 2071, it had appeared that mankind had finally come to grips with the issue of the overpopulation of its own species. The successful launch of the interstellar fleet had been a positive sign to most people. Of course, this was more of a political thing than anything: "Show the citizens that we mean business. Keep them hopeful with this mission, and we'll keep our jobs. Let the next guy in charge take the heat." Sure, everyone knew it was not going to be a real solution. It was a short-term solution to political pressure, but not the actual problem. In fact, many directly involved with the program doubted the fleet would even make it to its destination at all. Did it really matter? It was a show of doing something, and if it did succeed, well then, many politicians would be happy to take credit.

More tangible steps were taken, of course. Governments that were more enlightened had put new rules in place for the number of children a family could have. China went back to the one-child rule, and other countries adopted similar ones. In theory one child would be born for every person who passed away. The goal was to reduce the population, but if the population level remained neutral, that was better than nothing at all. Even the Catholic Church relented. The church had always preached that large families were a blessing and that anything but natural contraception through abstinence was wrong. Under Pope Francis III, a new, enlightened church proclaimed, "that while God had commanded 'Go forth and multiply,' he had meant that it should stop when the Earth could no longer support the population. "But," the pope had also said, "God intended his children to continue to 'go forth'—even beyond the bounds of Earth's gravity. And when that is accomplished with the mission of our interstellar fleet, man should once again return to the blessing that is children."

But even with these government initiatives, the church, and others with a voice, the world's population remained too large. Eight billion was the calculated sustainable level before climate change; yet the world's population reached over ten billion. There were too many people, and the quality of life in many parts of the world became intolerable. There simply wasn't enough to go around. Starvation, disease, and fighting for resources became the rule in many places. And then it happened. Mother Nature took charge.

The different religious factions in the Middle East had continued the fighting that had started to escalate around 2020. Every time a new government was established, the opposing factions would start another battle. The fighting was sometimes internal to a specific country or region, but often, it was waged with a neighboring country that considered itself to have been insulted in some way. In some respects, this turned out to be a benefit for Israel, which remained strong militarily. With everyone around it fighting each other, Israel remained reasonably isolated from the violence. But that didn't stop the inevitable.

With governments unstable, people moved constantly. Refugees crossing territorial lines back and forth just to stay alive meant health care became nearly absent. This was particularly true regarding disease. In late 2070, a particularly deadly flu strain spread like wildfire among the millions who continued to go back and forth across Middle Eastern national borders. From there it traveled around the world by unsuspecting international travelers. It was a particularly menacing bird flu that continually mutated with each person it infected. Nearly everyone who caught this virus, dubbed the "death flu," died within a couple of days. It was a horrible time. By the middle of 2071, two-thirds of the world population was gone. The world's infrastructure was so disrupted, even more people died. It took some time until those remaining could adjust. Many African nations all but disappeared, leaving survivors to form village governments reminiscent of those from centuries earlier. The jungle started to grow back, and wildlife that had been protected in parks started to repopulate the land.

Fanatical groups had added to the death toll. Governments at nearly every level could not be sustained. Political leaders and bureaucrats fell to the death flu. Police and other public-safety personnel succumbed. The public-safety forces that were left drifted to other occupations, trying to make a living, as no taxes were being collected to pay public employees. Military units that were able to stay isolated long enough to weather the storm became extremely powerful. Some remained as peacekeepers, but many in less disciplined nations went rogue, adding to the death totals.

Mass graves with sometimes only a single marker were created. Where whole communities had died, the areas were completely burned by the military to keep any animals from potentially picking up the disease and carrying it to other communities.

The United States and Canada fared better than some areas because of measures put in place as soon as the worst fears about the epidemic were realized. Having a little more time than those close to the epicenter, travel was severely restricted, and people were advised not to go out into public areas. Still, the cities were hit hard because of population density.

Some regions of the world were less affected directly than others by the death flu. Africa and the Middle East had a disproportionate percentage of their population die off. This was primarily because their governments weren't that effective in dealing with the flu in the first place. China and India were also disproportionally affected, but in their cases, it was because the population was so densely packed that it was difficult to avoid any area where someone had become sick.

Island nations like New Zealand, Australia, and Japan lost, on average, 30 percent of their respective populations. Interestingly, North Korea had the fewest number of cases because, in spite of the many decades of gradually opening its borders, it was still quite isolated, thus heavily limiting exposure. In addition, anyone even suspected of being sick was carted off to death-flu camps. Even starvation in North Korea was less of an issue than elsewhere. The country had been without resources for so long, the population hardly noticed anything was different.

Government in general began to change as well. Or, more correctly, reform. Big government was no longer so big. It decreased in the same proportion as the general population. But it changed in other ways as well. In the United States, the federal government shifted toward more of a military state. This was primarily a defensive measure against forces both within and external. The military was nowhere near the size it had once been, but it was very strong, and it controlled whatever resources it needed to stay that way. State governments became minor players in governing their populations, while governors took on the roles historically filled by congressmen and senators that the states had previously sent to Washington. In some cases, new states merged. All of the New England states and upstate New York, for example, merged to become the state of New England. The rest of New York merged with New Jersey, Delaware, and Pennsylvania to become New Pennsylvania. With the great powerhouse of New York City essentially wiped out with climate changes and death, the name *New York* nearly took on the aura of the fabled city of Atlantis. The Canadian coastal provinces became the Maritime Provinces and eventually merged with New England to become the new Maritime State of the United States.

As the states became less influential, county governments took on a new leadership role. Cities and towns elected delegates to county governments instead of electing local people for local issues.

The death flu naturally affected concentrated groups more than people who were living in reasonable isolation. And since very few actually survived the death flu once they caught it, it had some devastating effects. The flu made it into the Centers for Disease Control (CDC) in Atlanta, Georgia, and wiped them out. Many other concentrations of scientists and engineers, such as in the United Nations Stellar Commission, were also wiped out. A few scientists isolated in places like the Kitt Peak Observatory in Arizona did survive.

Colleges and universities were also hit hard. Students and staff died at a disproportional rate, leaving an average of 5 percent of the former academic populations. The knowledge base left behind was primarily in recorded form, creating a generational knowledge vacuum.

Industry beyond only the smallest scale ended. Power stations that had been so critical to the world's economies were no longer needed and became a new threat. Fortunately, in the case of nuclear power, operating-staff members were able to provide controlled shutdowns. In some cases, the operators did this work while they themselves were dying. Anyone in the general population who might have survived the death flu would have considered these operators heroes if they ever thought about it.

The death flu also affected colonies within Earth's own solar system. As these were primarily mining colonies with limited ability to raise their own food, they had depended heavily on deliveries. The colony on Earth's moon died out from starvation within a year of the flu taking hold. The colony on Mars fared better, as it had found water deep underground that had allowed some terraforming for crop production. By choice, the Mars colony had isolated itself, preferring to take its own chances. While most of its members died off, a small group of twenty-four was able to manage with the resources left to them as they developed their own survival techniques.

The colony on Jupiter's moon Titan also did not escape. While the Gate on Titan was under repair, a supply ship with a crew on board landed by autopilot. The crew had hoped to avoid the death flu by fleeing to the colony, but one member brought the disease on board, and all died on the way. Colonists only learned of the situation when the hatch was opened. Only thirty-six people out of a population of nearly fifty thousand survived—by locking themselves into isolation pods for over forty-five days. After that, they felt the death flu had run its course and they were safe to come out. But the fear of contracting the disease from those who had died and the need to dispose of the bodies forced the survivors to burn the central colony facility. They hoped that eventually they would be rescued, but in the meantime, the now-reduced population had ample food resources available if they put in the farming effort. They had no other choice. The Gate, still not repaired, became useless, and the colonists were isolated.

Back on Earth, another health issue that had previously been brought under some control raised its ugly head once again. The Zika virus spread by mosquitoes was infecting more and more pregnant women, resulting in a significant number of children born with physical and mental deformities. Added to the death flu pandemic, this provided an overwhelming general feeling of despair. It varied from location to location and from ethnic group to ethnic group, but its net result was that fewer people wanted to bring any children into the world. There were some births, of course, but the birth rate didn't come close to matching the death rate, and the Earth's population grew older. The population trend was definitely toward further reduction with no end in sight, and few seemed to care.

The death flu's course ran from the first person taking ill in Syria to the last person dying from the disease in Brazil over a period of nineteen months. Fear was so common among the survivors that few wanted to go back to the days of travel and intercommunity interaction.

Now in 2085, the world's population had finally started to adjust and was at about eight hundred million, less than 10 percent of the population before 2071. Travel was all but eliminated. Air travel was limited to military police action and rare diplomatic visits. Even then, quarantine was required to be certain something wasn't being imported. Even travel between neighboring towns was regarded as a bad idea. And, as a result of that mind-set, communities began to develop very differently from each other.

When the history lesson was over, Karl and Kim Sue actually seemed relieved. Len on the other hand now felt some inexplicable weight being added to his shoulders. With time to reflect, he felt he needed to do something, but what? He was nobody special.

Chapter 4
FarmVille

Around the turn of the century, a computer game called FarmVille had been popular. The concept was to build and expand a virtual farm by buying and selling virtual products with other players. It's not clear if there were ever declared winners of the game, but it was implied that if you had more than other players, you were at least ahead.

In 2037, Abel Fisher was born to Logan and Susan Fisher. He started off just curious, like most kids of the day, but as he got into his teens, he spent every spare minute playing computer games. In spite of that, his grades were always very good, and he outscored everyone on tests. Many considered him a genius, though his IQ was never measured.

His mother had died in childbirth, so his single parent, Logan, tried to get Abel out of his total fascination with computer games. Logan had also been a curious young man in his youth and truly enjoyed his time with his grandparents and their collection of historic automobiles, especially the 1914 Ford Model T. But that sort of thing wasn't high-tech enough for Abel, and he got bored easily. The day of reckoning came when Abel was a senior in high school. "Abel," said Logan, "you have to figure out what you're going to do to make a living. Playing computer games won't cut it, but maybe you should learn how these things work. If you are so hung up on being the best, learning how to reprogram and build these machines would give you a huge advantage."

Abel took the bait. "Why not!" he agreed, and he applied to one school: the Massachusetts Institute of Technology. His two older cousins, Ada and Karl, had both gone there, and they seemed to be doing well, so he gave it a shot. Much to Logan's delight, Abel received nearly a free ride, and he did as well at MIT as he had in high school.

When he graduated, he went to work for a start-up high-technology company that was getting into areas that some thought were scary but that Abel found fascinating. Abel couldn't get enough of this technology, but at the same time, he became more of a loner. He purchased property outside the city of Worcester, Massachusetts, and had a home built to withstand the increasingly bad weather caused by climate change. He loved his dad and spent time with him and talked with him daily, but he worked more often from home, limiting his interaction with others.

He startled his dad one day when he announced that he now had a neural implant that allowed him to operate his ever-growing collection of robots and drones without ever lifting a finger. It was then that Abel went back to an old love, the computer game FarmVille. Except this time, he did it for real—buying property, livestock, and planting crops. Of course, he never lifted a physical finger except to make occasional repairs to his robots and drones when they couldn't do it themselves.

Other events further reinforced Abel's isolation mentality. By 2050, climate change had progressed to the point where enough glacial ice had melted to significantly affect shorelines. In addition, the changing salinity of the oceans confirmed what ecologists had predicted for the past fifty years, and the Gulf Stream shut down. The freshwater intrusion was enough to disrupt the balance of flows within the Atlantic. For the northeast corner of continental North America and also Western Europe, the loss of the warm Gulf Stream waters resulted in harsher winters in the north. This was most notable from New Jersey up into the Maritime Provinces of Canada and across the ocean to Great Britain.

For decades, the city of Boston, Massachusetts, where much had been originally built on fill, tried to adapt. The Boston Society of Civil Engineers had first designed seawalls along a modified waterfront. As waters continued to rise, a different approach was implemented. First and second, floors of all buildings left standing were modified to exist belowground or underwater. Some of these buildings were encased in concrete at the lower levels. Fill was brought in, and the roadways and open areas were raised unto the fill. In other cases, the existing roads and parks were covered and became new tunnels. Many old tunnels had to be abandoned due to increased hydraulic pressures imploding the walls. In other cases, the ocean waters were allowed to take over, and a canal system reminiscent of Venice was established. This practice was followed in other cities that weren't abandoned completely. New Orleans, for example, ceased to exist after one particularly nasty hurricane overwhelmed the entire infrastructure.

These varied approaches seemed to have merit until the death flu of 2071 impacted the world's population. Boston, just like nearly every place on Earth, had a population that became too small to sustain the efforts, and eventually the capital of Massachusetts moved inland to Worcester. A few high spots in and around Boston became sparsely inhabited islands, along with some of the decaying hulks of the city's once-proud architecture. For a time, Worcester remained the capital even when all the New England states became the new state of New England. Later, when some of the easternmost part of Canada joined the United States, the capital of the even larger state of New Maritime was established in Albany, New York.

Abel, of course knew all of this was happening, but his interest was passive and rather detached, as it didn't affect him directly. The impact of the death flu only hit home when it took Logan, Abel's last living contact with a world outside of cyberspace. Soon after, his company disappeared as everyone who worked in the office succumbed to the pandemic. Abel had escaped the disease but was now more isolated than ever. Abel became a true recluse

Those whom he had known years ago had moved off, and there was no contact. His older cousin Karl Bickmeier had moved his family to Alaska, and Karl's sister, Ada, had signed onto the interstellar space fleet. Abel wasn't sure if any of them were alive.

He remained somewhat aware of what was happening in the world to some degree, but he never focused on it. His focus was on the technology that had been developed before the death flu. The technology innovators were gone, but they had left behind a technological legacy.

Just like Abel, the few people he did know through social media never went anywhere. As for Abel, he never physically ventured outside. Why should he? Everything he needed was a data thought away except on those very rare occasions when he felt a need for physical involvement. That's when he used the keyboard and mouse on his computer. It usually didn't last long. Pressing keys and moving a mouse was an unnecessary effort!

Abel felt comfortable meeting people online and staying connected with social media. People of the screen weren't really real to him and since he would likely never have to physically meet them, he was content. When the death flu hit and people were encouraged—actually, ordered—to avoid contact, Abel was almost euphoric as he barricaded himself in his cottage. Not surprisingly, he remained unmarried and untied to anyone in a physical way.

He still maintained some contacts with others that had survived, even those not considered traditional ones. Abel, in his own way, considered cyber contacts to be friends and thought maybe he was in love with Megan. She probably had a last name, but he never asked, and she never volunteered. He had no idea where she lived. He thought she might be a real person and not a computer-generated vision that had escaped from a game, but it didn't really matter much. It wasn't as if they would ever meet in person.

At least twice a week or when one of them was feeling especially erotic, they would have their media date. They would chat, have some kind of alcohol or drugs, and eventually take off any clothes if they happened to have any on, which was seldom, and entertain each other with increasingly erotic sexual maneuvers until satisfied. Always electronically connected, but in their own, individual homes. *One of these days*, Abel thought, *that physical effort is gonna kill one or both of us.*

"Megan," panted Abel after one extremely hot episode, "where did you ever learn to move like that?"

"Oh," she said, not embarrassed in the least, "I watched some old exotic-dancer clips from around the turn of the century. Did you know that women used to do this right in front of men in real life? I can't imagine what it was like in those rooms with all those people. How could anyone satisfy themselves with people around? Disgusting!"

Even without the sex acts, Megan was hot in Abel's eyes. Abel figured she might be twenty years old now, about six years old when the death flu hit. He guessed she was a little more than five feet tall and less than a hundred pounds. Her nice, straight lines with bumps for breasts were about as sexy as a woman could get, he figured. He didn't understand the fascination some had with shapely women. Almost milk-white skin typical of someone who seldom, if ever, went out of doors was set off nicely with short, flaming-red hair and bright blue eyes.

Abel had a slight built-in tan, probably from the leftover Portuguese genes he carried. Just turning on a light seemed to provide enough light for him to tan. Beyond that, he had similar traits shared with Megan and by most of his "friends." He was five feet eight inches tall and rail thin, with black hair and beard and dark brown, almost black eyes. He had no muscle tone; typical of someone who thought that eating and using the toilet were inconveniences. He would shower a couple of times a week, as it did feel good, but shaving almost never occurred. Occasionally, he would cut off a few inches of his beard. Oh, he remembered what it had been like to take care of himself. What a waste of time. Staying connected and building FarmVille was what it was about. This was living!

It wasn't that he was lazy. He just had a different idea of getting things done. His mind was in constant motion. By contrast, his body experienced minimal motion. Often, he wouldn't get out of bed. His handheld device and neural connections allowed him to control the robotic machines that tended to his wants and needs. He had his domestic machines that prepared his meals and took care of the cottage in general. So, while he was unkempt, his home was spotless. His shop was another story, however. It was where only broken technology went to be repaired. Occasionally, he would have to do the actual repairs with his own hands, but usually, they were carried out by a robot or nanobot that he controlled. Parts and unfinished projects were everywhere, in complete contrast to the living quarters. *What a great life*, he thought. And he sincerely believed it.

There were, of course, downsides to his existence. No one actually made intricate circuit boards anymore. Even a hundred years earlier, there had been only a handful of engineers capable of designing new circuits that went into microprocessors. Computers had taken over the design process. After 2071, the close proximity of people in production meant that the death flu left few in the workforce. The remaining population didn't provide enough of a critical mass to justify continued production, and all too quickly, companies simply disappeared.

Some people, referred to as geeks and nerds way back when, started to collect outdated computers and data processors to harvest useable parts from them. So, while there was little in the way of innovation, old units could be kept going. Even the military had been reduced to scavenging for scarce parts.

Another drawback was a lack of reliable power. Around the turn of the century and into the early 2030s, there had been a huge push for photovoltaic (PV) panels and wind turbines in an effort to reduce the dependence on gas, oil, coal, and nuclear power. At the same time, many hydroelectric dams were removed to open up rivers. The program was successful, and many large fossil-fuel installations were shut down. Then, by the end of 2071, it became nearly impossible to maintain any large installation because of the lack of trained labor, but there was also less reason, with the drastically reduced population. So the big power stations were nearly all abandoned in favor of the smaller PV farms and wind turbines. Nuclear installations were shut down and abandoned in place. Fenced perimeters around the power stations were the only safeguards. Decontamination and removal of hazardous materials was deemed impossible, so the problem was ignored.

When PV panels started losing efficiency about twenty years after installation, the availability of electric energy started to decrease. Wind turbines simply wore out, and there were few engineers or technicians left to keep them going. The net result by 2085 was a limitation of electric energy for powering computers and the many related devices in use. Hydropower was limited to hospitals and emergency services, as it was available nearly 24-7. Increasingly, people like Abel were limited to working during daylight hours and when the wind blew. If power was needed beyond that, it had to be stored in some form. It was inconvenient, but he made it work.

Because of his success with his real FarmVille, he was probably wealthy, but that wasn't important. The game was what was important. Playing the game, Abel made a living the same way as most people did—by providing what others needed. He was good at it even if he knew nearly nothing about the land or what was on it.

When New England and the Canadian Maritime Provinces had first been settled, fishing and farming were what most families did, but farmers found conditions somewhat difficult. The soil wasn't great, and the land was covered with what was really a rain forest, meaning generally poor soil. Trees were harvested, and the rocky soils seemed to produce more stones for stone fences and walls than they did crops. Within a hundred years, all the forests had been stripped, and the land was dotted with small family farms. When the Industrial Age had started and much better farmlands with more favorable climates were found farther west, northeast farms were abandoned one by one, and the forests once again took over in many areas, but this time with the old stone walls mixed in. Western farms had eventually become large commercial operations, and the concept of a family farm became an oddity.

As energy costs continued to rise exponentially into the middle of the century, it became more feasible for small farmers to again make a living on reestablished farms in the northeast, though crops had to be more in line with the cooler weather brought on by the Gulf Stream shutdown. That didn't stop Abel as he added to his portfolio. He now had three properties and was considering another. It was all part of the game. One was in the former state of Vermont; there was a small one near his home in Barre, Massachusetts, and nearly a thousand acres in South Dakota. With these three properties, he had enough crop diversity to satisfy most appetites and to produce a modest amount of alcohol for energy production and his own personal consumption.

In Vermont, he had a small herd of sheep—or maybe they were goats, or whatever. He couldn't remember. He also had a few dairy cows. The farm near his home had had peach, pear, and apple trees, and a number of acres for vegetable crops for his personal needs and local barter and sales. In what used to be South Dakota, he produced corn, oats, barley, wheat, hops, and grapes. Much of the corn was made into fuel for some old Honda generators he used to supplement the unreliable wind power. Farm products were used to produce beer and wine on a large enough scale and of good enough quality that it was in high demand. He was particularly pleased with his merlot. *Today*, Abel thought, *I better see how the wine is doing. The 2083 vintage should be good.* It took a few seconds, but finally, Abel was connected with Droid 1, his highest-level unit in the area.

Normally, the droid was self-directed, but with Abel's override, he directed it down a set of stairs carved into a cave directly accessed from within one of Abel's warehouses outside Sioux Falls. Abel thought, *Unlock the door*, and the door unlocked. It swung open, and Abel, through the droid, moved on past hundreds of barrels. Finally, in front of a barrel location labeled "Merlot, 2083," Abel had the droid stop. Abel had intended to tap the barrel, bottle up a good quantity of wine, and have it delivered to his home. But there was no wine. In fact, there was no barrel.

"What the—!" said Abel out loud. "How can a barrel of wine just disappear from a secure and a nearly secret storage location?" Through the droid, Abel scanned the storage area. Nothing else was out of place. Going back to the empty spot, he realized that he had overlooked what appeared to be gold coins in the spot where the wine barrel had been. *This is bizarre*, he thought. *Some gamesman is playing with me.*

Perplexed, Abel had the droid fill a case with bottles of this 2083 Merlot from another barrel and had it brought up out of the storage cellar, along with the gold coins. A drone was selected from a charging station, and the wine bottles and coins were handed off for the trip from ex-South Dakota to Abel's home.

In 2014, it had seemed that drones were about to be used for everything. Military and surveillance use was in the news the most. The machines ranged from very small to the size of a manned aircraft. A company called Amazon had experimented with the concept of drones delivering packages from their warehouses to the door of the customer. From a technical standpoint, it worked, but overcoming the regulatory issues and logistics of so many units buzzing around meant the plan wouldn't "fly."

But from Abel's perspective, the concept was perfect, and he embraced it. Abel was a big fan. He had his 2083 vintage merlot brought to Drone #4 along with a case of 2082 Merlot that had already hit the market. Activated, the drone took off toward his home. Its battery charge wouldn't last the fifteen-hundred-mile trip, but Abel was connected with other gamers who controlled recharging stations. He'd done deliveries many times before, so this was nothing new, and he could just about set his watch, if he had one, to the delivery time of twenty-six hours, plus or minus an hour or so based on wind conditions. That was fine. What wasn't fine was the mysterious transformation of wine into coins. Abel was pissed.

The next day, one of Abel's computers announced the arrival of Drone #4. The garage roof opened, and the drone settled in for a landing. House bot SAM collected the delivery and brought it to the kitchen, where a bottle was opened and the vintage 2083 wine was poured into a red-wine glass. SAM then brought the glass, along with the coins, to Abel, who was still lying in bed.

Abel examined the wine, swished it around to observe its legs, inhaled the vapor, sampled, and pronounced, "My God, this is good. This is probably the best we ever produced." SAM, of course, said nothing in return.

Abel looked at the coins, noting they had strange markings on them but that they did appear to be pure-gold coins. "So," he thought out loud, "someone took one of my barrels and paid in gold. Whoever did this must have really wanted the wine. They could have bought it at the market for a lot less than what these coins are probably worth. It would have been a lot less hassle, too. That barrel was heavy."

A few more sips followed by a drained glass put Abel in a party mood. "Hmm, I think I'll get hold of Megan."

Chapter 5
The Ships

By 2052, Earth's human population had exceeded ten billion even with regional conflicts, starvation, and disease killing people off. Planet Earth was suffering in virtually every context from this overpopulation. Realizing that Mother Nature might jump in and do something to "fix" the problem, world leaders decided that maybe they could be preemptive. They didn't really have a foolproof plan, but that has never stopped politicians. If nothing else, one does have to give them credit for being creative. Amazingly, they actually came to an agreement on action at a technological grand scale not seen since World War II.

World leaders, through the United Nations, took the initiative of bringing all the various government-sponsored and private space programs around the planet to accelerate the colonization of the moon, Mars, and the moon Titan circling Saturn. It looked good, but it was quickly realized that it wouldn't be even close to solving the population problem. The environmental conditions that these three colonies would face were too problematic for anything on a large scale. To have a great enough impact, a new initiative for the long term had to be devised—something grand and spectacular to match the size of the crisis. The fact that the world leaders were crossing the boundary into desperation was not relevant. They could position themselves as demonstrating bold leadership to the citizens of Earth in the face of a major crisis. Doing something, even if it proved wrong, was not an issue. Not for them, anyway. The program was going to be so bold and with the end result so far in the future that these leaders would be off the hook for decades.

The concept was simple enough, but naturally they left the details of actually pulling it off to scientists and engineers. The plan included an unrealistic schedule to build and send massive spaceships—really moving colonies—off to another solar system and to establish a foothold for the expansion of humanity. While the ships would hold a large number of people, the crews were only the means to an end, not the ultimate solution. Far more people would have to be transported off Earth to another planet to make this work, and that would be the second phase of the plan.

By 2052, technology had advanced to the point that a kind of wormhole could be used to transport people almost instantaneously between planets, but only if transmitters and receivers were at both ends of the wormhole. This had been the theme of the old *Stargate* movie and television series, except that in *Stargate*, the technology was credited to an ancient people so that no one had to build any gates. They were just there, waiting to be used.

In earlier times, no one would have believed that transportation through wormholes was possible, much the same way that it was once thought that Jules Verne's nuclear submarine, *Nautilus*, and flying machines were not possible. But as has been said many times, "If you can think of it, it can be built." So Gates were built on Earth and on each of the three colonies. They worked, but of course, they had never been tested between solar systems. They could only be tested and then used within Earth's solar system.

It was first thought that a Gate could be set up on a spaceship and tested as the ship moved away from Earth. Unlike in *Stargate*, however, these Gates required miles of power webs on and below the surface of a planet or moon. There had to be adequate gravity, and the grid had to be aligned with north and south poles. It had to be grounded, literally. So, in order for the plan to work, the ships would have to go to another solar system and build a Gate there. Then transport between Earth and the new colony would be nearly instantaneous. This was phase two of the plan and obviously would be for the long term.

In phase one, a fleet of interstellar ships would be built capable of reaching three-quarters light speed. They would be sent off toward Epsilon Eridani (EE), 10.5 light-years away. Three planets were in the habitable zone of this star, and it was believed that at least one planet, Epsilon Eridani b, was suitable for the endeavor. No one knew for certain if it was habitable, and if so, whether it already had life there. But having three planets in the solar system as options made the project seem like a reasonable gamble.

Of course, the gamble would be for the people on the ships, not the world leaders who had sanctioned the idea. Those politicians only had to show their bold leadership, leaving "the details" to others. Recruiting for phase one proved to be relatively easy. Many who signed up rationalized that life on the ships would be better than the fate faced by those left behind, so why not? Besides, it would be quite the adventure.

When scientists see something unexpected happen, they might exclaim, "Wow! Isn't that interesting?" When engineers experience something unexpected, they say, "Oh no! What went wrong?" Ignorant of those dynamics, the politicians recruited the best scientists and engineers to develop the program. The scientists were excited to have unlimited funds to play with, and the engineers were in a constant state of angst, trying to design components to minimize surprises.

Except for the size of the endeavor, some compared the program to what Christopher Columbus and other early explorers might have considered before sailing from Europe. "Follow me, men. What could go wrong (provided we don't fall off the edge of the earth, of course)?" What cynic could possibly think anything could go wrong with this new program?

As any good politicians would need to do, the world leaders established a bureaucratic committee to stand between them and anything that might go awry. The United Nations Stellar Commission or UNSC was given the ultimate responsibility for the program and most of the authority necessary for success. The ultimate authority came from the countries that actually funded their shares of the project. As a result, the UNSC spent a good portion of its time soliciting funding.

Even so, ship construction started in 2057. The ships were built simultaneously in orbit around Earth with materials transported to the assembly sites from Earth and moon-based facilities. It took ten years to complete the six ships. Each was sized to accommodate eighteen thousand men, women, and children. The initial crews, however, were fifteen thousand, with each ship providing flexibility for population changes. The ships each represented major powers and population centers that were respectively responsible for the cost of the construction of their ships, with the UNSC responsible for the designs and quality control. The leading regions for the ships were the British Commonwealth, Russia, the United States, China, India, and South America. The ships were called by these names with the prefix "Starship." Countries that didn't fit into the general categories were partnered with the leading regions. Japan and Israel, for example, were part of the United States program.

Not all countries participated. Originally, there were to be seven ships, with the last to be funded by the Middle Eastern countries and much of Africa. While none of these regions had technology to contribute, they had a large suffering population, and it was generally believed that participation in the program would at least improve morale. However, the factions of the Muslim world never stopped fighting among themselves long enough to agree on anything. And in Africa, constant war among tribal leaders over diminishing resources didn't permit many governments to stay in power long enough to consider anything that wasn't politically expedient or self-serving.

The ships themselves were huge, measuring over three thousand feet in length. They weren't exactly sexy-looking like those seen in old science-fiction franchises such as *Star Trek* or *Star Wars*, but they had an efficient design from assembly and operational standpoints. The main part of each ship was a cylinder four hundred feet in diameter; the middle three decks of the cylinder were expanded to a belt of five hundred feet. One of the expanded decks was the bridge and officers' quarters, and the other two decks were engineering. From these decks, connecting tubes were attached to the engine room pods that were another five hundred feet out from the main hull.

The base material for the ships was a new type of carbon fiber. Intensive research had found that carbon could be mined from ocean water to make this material. It was light in weight, both strong and tough, and, as an added bonus for the politicians, its use helped improve the ocean ecology. Not enough to make much of a difference, but scientific fact had little to do with the "significant" benefit touted by the politicians.

The ships had 150 decks with 120 living spaces each located around the outside diameter of most decks, providing approximately 150 square feet for every person on board. Each person was assigned one space. Couples and families had passageways between their accommodations, so a family of three, for example, had 450 square feet. The rooms were mostly for sleeping and downtime away from everyone else. One could make a very light meal there, but the main kitchens and dining areas were communal. The food service prepared the meals, and everyone was assigned times to eat. There were four meals a day: one meal every six hours to accommodate all shifts. There were day-and-night cycles built into the ships for convenience, but operations by necessity were 24-7. Shifts were different for the various disciplines, with a standard schedule of four hours on and four hours off, with every fourth day off.

At the top and bottom of the ships' hull core or central cylinder were armored cones that extended outward the width of the bridge and engineering decks. It was hoped that these cones might provide some level of protection by deflecting space debris that might be encountered. Because the ships would be turned around and going backward during a good portion of the journey, the back ends of the ships looked the same as the fronts. The cone areas provided the hangar decks for the shuttlecraft that moved between the ships and eventually to the surface of the planet or moon that would host the Gate.

The two reuse decks transformed everything used on the ships into something that could be used again. Wastewater was not considered "waste" but "used" water to be reused. The used water flowed to the reuse decks where reverse-electrodialysis stacks between chambers of microbial fuel cells cleaned the water while producing enough power to keep them operational. Other waste was diverted and made into fertilizer for plant growth. Still other wastes were used in the production of genetically modified shiitake mushrooms.

Water from the process was not always the best tasting, so it was further processed, similar to the way people in the sixteen hundreds and earlier had sanitized water by making beer. This came in two forms: near beer with little alcohol content and strong beer that provided welcome relief on the entertainment deck. Those who worked on the reuse decks found that beer brewing was a good compensator for their less-than-great environment.

There were freshwater tanks on the ships, essentially the equivalent of one deck, but this resource had to be rationed over the length of the trip and beyond. It was only tapped when there was a loss of water between use and reuse. Any loss in equilibrium was a major cause for concern, and finding the cause was always a very high priority. After all, it was uncertain what would be at the end of the journey, and onboard water might be critical to the colony's survival until the Gate was constructed.

There were four service cores that extended from one end of a ship to the other. Inside them were elevators, stairs, and utility tunnels for environmental and communications links. Air locks were frequent between decks in case there was ever a hull breach. Besides the physical-fitness deck, people were encouraged to use the stairs to help stay in shape. This was especially important when the acceleration/deceleration induced "gravity" was one half g.

There was no good substitute for gravity. Artificial gravity had been "invented" for the movies because people couldn't be floating around on movie prop decks. One way around this was to have rotating ships with the centrifugal force from the spinning keeping things in place on the circumference. There were three problems with this. One was the initial acceleration needed to get the ships moving. A second problem was the uneven gravity between decks and no gravitation force in the middle. The third and much more important factor was the engines. Once started, the starship engines had to stay operational. They wouldn't provide any major initial thrust but they could provide a constant one for the duration of the trip.

So, instead of rotating, the starships would continually accelerate, creating a downward force equal to 1.5 the force of gravity on Earth. This would continue until the ships reached close to three-quarters maximum light speed. Once top speed was reached, the plan was to have the ships experience a period of zero gravity while they were turned around. They would then decelerate at a rate of 0.5 g toward Epsilon Eridani until they reached near zero velocity, and the ships would be rotated again, repeating the cycle. It was felt that the occupants, including the vegetation, could easily get used to 1.5 and 0.5 g forces. It was certainly better than having everything floating around all the time.

The engines and their pods were massive. There were six per ship. Four were required for propulsion and a ship's basic energy needs. Two were spare engines pods providing redundancy. The redundant engines were left completely shut down until needed. If one was needed, a defective engine and its pod would be jettisoned, and a spare would be rotated into place. The six engine room pods containing the engines were each 850 feet in length and 75 feet in diameter. They were outboard of the bridge and engineering by five hundred feet. The engine rooms were attached to the main body of the ship through an elaborate slip-ring assembly allowing the engines to be rotated around the outer ring. The engines would be rotated around the central cylinder to maintain an even thrust. In theory, this system would allow a ship to function with only two engines, but it would not be able to reach the acceleration levels of four operating engines.

Propulsion was plasma based. The engine fuel source was a new technology utilizing a complex fission and fusion hybrid reaction producing nearly all its own fuel. The technology was so radical, in fact, that the periodic table had a few more elements added. Control rods kept each reaction from going critical. Once started, there was no known way to shut the engines down. When the ships were to turn around, the operational theory was to have the engines' plasma diverted temporarily so the engines themselves would stay operational. Though state of the art, the engines were flaunted as flawless—that is, except in the eyes of the operating engineers who had to constantly modify and adjust the reactions with control rods. Preventive and corrective maintenance was constant.

Not surprisingly, the UNSC knew this in advance, so the selection process for these operating engineers had been the most intense of all positions on the ships. They had been chosen for their skill and, even more important, for their discretion. Secretly, some were coerced. Their jobs were considered classified even after launch to avoid causing any undue concern among the ships' population. The stress level for the engine-operations staff was more than just intense.

On both ends of each ship were communication arrays. Those on the front and back of the ships were enormous and were mounted in front of the deflection cones. The logic was that the arrays had to be there to be effective, and if they were hit by space debris, that was better than a hull breach. With six ships, only one was really needed to communicate with Earth, and any information would be shared. With these arrays, communications with Earth was to be nearly constant initially, but as the distance from home increased, messages were scheduled less frequently. Unknown to the UNSC, however, there was one clandestine communication device on board known to only one crewmember that could communicate with no delays. That one system would remain idle for many years, with its owner wondering if it would ever be used.

The ships would move as one, providing support to each other as needed. Each ship was nearly identical in appearance, but there were major attempts to make each ship's interior closely represent its sponsoring region. This was most pronounced in the hydroponic gardens scattered around each ship representing fruits and vegetables favored within specific regions. It made a little break when a crewmember from one ship visited another.

There was a huge debate about whether animals should be included. But unlike Noah's ark, animals could be transported to the final destination through the Gate once it was established, so for the most part, animals weren't invited. There were some exceptions, however. A few breeds of dogs were added as service animals. While everyone recruited for the mission was healthy, it was realized that this would likely change over the decades that the ships were en route.

Another exception was canaries. For centuries, these colorful birds had been used in mines to detect dangerous gases as they were much more sensitive than humans. In spite of all the technology built into the ships to protect the occupants, the canaries were seen as a major safeguard. Besides, they added a little warmth and color to the enterprise. Originally, they had all been in cages, but as any caged animal would, they took every opportunity to get out, and in at least one ship, a rather large colony of free-ranging birds was established. Few seemed to mind the birds except for the occasional nests and droppings in the most inappropriate locations.

After considerable debate, honeybees had been invited. Besides the honey they would provide, they were still the most efficient pollinators of plants. Occasionally, bees were found setting up housekeeping outside standard-protocol hives, and the beekeepers would find that they would have a devil of time cleaning things up.

The last exception was chickens. These critters were relegated to an area on one of the reuse decks at the bottom of the ship. The chicken population was limited but important. Besides providing a much-needed, though occasional, source of protein through meat and eggs, they were efficient recyclers of waste from the kitchens into valuable fertilizer.

Nothing was to be wasted. Human and animal waste was used to grow genetically modified mushrooms. It was rather unpleasant working on the mushroom farms, but as this crop became the main "meat" on the ships, it was considered essential, so nearly everyone had a tour of duty there. Essential as it was, everyone understood the mushrooms were only a poor substitute for a cheeseburger in paradise. Everyone, that is, except for vegetarians and a new generation that was born on the ships and never knew what beef was.

There was concern that each ship's population would gradually become isolated from those on other ships. Continual interaction of varying kinds was considered crucial to maintaining harmony. It helped that each ship was decorated according to the region it represented, allowing for "vacation" time away from what people saw each day on their home ships. Scheduled shuttle trips between the ships provided transportation.

In addition to vacation visits, each ship had a soccer team and "field." There was one game a week, so each ship sponsored a team every three weeks. Home games were scheduled once every six weeks. In between home games, the entertainment deck would broadcast the games on the other ships in the main theater.

The soccer fields were about three-quarters the size of an earthbound indoor field and were used as a park between games. There was just enough room around the field perimeter to allow out-of-bounds. However, the thirty-foot ceiling was not out-of-bounds and allowed for some creative shots. Some shots could be very amusing after the ships went from 1.5 g to 0.5 g and vice versa before players got used to the new gravity. Each ship picked its team with tryouts. However, no player was allowed to play more than two years in a row. After a one-year hiatus, a player could get back on the team. This was intended to make the games less predictable. Team members took this seriously and practiced regularly after their normal ship duties. The general population needed the distraction and looked forward to every game. There was no money on board the ships, but gambling over game results still went on, with officers looking the other way. Work shifts and some privileges were the usual wagers.

Each ship carried heavy construction equipment and fuel for it. The Gate installation would require a massive construction effort, with huge excavations required over square miles of surface. Earthmovers, excavators, cranes, and equipment of every type was included in the inventory because no one knew what kind of soil or geological conditions the crew would find. It was hoped that a biofuel plant could be built early to provide fuel using local vegetation, but as that couldn't be counted upon, fuel had to be brought along. "Hope for the best but plan for the worst" was the equipment operators' motto. There were a handful of highly skilled equipment operators on each ship. Their job during the trip was to ensure that the fuel and equipment would be ready to go once they reached the end of the journey. They also trained other crewmembers who had other assignments now but would have little to do once on the new world. It had been estimated that no fewer than eight thousand workers would be needed for thirteen months, just for the site work alone. Construction of the Gate, gatehouse, power plant, and support structures would require another five thousand workers. Even more workers were required for support facilities and housing. A small city had to be built. To meet these demands, the starships had to carry everything they might need plus provide for wide margins of error.

Admiral Nimitz, a distant relative of the famous World War II naval admiral, had overall command. He had two vice admirals. The six ships' captains reported to the vice admiral of operations (VAO), Marvin Swartz. The VAO was to make certain that all the ships operated efficiently and maintained security, safety, and discipline. He also had overall responsibility for food production and preparation.

All scientists, research engineers, teachers, medical doctors, psychologists, and their support staff reported to the vice admiral of academics and science (VAAS), Ada Sylva. She had the overall responsibility for the health of mind and body for the combined population of the six ships. This was deemed critical not only for immediate needs but also for the long-term goal. Also critical to this position were all the calculations required to keep the ships on course and the timing of each turn. Thus it was critical to maintain a high level of education so the Gate would in turn be maintained and ready for deployment when the time came. It was deemed likely that many of the original crew would not survive the trip, so it was important that the youngest in the crew, including those born on the ships, received the best training in science, technology, engineering, and mechanics, collectively known in the early twenty hundreds as STEM. But to make sure that people were well rounded, the arts were included; thus, the general educational philosophy promoted universally was STEMA or STEAM. Just as the VAO had the six captains reporting to him, the VAAS had deputies on each of the ships known as chief academic and science officers (CASOs).

Admiral Nimitz, Vice Admiral Swartz, and Vice Admiral Sylva were stationed on the fleet flagship Starship *United States* initially, but every four months, the flagship designation of the fleet was moved to another ship to avoid any feelings of isolation or favoritism. While the vacated quarters were supposed to be left that way, the relatively luxurious accommodations somehow found occupants, a privilege usually granted by the ship's captain as a reward for some outstanding effort. The ships' captains had ultimate authority when the admiral and his staff were not on board, but if the ships' CASOs weren't consulted on anything controversial, there was usually hell to pay.

The ships were launched on June 29, 2067, with great fanfare. Just four years later, in 2071, the fleet received a garbled, incomplete message from Earth that seemed to indicate that the ships were on their own. There were no further messages from Earth or fleet command. After days of deliberation by the senior staffs of all the ships, they concluded that the message had meant the ships were no longer within a reasonable range for regular communications. Progress reports were still transmitted toward Earth every week with the assumption they would eventually be received. Once erected on the new host world, communications would naturally be resumed through the Gate. To avoid concern among the general population, the morale officers fabricated regular news from home.

So, the ships were now en route to a new world. Ship occupants were kept busy, and life was pretty good. For most of the ninety thousand occupants, the news from home showed that everyone back on Earth closely watched everything they were doing. Everyone in the fleet was supported, and almost everyone believed that all on Earth were proud of this major enterprise they had put forth. Ignorance was bliss.

Chapter 6

Awake

Kem-U-El woke with a start. Not that this was anything unusual. It was the way the stupid stasis pods were programmed. An electric shock, as a kind of defibrillation, would force hearts to reset and start pumping. That didn't mean Kem would be jumping out of bed right away, however. Oh, no. It would take a day or so for all the body parts to recognize that they were all connected and for the stasis fluid in the lungs, stomach, and digestive tract to purge. Kem knew what was coming. This was far from the first time he had been subjected to this misery. It was, however, part of the job.

How long ago was it that he'd said, "I really need to do something worthwhile. I don't like this feeling of aimlessness, and I don't do nothing very well." So he had asked the Boss, "What can I do?"

Kem had had an idea of what he might be called upon to do, and he had thought he was prepared when he popped the question. He knew of many in his family of El who had asked a similar question in its thousands of years of history, and they had been accepted into the Order. Kem had learned that no one was actually asked to join the Order. An individual had to ask and then pass through several degrees of learning before final installation. It was a commitment that redefined individuals as they would be separated from their family and friends. Family and friends would die natural deaths while members of the Order would be relocated and might live on forever, barring any catastrophic physical injury or an inability to return to stasis.

One could be free from stasis for many years, gradually growing older, but when returned to stasis, the body would be rejuvenated. It varied from individual to individual, but in Kem's case, thirty-three years of age was the baseline. Membership in the Order meant seeing life through windows of relatively short periods seldom longer than a couple of decades. Through these periodic interjections, history wasn't learned; it was experienced.

The Order was a secret society that got involved with things that were exciting and at times terrifying. Oh, life had been good for

Kem before joining. He had wanted for nothing. But the Order had promised to give his life purpose, and he needed purpose.

The Boss at headquarters was actually a mysterious committee of three but was always referred to in the singular, and, as such, it was the Boss that had considered Kem's application to the Order. Kem loved his work. Each time he came out of stasis, he would remember the family and friends with whom he had grown up and had some regrets about leaving them, but they had all encouraged him to join, believing it was his destiny. As before when he came out of stasis, these same thoughts returned, but not for long as his immediate condition required complete concentration. He had to focus on the here and now. The "here" he knew. The "now" he would learn later.

Within an hour, the vomiting and the convulsive discharges started. No passing thoughts now. This misery would last at least five hours, and there was nothing he could do but use a form of mental yoga to get past the pain and stench. A mask of sorts would take the vomit away while pumping nearly pure oxygen into his lungs. Tubes stuck into the most private of body parts would take much of the stasis fluid away, but the odor from the process and the general body odor from lying in stasis for God knows how long was less than pleasant. It simply felt so unclean and degrading. *But I guess its worth it* was his fuzzy thought. At least no one else could see what was happening.

At hour six, the convulsions stopped. What a relief! Now there was enough brain function to study the monitors above the bed to see what was going on with the purging and to determine how long he had been out of action. Instruments told him it was July 6, 2085. He had been in stasis for over a hundred years. *I'll bet a lot has changed*, he thought. Then, shaking his head and realizing that this was a dumb thought, he added, *Of course a lot has changed. That's why you're out of stasis, you idiot.*

At hour twelve, Kem started to feel his body responding, and part of that response was a developing hunger for food—real chewable food. This gave Kem something pleasant to think about and plan for in the immediate future. Protocol was to get the body functioning first, and fortunately, that meant food and drink. Though movement was still limited, he could at least plan a meal and later, through verbal commands, get the robotics to start gathering food and preparing a feast. Comfort food, that's what he wanted. But that would have to wait until hour fourteen, when his mouth could form some words.

Finally, at hour twenty-three-plus, the tingling in Kem's arms and legs subsided enough to allow him to slowly remove the mask and those miserable tubes. *Ah, much better!* he thought. *Man, am I hungry!*

He shifted his six-foot-eleven-inch frame so his feet could touch the floor. Using his hands and currently limited body strength, he steadied himself and looked around. There were no surprises. The soft glow showed the same dull gray walls he had looked at when going under. Though they and the somewhat darker floor looked cold, they were in fact pleasantly warm, a good sign that the environmental systems were working.

There were five other bed-type pods in the room. Each was occupied with a team member except for one. Schem-Hampha-Rae was missing from his. Kem figured that his friend Schem had been scheduled to be the next one up, explaining the empty stasis pod. Kem guessed that whatever was going on was more than Schem could handle, so Kem had been activated. He guessed the rest of the team would stay under until Kem found out from Schem what was going on. Maybe Schem and he could deal with whatever it was.

Slowly, Kem stood. He could smell his now-ready meal of shepherd's pie mitigating at least some of the odors that seemed to float around him. His meal was his own recipe of ground lamb and plenty of carrots and peas with a golden-brown piecrust made with real flour: no gluten-free stuff for him. He wondered, as a passing thought, if that had ended up becoming a fad! He hoped so. Food was in the next bay, maybe only a dozen feet away, but it seemed a mile. The ingredients, all freshly gathered by the robots and drones from someplace, had been carefully prepared. The aroma was heavenly. Kem mumbled, "I'm coming, food! Don't go away."

One stiff step after another, and he sat down in the galley. He put his head over the pie and inhaled, saying out loud to the kitchen robotics, "Thank you. This smells great." On the table was a tall glass of water with a little lemon wedge and goblet of deep-red merlot. Kem drank half the glass of water, and he felt it track all the way down. He let the liquid settle for a few seconds, and then he took a sip of wine. Swishing it around in his mouth, he could feel his taste buds coming alive. "Wow, this is great wine! Look out, pie, I'm going in!" he said with a smile.

After the first few bites Kem settled into a slow routine: water, wine, followed by a mouthful of pie. The water glass and the wine goblet were topped off by the kitchen robotics that served from above until Kem signaled, "No more for now, thank you."

Kem spent an hour at the table, relishing every mouthful, and at the same time wondering where Schem might be. He guessed Schem must be out on a mission as he wasn't there to greet him.

Once satisfied and slightly light-headed, he slowly got up from the table and moved to a reflective wall. He didn't really need to look. This wasn't the first time for him, but he supposed that deep down, there was curiosity. Maybe something was different this time. *Nope, same old thing*, he thought. The face was whiter than white, shallow cheeks, hair down to his shoulder blades, something of a beard, and no clothing. His muscle tone was in a sad state. His normally 280-pound body would bounce back quickly with proper nourishment, but right now he looked like crap. While in stasis, hair and fingernails still grew, though extremely slowly. When he had gone into stasis this last time, he had been forty-five years of age. He was now back to his baseline of thirty-three, but until he got cleaned up and back into condition, he really couldn't tell. So, with both stomach and appearance curiosity satisfied, Kem headed for the shower and dressing area.

"You know," he said out loud to uncaring robotics, "these adaptations to showers and baths are pretty nice. I like it!" First, the grooming robotics cut Kem's blond, nearly white, hair to the shoulders. The face was shaved and the nails clipped. With that and the subsequent washing completed, Kem dressed in the standard-issue uniform of white, loose-fitting, billowing shirt; loose-fitting white pants with cinch to match; and sandals. A gold-colored sash around the waist finished the ensemble. And now it was time to see what had triggered the awakening. "I hope it isn't another war!"

Following a short passage away from the living quarters, he climbed a ship's ladder into the control room. A quick glance at the stasis chamber monitors confirmed what he already knew: Schem-Hampha-Rae was missing. But everyone else in stasis seemed to be fine. *Maybe I can leave them there. Maybe this is an easy one*, he thought. *Or maybe not*, he added as he looked at the population, environmental, and natural-resources screens and printouts. "This can't be right," he mumbled as he tapped the monitors. Nothing changed. "Oh! This isn't good. OK, let's not panic." And he slid into a command chair.

A check of the remote sensors quickly confirmed that what he was seeing was in fact true, and he started to comprehend why he had been woken up. *But where is Schem?* Surely, as the first one up, he would have evaluated the situation and not waited until now to do something. With the realization that this was more than just routine, he headed for the stasis room. Everyone will have to be revived. It would take many collective hours to figure what was going on and then determine a game plan. Maybe the team would do nothing, but that would ultimately be the decision of the Boss after their commander and team leader, Gabe-Re-El, and the rest of the team completed the field evaluations.

"Gabe will figure it out. Besides, waking up once in a while is good for the soul." Kem headed down the ladder, through the living quarters, and to the stasis room. One by one, starting with the commander, Kem activated the waking sequence on each pod. For the next twenty-four to thirty hours while everyone else was being rejuvenated, Kem would analyze historical data to see if he could find trends. He would also activate the cloaking system. Though not needed just yet, it was good to have it in place. *Oh*, he thought, *and a bit more food. And I shouldn't let that wine go to waste!*

The team's quarters, or habitat, had once been a ship, but since settling into its present resting spot, its flexible technology had reconfigured to match the available space inside Augustine Island, a simmering volcano. The site had been chosen because the habitat's systems needed the volcanic heat energy. It ran a heat-sorption system to provide power for environmental controls and the rest of the quarter's operating systems. Nothing fancy, but it worked.

The cloaking system was nothing too sophisticated either. It was smoke from the volcanic activity combined with seawater to make a kind of thick fog that would keep anyone from seeing what might be happening on the island and discourage anyone from getting close. The artificial fog had extended out to a two-mile radius and up to about a half mile in height almost instantaneously.

It was tough on anyone who might be caught in it, but the potential risk of someone finding the habitat with team members coming and going would not be good. The system would stay activated as long as any team members might go in or out. While the island had been selected in part because of its remote location, human habitation in the area did fluctuate, and it was better to be safe than sorry.

In the past, the team members had made the mistake of being seen at the wrong times and then made poor attempts of disguising their intent. Everyone had been guilty of this at one time or another, but it was usually a rookie mistake. People had written firsthand accounts but without a complete understanding of what they had actually seen; the interpretations were speculative at best. A directive from the Boss thus had made the adherence to the policy of discretion much stricter. That didn't mean there might not be direct contact, but as Earth's native population became more and more aware of imaginative possibilities, any contact would have to be well thought out in advance or at least should be. Time would tell.

Kem was anxious to see the rest of the team, but for now, he would enjoy the next few hours with his own thoughts and some more dining pleasures.

Chapter 7
Situation Room

Kem-U-El stayed out of everyone's way as the rest of the team acclimated after coming out of stasis. It was now July 7, 2085; just thirty-eight hours after Kem had been revived. Gabe-Re-El and the remaining team members, Ara-Ri-El, Ere-Mi-El, and Na-Ki-Ir, were all awake, fed, and cleaned up. Their meals, much like Kem's, were of simple comfort food. Na-Ki-Ir, who was a transfer from another team and not an El, ate only nuts, fruits, and vegetables. Everyone else had some form of meat. All enjoyed the provided wine as it was one of the better merlots they had tasted, though, after stasis, most wines tasted good.

Only Kem had any idea of the issues as he had been up the longest, and so it was up to him to get Gabe, the team leader, and the rest of the team up to speed. Gabe sat at the head of the table in the situation room. He, like the rest, was dressed in the standard uniform of white, loosely fitting shirt, white trousers, and sandals. As a token of his rank, his gold sash was wider and trimmed with a deep purple. Not that anyone needed to be reminded of who was in charge. At seven feet two inches tall and with a normal muscular build of over three hundred pounds, he was formidable even among a group that was just as imposing when taken individually. No one was less than six feet seven inches, and all had muscular bodies. And except for Naki, whose hair was black and whose complexion was dark brown, all had white-blond hair, trimmed now to just below their shoulders. It was an El family trait.

Taking charge, Gabe said, "Kem, bring us up to date. What's going on? Where is Schem?"

Kem cleared his throat and simply gave the facts as he knew them. "Well, of course we only have the bare numbers right know, but something, or many things, seem to have gone off track. First, however, was anyone brought out of stasis for any adjustments after 1946? That might offer a little insight."

Everyone looked around as Na-Ki-Ir slowly raised his hand. "In 1960, I was brought out. People were going technology crazy, and it was getting serious with chemicals. Some of it was looking very good for a time with farming techniques, but the long-term problems were not well understood with the heavy use of herbicides and pesticides. It wasn't all bad as food production was up, but awareness was missing. A well-educated woman named Rachel Carson started to notice that some species of wildlife weren't doing very well. I nudged her along so she was able to see that wide use of certain chemicals had terrible long-term effects. In 1962, she published the book *Silent Spring*. The book created a new awareness, and subsequently, a new environmental movement seemed to be taking hold before I went back under."

"How long did you monitor things after the book came out?" asked Gabe.

Naki said, "Only a couple more years. All in all, those were pretty good years, and I would have liked to hang around a little longer. But I did follow protocol."

"Good," said Gabe. "Did you see any other troubling trends?"

"Oh yes," said Naki, "but there seemed to be enough people well aware of the dangers, and they seemed to have enough influence to keep things from blowing up. In some cases, quite literally."

"Anyone else? What about Schem?" asked Gabe.

Kem responded, "Schem was next up. According to the logs, he came out in 2067. The log entry was brief, basically saying that he had to make a judgment call and got involved with a space program. Since the program was taking a great many people on some sort of long-distance mission, he felt led to go and monitor. He believed that if anything else came up, the next in line would be called up, and—well, I was next up, and that was less than two days ago."

"Hmm," mused Gabe. "1946 to 1962 wasn't very long by our standards. Then not again until now, a hundred and twenty years later? That's not bad! This business with Schem, though, has me puzzled."

But Kem dampened any potential euphoria. "I think the calibration might be off with our systems. From what I can tell, there were a series of crises that we missed, and the system is just catching up."

Gabe interjected by saying, "I don't know what we're talking about yet, but remember, natural and predictable occurrences, no matter how bad, do not necessarily mean we're supposed to get involved."

"Right," agreed Kem, "but with your permission, I'd like to continue."

"Sorry," said Gabe. "Please go on."

"I don't have any time-frame details as yet," said Kem, "but here is what I do know. Somewhere around 2060, the world human population was around ten billion, probably more."

"What?" said Ara-Ri-El. "I thought Earth could handle eight billion!"

"Right," said Kem with a note of irritation. "Can I get a few words in without interruption?"

"Yes, Kem," said Gabe. "No more interruption. Please continue."

"Well, as I was saying," said Kem, not convinced he could finish without someone jumping in, "the human population was around ten billion, and as I was just reminded, eight billion was the magic number. Natural resources were stretched to their limits, which in turn started to limit advances in technology, which in turn made overpopulation worse. There was some off-world colonization, but authorities wanted to make a big show of leadership and decided to send a fleet of ships off to another solar system to establish some sort of transportation portal. This is where I think Schem went. And while it appears very interesting, I haven't gotten into the details yet.

"Wars and regional conflicts seemed to increase in Africa and the Middle East. I don't know what it is about the Middle East, but they have, or had, so much potential, and all they want to do is kill each other. Anyway, between the fighting and the pandemic, there weren't many left."

"Pandemic?" asked Gabe.

"Yes, I was getting to that," with Kem, noting that he had been interrupted again. "So, it appears Mother Nature initiated a population collapse. Bottom line is, we seem to have a worldwide human population of about eight hundred million, or less than ten percent of the maximum reached. In addition, it appears that the population continues to decrease. I suppose this could be heading for another mass extinction, like we had with the dinosaurs, but that's just a random thought.

"Now, not that that information isn't staggering all by itself, but it seems the world's population has evolved back into small, rather distinct, groups not aligned with any ethnicity or religion. There are still those who try to govern, but the large-scale governments of big countries are much less influential than they used to be. The military units still exist but certainly much smaller than before. There are now many pockets of humans that are far more isolated, in most cases on purpose, from the rest of the world. I haven't seen many population centers with over a thousand people.

"But it even gets better. There are some people who have completely isolated themselves from all actual human contact, relying instead on technology for communication with others like themselves. We'll need to get our heads together on this group. They rely so much on technology developed decades ago that the technology itself is maintaining itself, and with the self-imposed isolation, these people do not seem to ever connect and reproduce. Questions?"

"So, what's the problem?" said a smiling Ara, who only received disapproving looks from the group.

Ere-Mi-El asked, "So, what about this space fleet?"

Kem answered. "I'm not sure what's going on there. I assume it still exists, but there has been no communication with it since 2071 when the pandemic struck down nearly everyone in the program that was here on Earth. Records do indicate it was a large undertaking, with about ninety thousand people on six ships. It appears Schem sent messages, but I haven't had time to review them at all."

"How large a group is this techno group?" asked Naki.

"It looks like the hard core is about fifteen percent, with members spread out over most of the planet. These are the ones that almost never directly interface with another person. There are others that aren't quite this bad at different levels. Hard to say how many," answered Kem.

"So, is there any good news?" asked Gabe.

"Yes," said Kem. "There is a lot less fighting now. Any wars that break out seem to be of short duration and small in scale. I think people are finally tired of untimely death. Again, the exception seems to be the Middle East. They won't be happy until everyone there is a 'martyr.'"

"And—oh!" said Ara, the self-appointed comedian in the group, "The wine is really good. That's good news!"

Gabe, not impressed with these words of wisdom, just stared at Ara, who remained completely unfazed. Looking around to his companions, Gabe said, "This will be interesting. I don't recall this many apparently unrelated factors that seem to converge into a common theme. I don't want to jump to any conclusions, but certainly, we weren't brought back among the living just to watch things get worse. It is time we got to work."

Chapter 8
The Survey Begins

Following protocol, the team took a couple of days to regain strength and body mass lost during their long nap. They then prepared for a survey to get a firsthand understanding of some of the issues currently facing humanity. Each team member realized that although they were expected to observe firsthand, there was some manipulation that would be out of their hands and remain a great mystery. They would do their survey and allow themselves to be led to whatever and wherever. They did this without question. They were simply the initiators of whatever the Boss had in mind, and they operated on a need-to-know basis.

"OK, everyone," said Gabe, "it's time for field trips to see what the world is like. I have word that some of the other teams are out of stasis. No one knows yet why particular teams were activated, but I guess we're about to find out. Teams are coordinating their own efforts, so we'll be sticking with the geographical areas we know best. I'm going to spend some time in the local area from the east coast of Russia, over to Alaska, and maybe down into Canada. Kem, I want you and Ere to head to the east coast of Canada and the United States. Naki and Ara, I want you to head farther south to Texas and see if you can get more details on the space fleet and especially what resources are committed to it here on Earth."

With that, they all headed to the equipment room. On the wall were what appeared at first glance to be thin backpacks, except these had been on a charging station under the names of each team member. With no visible straps, each put on his pack. Then each team member entered the environmental lock chamber separating the always-comfortable environment within the habitat from whatever was outside. On this day, it was the immediate heat of the volcanic Augustine Island that greeted them outside the chamber.

The inner door closed, and Gabe checked a green light indicating that a thick, acrid cloaking fog had enveloped the island. With the fog confirmed, Gabe opened the outer door to the air lock. From here, the team could see a vertical tunnel leading up and to the surface of the volcano. It looked a lot different from when they had gone into stasis, as the volcano landscape had shifted over the years. Different, but the entrance remained open as the habitat systems maintained access. With intense heat now an instant issue, no one took the time to think about landscape changes but instead raced to the tunnel entrance so they could energize the packs that provided protective bubbles.

As the team members emerged onto the island's surface, they energized their packs. A golden glow emanated from the packs as they encapsulated team members with individual protective envelopes, and the volcanic heat became a nonissue. Outside the envelopes, they would have cooked, but inside, a cool twenty degrees Celsius was programmed in.

The tunnel wasn't long, and each team member was grateful for that. Ara said, "Man, this heat could ruin a perfectly good body if the tunnel was longer." The other team members looked at each other and shook their heads, to which Ara responded, "What?"

With the protective envelopes in place, the team members got their bearings, and antigravity panels unfurled from the packs behind each of them. There were actually close to a thousand small, interconnected panels, equal numbers of which went out to the right and left of each wearer. The small panels overlapped slightly, tapering to blunted ends. The left and right sides of the pack stretched for a length about equal to the height of each team member and slightly wider, based on each one's individual weight. Control was provided through a headband attached to the pack. A subtle look to the left, and the pack took the wearer to the left. The same was true for any direction or altitude.

Speed was limited to approximately 450 miles per hour, and the altitude was limited to approximately a thousand feet above the terrain directly below the wearer. This could make for a very uncomfortable ride if the terrain was rough and the speed high, but all the team members were proficient in the packs' use, and few ever wanted to get too carried away with speed. Besides, after all that time in stasis, viewing the world at a slow pace was something each enjoyed. Walking would have been nice and slow, of course, but no one really wanted to take it that slow. There were limits.

Usually when flying, both legs were together, slightly aft of vertical, and the arms were relaxed. In landing, the wearer would slow down, the legs would become vertical, and then the left leg was lifted slightly and the arms spread, with palms up in a more open gesture. These movements were all transmitted through the headband and harness to the pack. Once landed, the wearer could either furl the panels or not, depending upon his mood. Sometimes the wearer would forget to furl the panels or simply left them open to impress someone. The panels were pretty cool, after all! And the soft glow of the environmental envelope was a nice touch as well. Gabe wasn't too keen on show-off mode but understood the need to make an impression once in a while. Ara was the only one who seemed to make it a regular habit and had to be reminded from time to time to knock it off.

Kem and Ere headed to the east coast of Canada and the United States. Naki and Ara headed south. Gabe made the short trek across the Bering Strait to check out Russia's east coast. Later, he would return to Alaska. Normally, he would have paired up with one of the other team members, but with Schem off in space, that wasn't an option. He couldn't help feeling a little annoyed as he usually did this early in the process, not knowing exactly what he was supposed to be doing. He was somewhat on his own right now as he knew the Boss wouldn't be much help at this stage of the effort. It was always the same, with a lot of guesswork.

As the team members were about to emerge from the fog, they took a quick look around to make certain they wouldn't be seen. They would eventually be seen, of course, but they didn't necessarily want to get people more curious about the island than they might be already. Keeping their habitat location and entrance a secret was critical.

As Gabe headed west, the rest of the team headed east with a general flight path over Homer. They were all supposed to avoid being spotted this early in the process if it was reasonable to do so. Naki and Ara's path was more toward Homer, and Ara decided it would be good fun to fly down a little lower and maybe stage a little show if he saw someone. As luck would have it, he did see a couple sitting outside in Homer, and he flew to about five hundred feet above them, hovered, and then rejoined Naki as they flew off.

Naki asked, "What is wrong with you? Every time you do something stupid like that, you get people all stirred up. Weren't you the one who got the whole Roswell, New Mexico, rumor started?"

"No one knows that for certain," said Ara. "Lighten up, old buddy."

"I don't know why you weren't recalled years ago," concluded Naki.

Below Naki and Ara on this very clear night sat Don and Maria Bickmeier on the dock in some oak Adirondack chairs Don had made years earlier. The chairs were old and weathered but still perfect for sitting and watching the stars, especially while holding hands and with glasses of wine in their free hands. A newly opened bottle of local origin was on the ground between them next to one that had been emptied earlier that evening. "You know," said Don, "Leonard is never going to be satisfied until he's gone off and seen some of the world. I think the wanderlust gene was suppressed for a generation or two and has reappeared in Len."

"Yes," said Maria. "The new generation never witnessed the massive suffering we saw so are less content with the quiet life our generation enjoys. I suppose it is the sign of the times, and we may not be able to protect him."

"Maybe we're just paranoid," mused Don, adding with a chuckle, "but you shouldn't be paranoid just 'cause everyone is out to get you!"

"If Len were to go out into the world, maybe he could bring back some new jokes," said Maria, "and maybe you could retire some of your old ones!"

"Hey!" said Don, "It's a family thing. I was just a kid, but I remember my Great-Granddad Fisher and my Grandpa Bickmeier telling all kinds of stories. I didn't get most of them, but people either groaned or laughed. Someone needs to carry on the tradition."

"OK, OK! But you have to get some new material." And Maria smiled at Don. Then, still holding hands, they looked to the star-filled sky and noticed two strange, faint lights off in the distance among the stars, moving past them to the north. Then they saw two more lights closer to them. One of the lights came within about five hundred feet from them and stopped for perhaps a few seconds and then lifted up, joining the other light and disappearing to the east.

When the light had come close, the couple could see what appeared to be a smiling human shape inside the glow. From the glowing human shape, they had seen what looked like wings protruding from the vision's upper back. There was no discernable movement of the wings or the human shape. The vision had seemed to float. Curious and stunned simultaneously, Don and Maria had stood up and stared, instinctively moving closer to each other.

When the vision had gone, Don and Maria sat once again, with neither seeming to want to acknowledge what they might have seen. Finally, Don said, "I think I've had too much wine. Who made this stuff anyway?"

Maria said, "So, what did you see? Because I saw something that looked a whole lot like a flying person with wings, covered in a golden glow."

"OK," said Don, "I guess that's what I saw. So it wasn't just me. My mother is going to go nuts over this."

"Maybe we shouldn't say anything," said Maria. "Maybe it a military thing."

"Which military?" asked Don. "But yes, I think we'll keep this to ourselves; at least for now. Hmmm I wonder if it somehow connected with the weird fog around Augustine Island."

Chapter 9
Halfway to Houston

Naki and Ara headed southeast. A few people saw them go by overhead, and like Don and Maria, those who saw Naki and Ara fly by in a soft glow weren't sure what to think and kept the sightings to themselves. Occasionally, Kem and Ara would set down out of sight, the flight packs would contract, and they would look for a food store of some type, preferably away from people. It was bad enough that they were both tall, and well, generally large enough to stand out, but their clothing and hair made them a real attraction. Plus, each ate enough to feed three people of normal size. All of that, combined with the fact that most places these days had somewhat isolated themselves and didn't see many strangers, made it awkward enough for Naki and Ara that they decided they would visit food stores after hours when no one was around whenever they could. Access was no problem for them, and they left payment behind in the form of silver and sometimes gold pieces. Store operators were more than baffled, of course. Who steals and leaves silver and gold?

Their goal was to reach Houston, or more specifically, Houston's mission control, as the last place they knew of where space missions had been directed. The four-thousand-mile trip took them two days, with one stop for a little sleep—the natural kind of sleep and not the stasis type. For that rest, they chose a swamp in Minnesota, assuming they would be away from prying eyes. They left their environmental shields on, protecting them from water and mosquitos, but unbeknownst to them, the shield attracted some attention from a teenage couple out in a flat-bottomed johnboat who were also anxious to get away from prying eyes where they could generate an intimate environment of their own. As the teenagers rowed into the swamp, the dual glows raised their curiosity. When they got closer, they could see two large figures dressed in white with long hair, either dead or sleeping in what was some kind of soft light. The collective adrenaline of the teenage couple rose to such a level, all the original thoughts for the evening completely disappeared. Would they tell anyone what they had seen? Of course not. Why invite "What were you doing out there in the first place?"

When the sun came up, Naki woke first and jostled Ara awake. "You know," said Ara, "there just isn't anything as satisfying as waking up from a real sleep. I feel great!"

But Naki countered, "I place that as number two. Eating is number one in my book." And they headed off to raid a local diner they had spotted the evening before.

Unfortunately, it being a diner, it was open early for the breakfast crowd and occupied by a few locals. "Should we go in?" asked Naki.

"Um, I guess so. I'm pretty hungry," said Ara. "We'll just try to blend in."

"Very funny," mumbled Naki insincerely. "Maybe we should just tell them we used to work at a nuclear power plant and it stunted our growth."

As they entered, the waitress, cook, and eight customers all looked at the door. No one in the diner had seen a stranger for over a year, and here were two very strange ones indeed. Pastor Glenn tried to speak, but nothing came out. Was he seeing what he thought he was seeing? Naki and Ara sat at the counter as if they did this every day, and the waitress, Peggy, stuttered, "Co-co-coffee?"

When Naki and Ara finished their six-egg omelets, pancakes, ham steaks, and fifth cups of coffee, they felt much better. When Peggy, now almost under control, brought them their bill, Naki pulled out a gold coin and asked, "Will that cover it?"

This hardly went unnoticed as everyone was still staring at the strangers. "Is that gold?" one asked.

"Yes," said Naki in perfect Midwest English. "Is that OK? I don't have any local currency."

Peggy looked at them and quietly said, "That will be fine."

Pastor Glenn, gaining some composure and speaking for everyone, was finally able to speak. "Are you just passing through town?"

"Yes," said Ara. "We're heading for Houston."

"Really?" said the pastor. "There isn't much there, you know. I'm called Pastor Glenn. What are you called?"

"I'm Na-Ki-Ir, and this is Ara-Ri-El, but you can call us Naki and Ara if you like," said Naki.

With that, Pastor Glenn's jaw dropped, and Naki and Ara left the diner.

"That went well," said Ara.

"Yah, right!" chuckled Naki. "Did you see the look on that pastor's face? I thought he was going to faint."

And with all eyes in the diner now looking out its windows, Ara encouraged Naki to show off a little. They activated their packs' environmental shields, unfurled their antigravity panels, and lifted off the ground. *Sunday's sermon is going to have to be something special*, thought Pastor Glenn, *but what can I possibly say? I don't even know what we saw! Was it a sign? A sign of what?*

Chapter 10
Gone and Almost Forgotten

Even though the habitat systems back in Alaska had told of a population decrease, Naki and Ara were still stunned when they came to the edge of Houston. Ara turned to Naki and said in very soft voice, "This is unreal."

Naki responded the only way he could. "This is worse than I expected. I don't see anyone at all. Even with the huge population decrease, we should see someone."

As the team members came in from the northwest, they moved over the city toward the Clear Lake area where the United States' space missions had been controlled and monitored. This seemed like a logical first-step place to learn about the status of the international/interstellar program.

As they traveled over the city, they continued to look for people on the streets. As they got closer to the water, they saw more and more water where streets had once been. In some areas, entire blocks were surrounded with seawalls. Within the seawalls, some areas were still covered with water while others remained relatively dry. In the dry zones, Naki and Ara noticed a few people. Outside the dry areas and tied to docks were small boats and canoes, though in one area, they noticed a number of very large, luxurious watercraft that had apparently been brought together to form some kind of community. It wasn't clear if these craft were moored or resting on their bottoms, but in either case, it didn't look as though they ever moved. These isolated areas all exhibited human activity but certainly not anything large scale.

As they followed the major road through the city, Interstate 45, they noted that it was interrupted here and there with flooded sections, but it was still clear enough to get them close to mission control. When they reached their destination, they could see that a seawall had been built around the complex just like others they had seen and that it remained dry within. "Let's take a look," said Ara, and they settled down in front of a sign saying "Christopher C. Kraft Jr. Mission Control Center."

With their packs' panels retracted, Naki and Ara started toward the building, and Ara noted, "This place looks pretty good, like someone is taking care of it."

As Naki nodded, a seventy-something-year-old man came out of the building. He was about five feet ten inches and maybe 180 pounds, with a body that seemed a lot younger than what one would expect. Under his NASA-emblazoned hat was a ring of gray hair, and he was wearing dark sunglasses. He was moving pretty well for a person of some seniority, but it was the shotgun he had in his hands that got the survey team's attention. "Good choice," said Ara to Naki. "Much harder to miss with a shotgun! Probably best we turn on our shields."

"No argument here!" said Naki as the shields were activated, enclosing them in the warm glow.

"Stop right there!" yelled the man with the gun, seemingly not noticing the warm glow surrounding the intruders. "Who are you, and what do you want?"

"Don't shoot!" said Ara. "We're from the government, and we're here to help!"

"You are here from the government and are here to help?" repeated the holder of the shotgun, and with that, he started to laugh so hard, Naki and Ara looked at each other in bewilderment, thinking he might have a heart attack. But as suddenly as he had started to laugh, he stopped, raised the shotgun, and fired twice at each of them.

The sound was awful, but the impact was zero as the environment shield stopped on impact what appeared to be birdshot. Naki glared at Ara and said, "Obviously, being a comedian doesn't work. Let me try!" And then he turned to the shooter and said, "Hey, we're not here to harm anyone. Can we talk?"

The old man looked at the two glowing figures and then at his shotgun, somewhat perplexed with its obvious ineffectuality. His shoulders relaxed, but he held on to the gun. Finally he said in a very slow but still somewhat menacing way, "OK, you clowns, you're obviously not from the government, at least not one I ever heard of. What do you want? And it better be good, or we'll be joined by my friends with bigger hardware."

"OK," said Naki, "you are correct. We're not from the government, and maybe we can't help because maybe nothing is wrong. But we have reason to believe that the interstellar space mission may be in peril. We're on a fact-finding mission for a private agency. I go by the name Naki, and my not-so-funny companion goes by Ara. Can we talk to someone in charge?"

After a pause that seemed to stretch on and on, the man with the shotgun said, "First off, you can address me as 'Sir,' at least for now. Second, what makes you think I'm gonna trust a couple of odd guys I don't know dressed like that? And third, you offer me nothing except your word. Huh? Answer me that! And, by the way, how did you get here past the wall and gate? I see no boat or anything else. You don't look wet, so you didn't swim!"

Naki just knew Ara was going to say, "Oh, we just flew in," but cut him off with "Well, Sir, you have some points. First, if you promise not to shoot, we'll drop the shields." And he did so with only a nod from sir.

"Second, we're of Norwegian descent, so we're naturally a little bigger than some." The white lie continued. "We dress this way because this is comfortable and the cloth is a hundred percent natural. Finally, if we can stop shotgun blasts at close range, don't you think we could force our way in if we really wanted to?"

Sir responded coldly, "I think you're full of crap. But the last argument is good enough for now. So, for now, you can assume I'm in charge. What do you want?"

Naki started to wonder why Sir's friends hadn't appeared to back him up. Maybe there weren't any, but he decided there was no reason to call Sir on that assumption. Instead he said, "We have reason to believe that communications with the interstellar fleet have stopped. Why we suspect that is not important, but if it is true, we may be able to help restore that communication, assuming the fleet still exists. We are part of a larger survey group that has been sent out to gain information. Our origins are also not important right now. There is nothing more nefarious than that. Really. The two of us were assigned to find out what we can from here as it is only logical that mission control would have the best information on the fleet. We're not trying to cause any trouble. And if everything is fine, we'll be on our way, with apologies for our intrusion."

It was obvious to Naki and Ara that Sir was wrestling with something significant as he stared through them to some unknown spot on the horizon. It lasted so long, Ara wondered if Sir was OK. Finally, the distant stare refocused on the pair, and Sir spoke so quietly that Naki and Ara barely heard. "Oh, hell, I suppose I might as well tell someone. My name is John Carpenter. You can call me John. Follow me. This hundred-and-ten-degree heat is killing me."

The three of them walked about five hundred feet and entered through a foyer and into a conference room. It was cooler there, but it was obvious there was no mechanical space cooling. John asked, "Would you like some iced tea?" and another communication barrier seemed to fall.

While John was getting tea, Naki and Ara looked around the room. It was spotless. There were pictures of astronauts, presidents, spacecraft, and an assortment of other pictures everywhere. There was nothing out of place. Even the chairs set around the boat-shaped walnut conference table were all spaced evenly and pushed in just so. It reminded the pair of how servants for the aristocrats in ancient times had spaced everything on the dining tables exactly for each meal. The room was too perfect, like it was only for show.

When John returned, he had a large pitcher of unsweetened ice tea, three large glasses full of ice, and a basket of honey biscuits that for some reason were freshly baked. *How did he do that?* thought Naki. It was a sign that the communication barrier had dropped a little further still.

John poured the tea and started by saying, "I am in charge. In fact, I'm the only one here and have been almost since the death flu hit. You want to find out what's going on? Well, gentlemen—if that's what you are—I might as well unload on you. The government isn't going to do anything."

John looked at his glass, took a drink, wiped his lips, and launched in. "My wife and I came to this place in 2060. I was forty-seven years old, and this was going to be my big move. I was hired as director of facilities, and it was my job to make sure all the buildings and support systems for the upcoming interstellar-fleet ground control was maintained at the highest level possible. My department was well funded, and it was giddy times with the whole notion of sending tens of thousands of people off into space toward another solar system. All communications were originally to be maintained here. Things changed, though.

"As the ocean levels continued to rise, we realized that having all the eggs in one basket, especially a basket subject to the now too-common super hurricanes, was not a great idea. We built the seawall around the complex, and it does keep most of the water out. We still have enough power here from the electric grid and our own solar array that the pumps keep any infiltration under control.

"When the interstellar fleet was launched in 2067, the United Nations Stellar Commission wanted an alternative mission-control location with full redundancy. Politics entered the scene, as it usually does, so where to set up a second location became a problem. While everyone was arguing, NASA decided to work quietly outside of the UNSC and set up a second station. They did that without sharing that information with the rest of the world. After all, if there ended up being multiple stations, what would be the harm? Some did fear that control of the mission might be compromised if too many were able to communicate, but ultimately, it didn't matter.

"NASA started things moving in 2068. Not well known outside of the space community, the only university-owned rocket range was in Alaska at a remote location called Poker Flats. It already had a mission-control center for their Aurora research program, and it was isolated enough that it was believed the location would be a safe haven. Redundant equipment was built and shipped to Poker Flats, and apparently it was about to be assembled when the death flu hit in 2071. I have no idea how far along they got with that effort.

"As luck would have it, I was on vacation in Alaska, halibut fishing, when the flu hit. My wife called and suggested I stay a little longer. She kept from me that she had the flu and died shortly after her call. The flu spread fast and out of control, but you probably know all about that."

Naki interjected. "No. I'd like to hear your story if you're willing to share. And, of course, we're sorry about your wife. How did you learn about her death?"

"The flu caused so much panic and confusion," said John, "that virtually everything stopped. No trains, boats, or planes. Phone service quickly followed. I understand they found cruise ships and even warships years later out in the ocean with nothing but corpses. For those of us who were reasonably isolated, as I happened to be at the time, the degree of death caused by the flu was completely misunderstood. What news media was still functioning was not trusted as the media always exaggerated every disaster. Finally, I couldn't take it anymore and found a car I could buy and started driving south. The drive is over four thousand miles."

"Yeah, we know," interrupted Ara while receiving a stern look from Naki. "Sorry," he added. "Please continue."

What an odd comment, thought John, but he resumed. "I knew the flu was contagious, and as I try to avoid colds and flu anyway, I took all the precautions I could. The car I bought was a hybrid, so I didn't have to stop to fuel up as often. I loaded it with enough supplies so I wouldn't have to buy much food. When I did stop for fuel, I put on a mask and gloves and soaked my hands in sanitizer before and after pumping gas. I made stops in the most remote locations I could find. When I did pass through congested towns, there seemed to be bodies everywhere. It was horrible, and I was getting more and more panicked.

"When I reached Houston, I found nearly everyone I knew dead. The flu had passed but left devastation in its wake. My home was now flooded as the city infrastructure that kept the waters at bay was unmanned. My wife was gone. A preprinted notice on the door said the house had been sanitized. I learned later that it meant dead occupants had been cremated. We had no children, so I lost my best friend, and my life changed forever. I was truly alone in my personal life.

"I ended up finding my way over here. I don't know what I was thinking. I guess I thought I would see things here as I had left them. But instead, as they say, 'the lights were on, but no one was home.' I found a handful of support staff dressed in protective gear removing corpses, my friends and colleagues, from the buildings. When they saw me, they couldn't believe it but had the presence of mind to get me into protective gear. I probably would be dead if that hadn't happened because I sure wasn't thinking clearly. Some people must have died at their stations. It was overwhelming. Mindlessly, I helped with the last of the bodies as they were placed in an old wood admin building. We then set it on fire and added as much fuel as we could find for complete incineration. We isolated ourselves, and after a week of no more outbreaks, we started to relax and take stock of where we were.

"What we had was a completely functioning system with no one left to operate it. This is pretty sophisticated stuff. After all, signals were being sent and received much farther than anyone had even considered previously. Being the senior man in charge, I took it upon myself to try and send a message to the fleet. I'm not sure if I actually sent a message, and if it did go out, I have no idea if they ever received it. I tried to tell them what had happened here and that they were now on their own.

"Of the handful of staff members that survived, some moved away, and the rest of us decided to move in. Eventually, what was left of the government sent someone here to see what was left of us. We had kept the place maintained, and the government told us we could stay and would continue to get paid. I was told that eventually, someone would come and get the place functioning again. 'Don't worry,' they said, 'the government is here to help.' I'm the last one left, and I still get paid, though the postal service is a lot slower these days. It doesn't matter. I've got nothing to buy. Anyway, no one from the government ever returned. I stay because I have nowhere else to go, and maybe, just maybe, I can eventually contribute to getting things up and running again. Until then, I have shut down everything I dare to and try to keep the place ready to be reactivated. Keeping the ocean out is probably my biggest issue, but so far, so good, though I think the humidity and salt air has done a good job at compromising the communications circuitry. That's only a guess. The antennae and its directional hardware were destroyed in a hurricane a couple of storms ago. That could be rebuilt, but honestly, I think this place is on borrowed time as far as flooding is concerned."

Naki asked, "Do you have any contacts outside of this place?"

"I'm not sure I know what you mean…but, yes," said John. "Sometimes I leave to get supplies, and there are a few people who stop by once in a while for a visit. We estimate there are about two thousand in the greater Houston area in scattered pockets of maybe no more than two hundred. Most of them make items in converted mills and shops to be sold to the farmers outside the city and some local fishermen. That's how we get our food. The farms have reverted back to small family farms. The big industrial farms—around here, anyway—are all gone."

Naki inquired, "What can you tell us about the overall mission of the interstellar fleet?"

John responded with a bit of curiosity in his voice. "You guys don't seem to know very much about anything. Who did you say you work for?"

Before Naki could stop him, Ara said, "Oh, let's just say we work for a very powerful guy that make things happen."

"Ignore him," said Naki. "He thinks he's funny. We do work for someone who can make a difference, but all the facts aren't known, so we're trying to get those facts from many sources. Then an evaluation and recommendation can be made. Once that happens, we'll try to find the human resources that might be available to make changes if it is deemed necessary. We're mostly organizers and coordinators. But we need to know what we might have to organize and coordinate first."

John still wasn't satisfied, but he answered, "The real mission for the space fleet, from what I've deducted, was to get the world's population to think the various governments around the world were actually doing something to address overpopulation and the impact of climate change. You know, refocus the world's attention away from the real issues. A grand plan! So, what was put forth was certainly grand: 'We can use a wormhole gate for the transport of many people to another world, reducing the stress on Mother Earth.' The only problem was the construction of the Gate. We would transport a sizeable number of people and supplies to another planet in another solar system on giant ships so they could build it. Keep everyone thinking about that, and then no one would expect the politicians to do anything else. Of course, the politicians, who had little to no scientific evidence to prove their theory 'knew this would work because we've done it here in our solar system.' So, through extrapolation, the political masterminds convinced everyone that it would work light-years away. It would be decades before anyone would know if it worked, thus giving the politicians decades to procrastinate.

"I know that is a very cynical view, but look at what we did. We took the best and the brightest, stuck them in pressurized, cylindrical tubes, and sent them off. Oh, we made sure they had everything they would need to build the Gate on the other end. After all, it was cleverly surmised, there might not be any hardware stores there. Little is actually known about the planet, and no one would want to have a problem looking for a screwdriver. Right? And, 'Oh, by the way, we'll have everything in place here on Earth when you get set up. Not to worry.' I mean, really! It was exciting and all, but would it work? What could go wrong?"

Naki said with mild sarcasm, "You don't seem very optimistic."

"Well," said John, "does it look like we're ready here? For all intents and purposes, it looks like we have tens of thousands of the best human minds hurtling through space for no good reason. Certainly, the stated reason for the mission has evaporated. I'm not sure anyone knows how many people are left here on Earth, and as far as I can tell, there seems to be little interest in adding to it. So the ships are gone, and except for a few of us, I'd say the fleet is almost forgotten. Out of sight and out of mind."

Chapter 11
The Gatekeeper

Before leaving John Carpenter in Houston, Naki and Ara learned about the general principles of the wormhole gate. John had never seen it, and only due to sitting through numerous meetings did he even know it was in Ziebach County, South Dakota.

According to John, each of the major countries of the world had wanted to host the Earth end of the Gate for the prestige and economic impact, but when it got right down to it, often, the "not in my backyard" (NIMBY) syndrome had kicked in at the local level. There were criteria for the Gate location from a technical standpoint. It had to be between the forty-five-degree parallels of latitude for the Earth's magnetic field to be reasonably balanced between the north and south magnetic poles; the land needed to be flat enough to avoid additional construction costs. It used nearly sixty megawatts of power when it was in receiving mode and nearly eleven hundred megawatts in the sending mode, so its location had to have that kind of power available to be tapped.

From the human perspective, the Gate had to be remote enough to avoid NIMBY but close enough to transportation routes so equipment and building materials could be brought in. The locals would have to buy into the project. To avoid NIMBY, the Gate Commission had been formed to solicit proposals from communities. The process was very reminiscent of the way communities were selected for the Olympic games, except the criteria for the selection were almost the complete opposite.

The theory for the Gate had been tossed around for decades. The *Stargate* movie and TV series had actually been based on a secret research project within Russia. Rather than try to deny the research when some information leaked out, the United States had agreed with Russia to hide the project "in plain sight" by turning it into a science-fiction story. It had worked. No one believed it was true, but on the other hand, it had gotten into the general population's imagination, and people started to consider the possibility. So when the program was actually announced, most accepted it with a nod and a general "No kidding?" in 2047 when a site for the eventual Gate on Earth was being sought.

Typical of everything humanity does of significance, it took a major event to get the program off the ground—or, more correctly in this case, in the ground. In 2050, when the freshwater intrusion into the Atlantic Ocean from glacial melt shut down the Gulf Stream, environmental scientists were not surprised. They had predicted this event since the beginning of the century. Complex math models had showed that it would happen, but the timing was never clear. It turned out to be August 2050. It took only six weeks from when the Gulf Stream started to slow until it stopped. The disruption of the Gulf Stream ocean current, as one of many interdependent ocean currents, triggered major changes in how the ocean currents flowed. Some increased, some changed direction, and new ones were formed.

The net result was overwhelming in some geographical regions. Politically, it caused all stable governments to accelerate whatever projects they could think of that would remove some of the human stress on the planet that was now universally understood to be the major cause of climate change. So, with huge pressure now placed on the Gate Location Selection Committee, Ziebach County, South Dakota, was selected. When Chief Robert Builds With Hands had presented the proposal, it wasn't very elegant. But, as it turned out, that was one of the things noted as a plus by the committee. They wanted nitty-gritty, not fancy.

Ziebach County was the home of the Cheyenne River Sioux Tribe. In spite of the overall surge in the world's population, the local population for this entire county remained below three thousand. It had undeveloped barren grasslands where construction would be relatively easy. People didn't have to be displaced. The county had always been one of the poorest in the country, yet there was a more than willing workforce eager to change that. The tribe wanted this. The committee found few downsides, and a deal was signed.

John told his visitors, "I understand that when the documents were signed, one junior member of the committee quipped, 'It looks like we're now in the good hands of Bob the Builder,'" and from then on, Chief Robert Builds With Hands went by the new nickname. Construction started immediately. At the same time, another Gate was being shipped in pieces to the fledgling Mars colony, where work moved at a snail's pace. It's difficult to know what the brain trust had been expecting, but construction equipment didn't work well in the next-to-zero atmosphere. It wasn't until 2052 that the first use of the Gate between Earth and Mars was made. To everyone's shock, it worked flawlessly—or at least, that is what everyone was told. And with the Gate open, more people and supplies went to Mars, and exotic raw materials from Mars started to arrive on Earth. Other Gates were built on Saturn's moon Titan and on our own moon. All were to support new colonies, but it was not an economical success."

Finally, John finished his lesson saying, "I never went to the site. I don't know if it still works or even if there is anyone there still alive. I just don't know. But I suspect that the interstellar fleet, if that still exists, is moving farther and farther from Earth, still believing that the Gate here and the one they are to construct will save the day. It makes me very sad."

As Naki and Ara took their leave, Naki asked, "Is there anything you'd like us to do for you?"

John simply said, "I'm not planning on dying any time soon, but I would go a lot more peacefully if I knew that the human population hadn't screwed things up so bad that we killed Earth. I'm not sure why I trust you, but if you really can help, please do so, and let me know from time to time what's going on."

"We will," said Naki, and the three of them walked back out through the foyer onto the grounds.

Naki and Ara activated their packs. A soft glow surrounded them, their antigravity panels spread, and they floated into the air. John hadn't seen them land, so this took him completely by surprise. His mouth dropped, he started to tremble, and he fell to his knees. He suddenly, somehow, knew all would be well.

Naki and Ara were considered equals. Only Gabe had any seniority within the group. Even so, Naki said to Ara, "You have got to keep what you think is funny to yourself. That crack about 'we're from the government' could have got us killed."

"I know," said Ara, "but it was funny."

Naki laughed in spite of himself and agreed. "Yes, it was funny. I'm hungry. Let's find something to eat."

This time, they waited until late evening. They spotted a small store with "Closed" on the sign out front. They entered with their usual ease; they each took three roasted chickens, premade salads, twice-baked potatoes, a gallon of ice cream, and a bottle of merlot. Standard travel kits included sporks and knives, so all they needed to add for their dining pleasure were some napkins. They left four silver coins on the counter and retreated to a secluded, overgrown, lakeside park outside Eureka, Texas. This time, no one saw them.

As they finished their "snack," Naki said, "I think for this first round, we got lucky and learned a lot. John gave us a pretty good overview of the death flu and interstellar program."

Ara agreed. And stating the obvious, he said, "It's too bad we can't just send a message to Gabe. You'd think after all this time, we'd have communication capabilities without relying on the systems in the habitat."

"Well, we can't, so we're heading back. But since this Ziebach County is not far out of our way, we should pay a visit," said Naki. And with nothing more to say, they left.

Before entering Ziebach the next day, the team stopped to rest for the night. Again, people on the ground did not see the pair as they flew overhead. Naki and Ara were too far up for clear identification.

Breakfast looked like it was going to be a problem. The pair didn't spot any diners or food shops. Finally, when they crossed the Ziebach County line, they spotted a man and woman selling breakfast sandwiches out of a cooler, in this case used to keep the sandwiches warm. Naki and Ara landed on the other side of a rise from the couple, collapsed their packs, and walked down the road to the stand. The couple as well as the one customer who had apparently arrived by horse watched Naki and Ara approach.

The three at the stand were of Native American descent, with dark hair that was a little on the long side. They had rugged good looks. They wore old baseball caps, colorful long-sleeved shirts in spite of the early heat, jeans, and sunglasses. As Naki and Ara approached, there was no indication that the trio saw anything unusual in the pair. "Want something to eat?" said the women. "Made fresh this morning. I have plain egg sandwiches; egg and ham; and egg, ham, and cheese. I made the bread. I've got some coffee in the thermos if you want some."

Naki said, "I'll have one of each and a cup of coffee."

"Me too," said Ara.

The woman thought, *That's half of my sandwiches*, but said, "You got money?"

Naki pulled out a couple of silver coins and asked, "Will this cover it?"

The woman took the coins and looked to see if they were solid silver and said yes without any sign that she thought this unusual. The two male companions never said a word or indicated the slightest interest until the horseman said, "Where you from, and where you going?"

Ara started with "We're from the g"—before Naki cut him off with "We're pilgrims seeking enlightenment. We have learned of Chief Robert Builds With Hands and would like to meet him."

That statement generated an immediate reaction from the local trio. And the horseman said, "We knew him as Bob the Builder. He was a great man who brought prosperity to our people before the death flu. He brought our people together to lay the foundations for the Gate and then became the gatekeeper. He died from the death flu while in Washington in 2071."

Naki said, "That truly saddens us. We had hoped to meet the great man. Who is the gatekeeper now?"

The woman said, "That is Summer Snow, Chief Robert's daughter. She lives at the Gate. It is about four miles from here."

"I can take you. I work there," said the horseman, "but I have only one horse."

"We can walk," said Naki, and the three walked off, with the horseman leading his horse.

They had actually walked only about one mile when they came up to the top of a rise and a very intimidating barrier of two twenty-foot-tall, heavy chain-link fences separated by another twenty feet and both topped with razor wire. Between the two fences was barren ground, perfectly groomed except for occasional paw prints. There was not any trace of vegetation. Here and there between the fences were small houses with food dishes, water bowls, and very large dogs. When some dogs saw the three, they raced over, sat, and watched. They made no threatening sound.

The barrier stretched in both directions as far as the eye could see. Well within the barrier, the team could see swales and ridges that seemed to emanate from a central point still out of sight. Above each swale was wire suspended from poles that started at the edge of the barrier about twenty feet up, the height of the barrier. As the suspended wire stretched away from the barrier, the suspension poles' height seemed to increase geometrically. In the distance, Naki and Ara saw poles that were at least five hundred feet tall. It appeared as though little effort had been made to level the entire area within the barrier, but it was obvious that the lines had been set to some imaginary plane.

Ara said to Naki, "This reminds me of a large-scale Marconi transmitting station from the turn of the twentieth century."

"Yessss…" said Naki, his voice trailing off.

The horseman interrupted any thoughts the pair might have with "An entrance is over there. Few people come here, so we let just about everyone in as long as they are escorted. Between the fences, we have four-legged security, and inside the barrier we have legalized hunting for anyone who is not invited. I am one of the guards. You are now invited."

As they moved to the security entrance, a sign read,

WORM HOLE GATE

SOUTH ENTRANCE

HIGH SECURITY

TRESPASSERS WILL BE SHOT ON SIGHT

The dogs watched. At the entrance, the horseman pulled cables to close off the space between the fences on both sides of it. He then opened the outer entrance for the visitors. Next, the inner entrance was opened and the outer one closed. Finally, the inner entrance was closed, and the area between the fences was reopened, allowing the dogs to move freely. They seemed disappointed to be shut out of some potential security work. "It looks like anyone could get in," said Ara.

"Yes, it does," said the horseman, but with a subtle smile, he added, "Would you like to see the burial ground for those who thought that previously? Stay close to me until you are in the headquarters."

And they did for the next three miles, moving ever closer to what must be the center. The poles continually converged and increased in height until they were about 150 feet from the center. There, the poles stopped, forming a three-hundred-foot circle of thousand-foot-tall poles. They were probably three feet apart. From the top of the poles, the cables fed down to a center concrete building that looked to be four stories tall. It was round, looking very much like a low water tower. About a hundred feet from the concrete structure was a log cabin of about two thousand square feet marked simply HEADQUARTERS. It didn't look like it fit in at all.

When they entered the cabin, the horseman stayed at the door and stood watch. The inside of the cabin was decorated with colorful blankets, pictures, flow charts, and protocol posters. Above the foyer door hung a mission statement: "Protect the Gate from Man to serve Mankind." It was signed "Chief Robert Builds With Hands, June 29, 2066."

Past the foyer was a very large walnut desk. Behind the desk was a black-haired beauty with smooth skin and black eyes. She stood to greet the pilgrims, showing that she was about five feet two inches tall, in excellent physical shape, and wearing jeans with matching jacket.

She came around the desk, smiling, and shook the hands of the pilgrims, apparently not noticing that they were at least twice her size. And then, without skipping a beat, the smile left her face, and she said, "I am Summer Snow. I am the gatekeeper. What do you want?"

Oh, great! We're off to another not-so-smooth start, thought Naki, but also thinking this "pilgrim" thing might be working, he said, "Our commune has taken upon itself the mission of documenting the history of great people and what they had contributed just before the death flu destroyed so many lives. That is our pilgrimage. One of the people we were hoping to find was Chief Robert Builds With Hands, or as he later became known, Bob the Builder. Today, we learned that he has died and that you are his daughter and have been named the gatekeeper. Would you provide us with few moments of your time for an interview? My name is Na-Ki-Ir, and this is Ara-Ri-El. We go by Naki and Ara."

Showing some annoyance, Summer Snow simply said, "OK. You have thirty minutes."

Naki expected a break in the apparent ice shield as he'd seen in most cases when they were interacting with people. Giving more time for the ice shield to drop, he started with "We understand how your father got his name, being the one responsible for building the support infrastructure here. How were you given your name?"

"OK, if that's how you want to waste your time. I was born in 2060 on July twentieth. As I'm sure your commune knows, the ocean currents had stopped, resulting in a disruption of nearly all predictable weather. It happened to snow on July twentieth. I'm told the snow came in like a winter blizzard, and there was nearly two feet of it on the ground when my mother gave birth. It didn't take a genius to figure out a name for me."

And, thought Ara, *you've been frosty ever since, would be my guess*. But instead, he said, "You seem to be quite young. How did you end up in charge?"

Summer bristled with that comment and said rather firmly, "Maybe because I know what I'm doing!" And then, a little more calmly, "My mother was left in charge when my father died. People were working in pretty close quarters back then, so when one got the death flu, just about everyone else got it and died. My father was one of them. Many of us on the reservation have always remained somewhat isolated, so, while devastated, the Cheyenne River Sioux Indian population stayed relatively strong. There are over six hundred of us here in Ziebach County. Half of us watch this facility, and the rest provide support with farming and such.

"In answer to your rude question, my mother wanted me to be prepared for the future and encouraged me to go to one of the few schools left with instructors. I went to the Massachusetts Institute of Technology and earned a degree in civil engineering. So, while I have only the most basic understanding of how the Gate works, I understand the engineering principles behind the cabling system that is spread out over the county. I am not the chief, but when my mother died, the chief and the elders looked for the best person to be in charge of the facility. I had the best qualifications. Since the government has left this facility in the hands of the Sioux, no one argued. I have been in charge for the past eighteen months with a staff of about two hundred and fifty. We maintain what we can and protect the facility. We assume the actual technology still works, but who knows. There are no operators. I thought you wanted to know about my father."

"We do," said Naki. "He obviously knew what he was doing to get the Gate location here. Did he build the Gate as well?"

Summer, showing a great deal of pride and seeming to calm down further, said, "My father was a contractor and organizer. The site-award language included a guarantee that the residents of Ziebach County would have the right of first refusal for any jobs. No one had any high-tech skills, but most people here had a lot of experience with mining and the heavy equipment that goes along with that. So, installing the cable system and gatehouse was a natural."

Ara said, "It just looks like a bunch of poles with cables. That seems pretty simple."

"On the surface, yes, but think of the big picture," said Summer. "The entire layout is about six miles in diameter. Just below the ground surface is a horizontal mat of cables laid with a tolerance of no more than two hundredths of a percent from horizontal. After a severe winter with deep frost, it has to be checked and in some places reset. You can see the aboveground cable system, but below the surface is a mirror image with cables going into the ground up to a thousand feet near the center of the array. All of that feeds to the actual Gate located in the concrete bunker next door.

"The actual Gate through which people and things pass is in one floor, oriented so that it is split by the surrounding landscape grade. Support systems and controls are in the remaining four levels. The power needed to feed this monster enters through tunnels that were carved into the earth below the lowest transmitting cables and then brought up to large transformers and coils—actually a huge bunker full of transformers and coils. The coils actually pulse out rings of power through a wormhole rather than a continuous stream of energy. I'm told the temperature level in there when it was in operation was unbelievable in spite of the massive ventilating system to keep it cool. In fact, everything outside the central bunker and within the diameter of the cable array can get so hot the ground has been known to burn. This office will be moved if—I mean, when—the Gate is reactivated. If it stayed here, it would be toast. Don't waste your time asking me how it works. I don't know and wouldn't tell you if I did."

Naki asked, "When was it last used?"

Summer said, "Well, that would be 2071. In spite of what were thought to be prudent precautions, a death-flu carrier made it through the Gate to Mars. As far as we can tell, no one there in the colony survived."

"And no one has gone to Mars to check things out?" asked Ara.

"Do you guys know anything at all? Where the hell is this commune of yours that you are so ignorant? When the death flu was introduced into any cluster of people, they almost all died. Technical groups that worked closely together died. That's why we have none here. School populations stood no chance. Neither did city dwellers. I don't think there is anyone left who can operate this thing, but our mission is to protect it in case there is someone and when the space fleet dials home. I hope when they dial home, we can answer the call. So no, no one has gone to Mars to check things out. Now, I think you've wasted enough of my time, so you can leave now." Summer had mellowed considerably since Naki and Ara had arrived, but even so, she abruptly stood up and left the room.

The horseman came into the room and, as the pilgrims were being escorted out, Ara asked, "Do you like working for her?"

Without any change in facial expression, the horseman said, "She is a very tough cookie but very fair and very, very smart. I think she spends all her free time trying to figure out how to the run the Gate."

"So," started Naki, "you all still get paychecks?"

"Cash, not a check," said the horseman. "Someone from the government comes here once a year in April to count noses and hand out money. No one from the government seems to do much beyond that. Oh, and we pay our taxes during that same visit. They give and then take back."

When the pilgrims were outside the barrier and out of sight, Naki said to Ara, "This is turning into something quite extraordinary. I'm beginning to get a sense of what we're supposed to do, but I don't know why. I'm glad it is Gabe who has to figure it out and not me." With that, they activated their packs and headed for Alaska.

Chapter 12
East Coast

On July 14, 2085, when Naki and Ara went south, Kem-U-El and Ere-Mi-El had headed toward the East Coast of North America, flying over a good portion of Canada and the Great Lakes. Like most of the Els, Kem and Ere were relatives; in this case, cousins. It was common for relations to be placed on the same team as they seemed to agree more readily. Only Na-Ki-Ir and Schem-Hampha-Rae were unrelated, but there had been an opening on Gabe's team, and Naki had been assigned. Schem had been there for so long, no one knew anything different. Naki blended in quite well, but still, Kem and Ere were glad to be on this mission together.

When they had reached the town of Superior, Wisconsin, they'd settled in for a landing. So far, they had attracted little attention as they flew from Augustine Island. They had stopped briefly at an abandoned filling station/convenience store and had found a few cans of beans and corned-beef hash. With a pan they had also located, they built a small fire and cooked themselves a meal. It didn't really satisfy their appetite, but it stopped their stomachs from complaining so much. But now, they were tired and needed a more filling meal.

Superior seemed to reflect what they had been seeing nearly everywhere, with not much in the way of population. The ore terminals looked like they had been abandoned for a hundred years, and while the rest of the town also looked to be nearly abandoned, those abandoned structures looked like they had been vacated a lot longer. Kem and Ere landed in a quiet location near the train yard, furled their antigravity packs, and walked into town.

As they walked, a few people saw them and stared. After all, it isn't every day you see a couple of very large people with long, silver-blond hair, dressed in white from head to toe. Kem asked one older gentleman, "Excuse me, sir, we're looking for a good place to eat. Nothing fancy, just good food. Do you have a suggestion?"

The old gent, observing the obvious: "You fellas ain't from around here, are yah?"

"Well, no," said Ere, "we're just passing through, heading east."

"We don't see many outsiders around here. How'd yah git here?" asked the old gent.

"Oh, we hitched a ride on the train," said Ere, trying to think fast.

"What train?" said the old gent. "There hasn't been a train through here in years."

"Really? Well, it's not important," said Kem. "We just want to eat. Where's the problem?"

With a few more people gathering around, the old gent must have figured he was on a roll and continued with "I'm not sure we want a couple of weirdos like you two in any place we might like to go." And then he stared up at Kem and Ere, his eyes squinting.

"OK," said Kem. "Don't get your tail feathers ruffled. I guess we'll just move along and find someplace to eat on our own."

And as the old gent was starting to get annoyed and was now attracting more attention, Ere motioned to Kem, and they simultaneously unfurled their antigravity panels, turned the palms of their hands skyward, raised their heads slightly, and lifted off the ground. All that took less than a second, and as they lifted off, they looked below to see a dozen faces upturned toward them with mouths wide open. "Hmmm," groaned Ere, "that didn't go so well, did it?"

"Nope," agreed Kem, "and I'm still tired and hungry. We should probably start thinking about carrying some food with us."

"I suppose," said Ere, "but it cramps my style when we don't travel light."

"'Cramps your style'? What style would that be?" retorted Kem.

Ere smirked. "I shall not dignify that comment with a response."

They flew on until they came to what seemed to be a well-traveled highway. Following that, they eventually found a roadside diner with a very large tractor-trailer rig outside. "I haven't seen many of those being used," observed Kem.

"It looks like it's military," said Ere, and they landed out of sight of the diner.

When they entered the place, it was confirmed that the truck was military as there were two soldiers dressed in fatigues sitting at the counter, eating apple pie and drinking coffee. There were four or five civilians in the diner as Kem and Ere went in, and, as usual, everyone turned to stare at the newcomers.

Without saying a word, Kem and Ere went to a booth and sat down. A very pretty, middle-aged waitress pensively approached the pair and asked if they knew what they wanted. Ere asked, "What do you recommend?"

And the waitress responded with huge laugh, "I recommend you not eat the food here. But since there isn't any place else around, I'd go for the pork chops, unless you guys are vegetarians. Or maybe something else." She eyed them from head to toe.

"We'll start with that," said Kem. "An order each, and maybe some iced tea?"

"Raspberry iced tea?" asked the waitress.

"Excellent," said Ere.

As the waitress left with the order, Kem asked, "Hey, did you notice how the old guy got uptight around us? That's a little off, don't you think? Usually, people mellow out when they are with us."

Ere responded with, "Yes, but I've noticed in the past that if someone is generally angry about everything, they may mellow out around us, but relative to everybody else, they are still uptight."

"Man, then he must be a charmer."

When they finished off the platter of food left in front of them, they ordered hamburgers and then split an apple pie.

The soldiers who had been finishing their meal when Kem and Ere came in didn't seem to be a hurry to leave, and they kept looking over their shoulders at the pair. When Kem and Ere finally appeared to be done, the soldiers came over and invited themselves to sit in their booth. Both soldiers appeared to be in their late forties.

A little unusual for soldiers to be this old, thought Kem, but he said, "Hi, can we help you?"

Soldier number one, whose tag displayed the name "Falkner" and whose uniform showed he was a master sergeant, said, "Well, sir, we were just wondering where you two are coming from and where you're going. You sure aren't from around here or anywhere else we've been. Not many people travel very far these days, so we're the exception, and gotta say, we never ran into the likes of you two before. So we're just wonderin'."

Kem said, "We're nothing special. We're from a commune in Colorado Springs. We're heading east, no place special. We thought we'd like to see the Atlantic Ocean and maybe pick up some culture. Maybe Boston, Massachusetts."

Soldier number two, whose nametag said "Roberts" and who was also clearly a master sergeant, nearly yelled out "Boston! If you go to Boston, you'll see the Atlantic, all right. Boston was flooded out years ago, and only a handful of people have stuck around, living in the tall buildings like they were islands. Islands with no power or freshwater, that is. Must be great. I guess they think the tide will be going out soon." And he laughed.

"Oh," said Kem. "I suppose we should have thought of that. Any suggestions?"

Falkner wasn't sure why he said it, but he did: "We're going to Andover, Massachusetts. There's enough room in the rig for you guys if you want to tag along. It's a long haul, and a couple of riders can make the trip seem shorter. You can bail any time you'd like."

Roberts nodded in agreement but added, "You're on your own for food and lodging. If you eat like this at every meal, I'd hate to pay the bill."

Kem honestly said, "That's very generous of you. We accept. But if you think we're becoming a bother, let us know. We'll bid you farewell with no hard feelings." And then he added, "Isn't giving us a ride going to get you in some kind of trouble with your commanding officers?"

"Ha!" said Roberts. "No one else wants this job, so they leave us alone. As long we get the job done, they don't care how we do it."

When the waitress came over with the bill, Kem handed her two gold coins and asked, "Will that cover it?"

"Uh, uh…" stuttered the waitress. "I don't think we can make change on these. Are they for real?"

"Oh, they're real. You can keep any change. Great service and all that," said Ere as he, Kem, and the two soldiers got up and left.

Falkner asked, "You always pay your bills like that?"

"When we can. It seems to be accepted everywhere we go," said Kem.

"Really?" Said Roberts sarcastically. "I can't imagine why."

The truck cab was massive, with five very comfortable captain's seats—two in the front and three just behind. As the four got into the truck, Roberts asked, "You guys ever worried about getting robbed? I assume you have more of those coins, and they're worth a fortune. No one carries that stuff around."

Kem answered, "We find the coins are good currency anywhere and at any time. We have never been robbed. If someone were to attempt such a thing, we'd hand the coins over but with a warning. We have ways of getting the coins back, and there would be consequences. Not many people express aggression toward us, though we did have a small incident earlier today. I suppose anything is possible."

Falkner said, "I think this is going to be an interesting ride."

The roads the truck traveled had been at one time the envy of every nation. The Eisenhower Interstate Highway System had connected every major city in the country. It still did, for the most part, but some bridges had failed, and the road surface in many places was in a state of decay as Mother Nature did her best to reclaim the ground below. Still, the truck was able to make pretty good time, reaching Massachusetts in five days.

The soldiers obviously knew the route, where to stop and eat, and where to stay at night. They could have slept in the truck, but they had no reason to do that, so they didn't. Kem and Ere would also get a room each night and continued to impress everyone who saw how much food they could consume. At one point, Falkner said to them, "You guys eat like you haven't eaten in decades," at which Ere and Kem just looked at each other and roared with laughter but never responded to the comment beyond that.

Kem and Ere entertained their companions with stories, many touched with humor. As the trip progressed, the soldiers became more and more relaxed, though even from the beginning they had seemed quite comfortable with everything around them. The sergeants seemed more than willing to talk, giving Kem and Ere an opportunity to learn a lot more about the world they had reentered.

Falkner and Roberts had joined the military back in 2057, the same year the interstellar space fleet left Earth's orbit. Back then, the US military had been the most dominant force on the planet. The US military had been in just about every corner of the globe, but its mission was to intimidate with its might without going into combat. It was tricky but it seemed to work. There were exceptions, like in the Middle East. There, just about every country outside of the region had decided to leave it alone and let its factions continue to fight among themselves and kill each other off. Apparently, they did a pretty good job at it, and the population of that region and parts of Africa kept falling as the rest of the world's population exploded.

In 2071, the death-flu pandemic had struck, and suddenly, the world had a renewed interest in the Middle East. With little to no health system left in place because of the continuous fighting, the death flu really took hold and reduced the population to such a level, anyone would have thought there was no fight left in the region. While that might have been seen by some as an exaggeration, the close proximity of the fighters to each other meant the disease spread rapidly and with no hope of a cure, militant numbers did dwindle. Citizens already isolated fared comparatively well while the militants nearly disappeared—but not quite—and those left kept fighting. It was pathetic.

The scenario was similar in parts of Africa as well, and to a lesser extent around the globe. The United States and the European Union had a different kind of problem. Concentrated population centers such as cities, large towns, and military complexes were also transportation hubs. The death flu moved quickly from one area to another and then within these population centers, leaving little chance to avoid the disease. There were few, very few, who survived once they caught it and by default ended up left with the grim task of disposing of the massive number of bodies. The preferred method was incineration in an attempt to destroy the disease. Barges in New York harbor, as an example, were loaded with bodies and then set on fire. It was hell on Earth.

The military establishment had had mixed results. If the death flu made it into a unit, few survived. Other units that went into isolation mode kept the disease out. Ships at sea were a prime example. Aircraft carriers fared worst, as pilots unaware they had the disease would bring it back to the ships, where it spread. Crews on escort vessels and submarines were usually isolated. While the pandemic didn't reach their ships, they could only watch in horror as the sailors on other ships within their fleet died, leaving floating graveyards. Many jumped overboard, preferring to drown rather than suffer from the illness.

When the death flu had completed its devastation, most government structures changed. After all, politicians weren't immune. In the United States, martial law was put in place, and senior military officers took charge at the state and federal levels. The average citizen who survived the pandemic didn't see much of a change as far as interaction with government was concerned, except there was less of it.

In many cases, local government completely disappeared, as did health care and grade schools. This meant no taxes at the local level. State taxes plummeted, but federal taxes remained the same as the military now had a new mission, and money was needed to keep it relatively strong. Internally, militant groups sprang up. Drug lords in Mexico and other countries farther south had taken over their countries and were now flexing their muscles toward the United States. North Korea, which had been isolated from the rest of the world, had remained reasonably intact and was now a world power looking to expand its own idea of government. The US military, though much smaller than before the pandemic, was still strong and quite determined to protect the country.

There was a major problem for the military, however. The defense industry that had supplied it had been devastated. Much of the problem had started as far back as the 1970s. Technology, especially in the field of computer-chip design, had become so sophisticated that only computers could design new computer chips.

Engineers dealt with concepts, not design. Manufacturing that had relied on computers and robots was hit hard as equipment failure became the new reality. The entire technologically run world was operating at such a precarious level that it didn't take much for it to topple. The death flu was an extreme blow, setting humankind back decades and with a further decline forecasted by the few who cared.

For the technology-dependent military to keep functioning, it had to salvage parts from donor equipment for reuse. One company, Raytheon, in Andover, Massachusetts, had been a technological leader for the military before the death flu hit. After the pandemic passed, they found they had few human resources left. A few clever engineers who did survive knew that they couldn't rebuild the company to what it had been previously, so they devised a new business plan to reverse engineer equipment when possible and use salvaged parts to maintain the military's needs. This wasn't high tech, and it didn't always yield satisfactory results. They would take parts out and put parts in. They would make some mechanical parts, but anything with a circuit board was simply a puzzlement, so if a replacement electronic part looked good, they would try it out. If it wasn't any good, they soon found out, but sometimes with disastrous results for a pilot or equipment operator.

This is where Falkner and Roberts came in. They were one team of soldiers that would salvage parts and transport them to the Raytheon facilities for reuse. Or if rebuilt equipment was small enough, they would transport it back to a military base to be used. It was the army that had been tasked with this mission for all the military branches as most items were small and could be transported over land. That was what the sergeants were doing now. They had a full trailer of components that had been removed from nonfunctioning fighter aircraft and were heading to Raytheon. Some would be used right away; some would be placed in inventory. This was all they did, and they found it to be a pretty good job.

Both had been married with families but lost everyone to the death flu and now regarded each other as their only family. Their common roots were the military, and their truck was their base of operations. One might think that this relationship, combined with their unique talent for finding the right part, was why at their age, they were still in the army. As Kem and Ere learned, however, that wasn't the only reason.

Early in the century, it was becoming obvious that the human population was getting too large for the planet. The Chinese had experimented with planned parenthood, trying to mandate one child per couple. That had had some success, but other ethnic groups and religions saw children as a blessing, professing that more were better, as it was what God wanted. By the 2030s and 2040s, nearly every organized religion and legitimate government started to push for birth control, and it suddenly became the new normal. In fact, those who wanted to have children were often shamed into not having any. This attitude became so prevalent that not only was marriage no longer considered essential, couples seldom remained couples for very long. Friendship groups took over, and casual sex was the norm.

Even those who wanted to get married or have children had second thoughts as the birth-defect-causing Zika virus had expanded along with climate change. Few were willing to take the chance of being burdened with a child who would require massive amounts of care for life.

This mind-set had been carried through to the present day after the pandemic to such an extent that instead of the human population rebounding, it was continuing to decrease. Young recruits for anything were rare, and just like the rest of society, the military was adapting as its forces began to gray. People were required to stay on active duty longer. This tidbit of information just came out in a casual exchange with Falkner and Roberts, but it was the most distressing of everything Kem and Ere had learned up to this point. What was the human population's current direction? Why had the habitat systems waited so long to usher in assistance?

When the truck was within fifty miles of Andover, Kem and Ere thanked the soldiers for the ride and said that they needed to go on their own from there. Falkner and Roberts both said that this had been the most relaxed drive they had ever taken and thanked Kem and Ere profusely. "You two are the strangest guys we've ever run into, but we had a great time. We certainly hope to run into you two again sometime." The sergeants were nearly in tears when Kem and Ere bid farewell.

Kem and Ere found an abandoned park not far from where they had gotten out of the truck. Their original plan had been to reach the East Coast and have a look around and maybe interview a few people. After listening to the soldiers, they now thought this would be a waste of time. They knew, however, that Gabe would not be happy with them if they didn't at least take a look. They decided to camp out in the park for the night, and as the sun was rising in the morning, they would fly over to Boston Harbor and take a look from there. They figured that the sunrise behind them would mask most of the golden glow their antigravity packs produced.

At dawn, they deployed their packs and headed east. They hadn't had any breakfast yet, but they decided to suffer a little. When they reached Boston, they weren't shocked, as they'd had plenty of warning, but it was still very disquieting to see what had become of the city. Most levies that had been built decades ago had been breached, turning Boston streets into canals. Maybe half of the buildings looked to be in pretty decent shape, sticking up out of the water. Others were in various states of collapse. Some had fallen over, some had collapsed into the subway tunnels, and some looked as though they had been hit by fierce winds and simply left as they stood, with broken windows and damaged roofs and walls. Many of the better-looking buildings had small boats of different types tied to makeshift docks, and there were some signs of life but not much. "I've seen enough," said Kem in a quiet voice.

"Yeah," agreed Ere. "Let's get out of here. Let's get something to eat and head for Albany, the apparent center of government for this part of the continent."

They flew west, running the risk of being seen flying by a few people. They would stay high and move quickly, causing anyone seeing them to get an unclear image. Once past the beltways of the greater metropolitan area, they decided they would cook up a meal of things they could scrounge up. They settled into a remote area in the middle of the state. An old signpost by the road said it was Barre. In Barre, they found a well-tended field with no one around. They made up a meal of summer squash, tomatoes, lettuce, and strawberries. *We don't have to have meat with every meal*, they thought. Silver coins were left on the seat of a very old John Deere tractor that was obviously still being used to tend the fields, in spite of the fact there were no visible control levers or steering wheel.

While relaxing under a shade tree, they were wondering why a farmer would go to the trouble of removing a steering wheel, when the tractor started up. It moved over to a raised tank and stopped, seemingly guided by no one. The fuel cap on the tractor opened, and an arm swung down from the raised tank and seemed to fill it. Once this task was completed, the tractor moved into the field, lowering some type of rototilling apparatus. As it went down the rows, weeds no longer showed. "Well, now," said Ere, "that's different!"

As they watched in fascination, still munching on their meal, two flying objects entered the area and, while hovering over crops, picked what seemed to be the best-looking fruits and vegetables and placed them in attached baskets. When the baskets were filled, they were gently emptied into larger ones along the sides of the fields. Kem and Ere were now done with lunch but watched with even more fascination when an even larger flying machine came onto the scene, dropped a hook, picked up the larger baskets, and headed off.

Kem stated the obvious. "Um, this is a tad more sophisticated than anything we've seen up until now. Let's see where that thing goes."

They deployed their antigravity panels and followed the drone for several miles before reaching what seemed to be a fortified warehouse. The drone dropped its load outside the door and headed back from where it had come. Wheeled robots brought the baskets inside the warehouse. Kem and Ere looked at each other, shrugged, and headed for the door, thinking someone would be inside. As they approached, they noticed large cables heading skyward. Maybe a thousand feet in the air, they saw what appeared to be odd-shaped balloons about sixty feet in diameter. From each, one cable appeared to be a power cable connected on the ground to a series of power transformers.

Inside the warehouse, there were only robots moving, sorting, and repackaging. On the other end of the warehouse were unmanned utility trucks taking the repackaged goods off down the road.

At the front of the warehouse, different-sized drones seemed to come in from all directions, dropping off goods. The inside of the warehouse was packed to the ceiling with fruits, vegetables, and barrels of wine, beer, and alcoholic beverages of all types. In one corner, were several robots that were obviously being recharged. Nowhere did Kem and Ere see anything that was broken or out of place. What they also didn't see were people. There weren't any.

As they watched in fascination, one of the warehouse robots stopped with a groan, and a puff of smoke came out from its lifting arms. Everything in the warehouse stopped momentarily. Two robots moved from the charging area. One took the apparently injured robot to the front entrance, and the other took its place. Everything in the warehouse started up again just as suddenly as it had stopped. One of the larger drones hovered over the stricken robot and hooked it, but before it took off, a voice emanating from speakers within the warehouse boomed, saying, "This is private property! You have no business being here. Please leave immediately, or there will be unpleasant consequences for both of you."

Kem turned to Ere and said, "That sounds like an invitation to me. We need to follow that drone. Something or someone is going to fix it. I'm betting it is the same someone who has invited us to leave. I'd be willing to bet a real, live someone, because last time I checked, robots didn't eat vegetables—at least the ones I'm familiar with."

"Sure, let's follow," said Ere. "Maybe we'll be invited for dinner."

Chapter 13

Unwanted Visitors

When Kem and Ere left the robot-controlled warehouse in Barre, they followed the large drone carrying the damaged warehouse robot. They didn't bother with any subtleties and flew no more than a hundred feet from the drone. It traveled at less than 150 miles per hour at about two hundred feet off of the ground, so it was easy for Kem and Ere to stay with it. The drone flew for about six miles before moving down into a small open area. At one end, protruding from a hillside was the front of a house. To the left and protruding a bit farther into the opening was what appeared to be a small garage. To the right was a sizeable solar array, though it appeared to be close to the end of its full effectiveness. All structures faced south, catching the warm summer sunshine though the house and garage had no windows.

As the drone approached, the garage opened up. Not from the front doors but from doors in the roof. The drone hovered, and the robot was gently lowered. Once it was detached, the drone took off. The roof doors started to close but stopped and reopened wide as another drone appeared with a fifty-gallon wooden barrel. On the side was the single word "merlot" and the date of 2081. Once it was left in the garage, the second drone left, the doors closed, and it was quiet.

Ere and Kem weren't sure what to do next. Go knock on the door? A door that looked as though it hadn't been opened in years? After what seemed to be an eternity, the same voice they had heard at the warehouse boomed out, "What do you want for those flying things you have?"

"They aren't for sale," a somewhat startled Kem answered.

After another eternity, the voice said, "What do you want? You are not welcome here. Go away, or there will be unpleasant consequences for you both."

"Well, sir," said Kem, "if you wouldn't mind listening for just a few minutes, we may have something that would be helpful to you. After that, if you're not interested, we will leave quietly."

"Fine, make it quick," said the voice.

"OK," started Kem. "Based on what we've seen of your operation, you have a number of resources at your disposal. We can only assume right now that you also have people who repair your robots and drones in order to keep you operating. This probably includes rebuilding circuit boards and programming. Is that right?"

"Maybe," was the terse response.

"Um, OK," stammered Kem, not sure where to go from there.

But Ere picked up the train of thought, saying with some exaggeration, "We have been traveling the country, and we have identified sources of parts that might be useful in your enterprise. Also, we know of places that could potentially use the technological skills your operation employs."

"Not interested," said the voice but then adding, "you willing to rent those flying things that you have long enough for me to copy?"

Whoa! thought both Kem and Ere, wondering if this could be an opening, but Kem said, "Maybe. What kind of a deal are we talking about here?"

Still another eternity passed before the voice said, "You hungry?"

Never one to pass up a meal, Ere said, "We could use a good dinner. We've been on the road for some time."

"Wait. We'll talk over some food," said the cold voice. "Give me—us—a little time to prepare something."

Five minutes later, Kem and Ere were sitting in chairs at a large maple table that had been brought out by a couple of robots on tracks. A third robot followed with a tray. On the tray were wine goblets, a carafe filled with red wine, another filled with lemonade, and a third filled with ice water. The robot, sounding very much like the bodiless voice, said, "Please help yourself."

Kem and Ere each poured wine into their goblets, swished it around, put their noses in for a whiff, and took a taste. Ere stared at Kem and said, "We've had this before. Recently!"

Kem agreed very quietly, saying, "This is fine merlot. What do you think the odds would be this made it to the habitat?"

Kem and Ere enjoyed their wine. When they had polished off the carafe, the robots reappeared with more wine and food platters of chicken, lamb, fresh corn, fresh beans, fresh squash, hot rolls, butter, and honey. "Are you joining us?" asked Kem.

"I—we—have our own," was the reply. "There is no reason to go outside. How much to rent one of those flying things?"

"We don't want any money. We have all we need," said Kem. "I will loan you one after I get permission from my supervisor, provided you do us a favor in the future."

"When can I have it? What kind of a favor?" said the voice.

"Since I need this thing for now, I will have to come back. Give me one month. As far as the favor is concerned, I'm not sure what that will be. But when I come back, I'll tell you then. If you are not happy with the arrangements, we can call off the deal. Is that OK with you?"

"I can wait," said the voice.

"I have a couple of questions, if you don't mind," said Ere.

"I do mind, but go ahead," said the voice.

Ere thought, *This guy is a real beaut*, but he said, "Can we have your name?"

"My name is Abel Fisher," was the answer.

"OK, Abel, just out of curiosity, do you have your own winery?" asked Ere.

"Yes."

"Did you by chance miss a barrel of this fine vintage?" Ere continued.

"Yes," said Abel. "How did you know about that? Some gold coins were found where the barrel had been. How did you get in to do that?"

"Oh, it wasn't us," said Kem, knowing the statement probably wasn't completely accurate, "but we might tell you how it happened when we return."

"Fine. You can leave now," said Abel.

As Kem and Ere unfurled their antigravity panels and lifted off, Ere said to Kem, "Do you really think Gabe will let you loan this guy an antigravity pack?"

"Maybe," said Kem. "It isn't like he could ever figure it out and actually copy it."

From inside the house, Abel watched the monitors as the unwanted visitors left. Something inside of him hoped they would, in fact, return. The thought of getting his hands on something like those flying things was almost more than he could stand. For the first time in years, he felt excited. Forget that the size of those two was daunting and the clothes they wore were strange. They had something he wanted.

Something else was now strange. Abel seldom got out of bed, and he hadn't worn any real clothes in years, but suddenly, for no apparent reason, he felt a degree of self-consciousness. He actually felt a need to get out of his bed. He went to find some pajamas. What was happening to him? Did those two guys exercise some sort of mind control? Abel didn't know what to feel, but somehow, wearing clothes for the first time in many years, he knew he was feeling something, something very different and not part of the game.

Outside, the sky was getting darker, and the barometric pressure had started to fall. Within a couple of hours, another legacy of climate change came home to roost with the third hurricane for the summer. This one would deliver 232-mile-per-hour winds and leave five inches of rain in its wake. Abel took this in stride, however. His home and warehouse were well fortified, and his army of robots and drones would repair any damage to his holdings. It was just part of the game!

Winter, he knew, was potentially a different matter. The prediction of a miniature ice age following the interruption of the Gulf Stream had come true. While there was actually no detectable movement of any new glaciers being formed in the north, the massive amounts of snow that had fallen for the past decade was having an impact, especially on the other side of the Atlantic Ocean. But even in the state of New Maritime, people were gradually moving south to Abel's region to escape the seemingly never-ending winter. He didn't like the thought of people invading his game zone. *Why does life have to be so complicated?* he wondered. This was followed be the startling thought of, *Oh no! Were those two guys part of an advance party? I had better be on my guard.*

Abel went and found some anxiety medication. Some pills and some wine were a good fix.

Chapter 14
Sherman Hamer, the Finn

Sherman Hamer was easy to spot in any crowd. Being six feet eight inches and weighing in at 250 pounds would probably be enough to set him apart from the rest of the crew. But his shoulder-length, nearly silver-blond hair and smooth white skin made him seem to glow when he entered a room. With his believably Finnish name, it was easy for people to buy that he was from Finland, hence his nickname "the Finn." And, typical of most Finlanders, he was not very talkative. On the other hand, he was a great listener, and as the Starship *Russia*'s chief brewer and bartender, he was in great demand for that. A couple of strong beers in a crew member would tend to loosen him or her up and encourage the sharing of thoughts and feelings, with the understanding that the Finn wouldn't compromise any confidence.

When the UNSC had put its crews together, its primary focus had been on the technology of the ships and the Gate. It did not overlook the needs of the crews for the long haul, however, and had gone out of its way to find the best people in support roles. Everyone had to show that he or she offered something special. The Finn had showed up at the interview speaking fluent Russian and with his version of Trappist beer that he had brewed. And since he had potentially been signing up for the Starship *Russia*, he clandestinely demonstrated his ability to make drinkable vodka out of almost thin air. The official policy was nothing stronger than beer and wine on any of the starships, but, people being people, it had been expected that rules would be bent, and the predominantly Russian crew on that particular starship liked their vodka, even if it was "Finnish" vodka.

Just like everyone else's, the Finn's background had been carefully checked. Nothing anywhere, from local law enforcement to Interpol, had showed any issues with the Finn. In fact, there was little information on him at all. Listed places of employment had either failed financially or been destroyed, so references were sketchy. But there was something about the guy that made everyone feel at ease, and the Finn was welcomed aboard.

Who knows what the interviewers would have thought if they had known the truth. Oh, it was nothing bad. In fact, as far as his recent history, there really wasn't any at all. The Finn's made-up background as Sherman Hamer had only been a few days old when he'd appeared for the interview as a possible replacement for the man who had been selected years earlier but suddenly left the crew. Since the starship fleet had been only a few days from departure, the interviewer had had to fill all newly opened positions quickly, and there in front of him was what appeared to be the perfect man for the job.

The Finn could have applied for any job, and he would have been qualified based on his background and training, but he thought that as chief brewer and head bartender, he had found the best way to maintain a quiet persona while keeping his ear open to virtually everything that went on in the ship and the fleet.

One month prior to the fleet launch, Schem-Hampha-Rae, or Schem, as his teammates called him, was woken from stasis. It was his turn to be the first awake. He had endured the twenty-four hours of stasis cleansing finding himself in a very different situation from anything his team, or any other team, for that matter, had ever experienced. The world leaders were about to send off nearly a hundred thousand people on a voyage to another star system. It seemed to Schem that the habitat's system should have woken him earlier, but on the other hand, he wasn't sure there was a crisis.

Schem had checked the habitat's logs and saw that Naki had been called out in 1960 when the world was killing itself off with chemicals. "Better living through chemistry" might have been the mantra, but with a little push from Naki to the author Rachel Carson, the world woke up to the fact that while living was possibly better with them, not all chemicals were good, and overuse of the good ones was just as bad. The direction the planet had been going in was changed for the better.

This was something different. The alert was for the fleet, but Schem wasn't sure what, if anything, was wrong beyond what seemed to be a desperate attempt by the world leaders to distract the world population from the grim reality of too many people. Schem felt led to a decision. Right or wrong, it was his decision to make, and make it he did. Before heading off to join the fleet, Schem had entered into the habitat's log:

May 4, 2067. I was woken from stasis with an alert that the world leaders were making what could be considered a desperate move to pacify the world population but could also in fact move humankind beyond the bounds of Earth's own solar system. After reviewing options, I determined that one of us, in this case me, should become part of the crew of fifteen thousand on one of the six starships being launched on June 29, 2067, toward Epsilon Eridani. My intention is to monitor the progress of the fleet and the well being of the crews and to transmit updates when possible. It is my belief that the habitat systems will wake more team members from stasis if the situation on Earth requires it. As for me, I believe my place is with the fleet, as that is where the alert was focused. However, I am suspicious that the habitat system's sensitivity calibration may be off and recommend that recalibration by headquarters be requested. My one concern is that no one else will be removed from stasis, and I will be left alone.

My blessings to you,
Schem-Hampha-Rae

When the ships launched, Schem had used his portable transmitter to update the log:

Today, June 29, 2067, the fleet was ordered to cast off. All systems on the ships appear to be functioning as designed. The general mood of the crews is extremely upbeat. In spite of the prospect of such a long voyage, there is an air of excitement bordering on euphoria.

My blessings to you,
Schem-Hampha-Rae

But that was then. For the next eighteen years, Schem sent out monthly updates, never certain if the messages had been received. He assumed that the rest of the team was probably still in stasis and not reading his messages, as he did initially receive acknowledgments that his messages were being logged for later reference. However, as the fleet moved farther from Earth, the more traditional communications system he was using became less reliable. He hoped by all that was mighty that his own portable transmitter wasn't too weak to receive anything. He wondered if he was now completely isolated from the team, and, should they awake, what they would think. Eventually, he thought his clandestine communications device might get some use if and when Gabe came out of stasis.

Right now, here in the present, he supposed he had enough to think about, and it was troubling. Just about everyone on his ship seemed relaxed, comfortable with their duties, and generally leading normal lives—as normal as they could be, living with 14,999 of one's closest friends in a pressurized cylinder.

Sergey sat at the bar with his sixth tall, strong beer with a little something on the side. Normally, Schem, taking on the role of the Finn, would shut someone off before this, but this engineer had something on his mind, and he felt it was important to learn what it was. "Sergey, you seem to be very bothered tonight. What's the trouble?" asked the Finn.

"You mean other than the day/night bull? They should come up with something else. Maybe work everyone on the eight-bells cycle of the old sailing days. Maybe toss in a gong to indicate which four-hour sequence we're on," mumbled Sergey, making a little sense.

Sergey was the third-class engineer on Schem's ship. Most all of the operating engineers demonstrated an exception to the upbeat attitude shown by the rest of the crew. The engineers never relaxed. Most worked long hours, and when they weren't working, they spent an inordinate amount of time in the bar. Almost all of them had a regular source for their beloved vodka in the Finn. Sergey, however, was even more uptight than the rest, and the Finn thought that Sergey might be the one to confide in him as to what was wrong in engineering. "Yes," said the Finn, "you guys in engineering are always uptight. Is the chief engineer that hard of a taskmaster?"

At bit more alert at that comment and taking his time to respond, Sergey said slowly, "Well, no. The chief is fine. Did someone say something?"

"No, no one said anything," said the Finn, "but every one of you guys comes in here between shifts, and every one of you, including the chief, by the way, is uptight and then drinks too much. You guys must be a blast in your quarters. You're married, right?"

"Yah. And my wife nags me about the drinking." And, looking around the room, Sergey added, "especially with the vodka you brew up."

"I don't give you that much vodka," said the Finn.

"No," said Sergey, "but there are other sources. There are those who will swap it for a favor. Especially those who have time for a hobby and need something special from engineering. And how come you're so nosey tonight, or today, or whatever it is? You usually just listen."

"Oh, I'd listen," said the Finn, "if you and your buddies had anything to say. But all you guys do is drink. I figured if I asked, maybe the *engineer* in one of you guys will act more human and let it out. You wouldn't believe some of the crap I listen to."

"Like what?" asked Sergey.

"Oh, come on, you know I can't divulge bartender-customer privileged information. It would be against my sacred bartender vows of confidentiality," said the Finn with a wry smile.

"You are so full of crap," said Sergey, but he smiled a little, too. "Come on, give me some dirt."

"OK…did you hear that they want some volunteers to swap places with people on other ships? The counselors think it will be good to have the crews interact more beyond the soccer games. Don't you guys in engineering do something like that already?"

At that, Sergey got visibly upset and said, "We only go to another ship for cross-training! Nothing more!"

Pushing more than he probably should, the Finn asked, "Cross-train on what? Aren't the ships' propulsion systems all the same?"

"We learn new things." Sergey got up, looked around the bar and then back at the Finn, and left.

"*Engineering is wound up way too tight. Something just isn't right*," thought the bartender, now thinking as Schem and not the passive Sherman Hamer.

Chapter 15

The original schedule for the interstellar fleet to leave orbit had been early 2067, but the inevitable delays in any large project had pushed the launch off until June 29. Still, that wasn't bad for an endeavor of its size. Trajectory calculations did not make this an ideal date, but because of the distance involved, it would work. Scientists and engineers on board the fleet had the ability to modify the flight plan as they moved toward their target. In fact, they could change the target when they had a better idea of the exact conditions on the ground.

At 265 days from launch, the fleet was close to three-quarters light speed. Scientists had calculated that the ships could probably go even faster, but since they were dealing with a huge unknown, they had set a conservative maximum. With all the other unknowns with this adventure, adding a little safety factor had seemed prudent.

With the engines temporarily diverting the plasma drive and reduced in power, the auxiliary thrusters on the bow and stern of each ship turned the vessels around very slowly. A fast turn would have created too much centrifugal force at the ends of the ships, forcing people and things into places where they weren't supposed to be. But the essentially zero-gravity period during the turn also had consequences that required full crew cooperation. Everything that wasn't "nailed" down had to be secured. This included any soils and vegetation.

Nets were spread prior to the turn and ratcheted down. People who couldn't stand being weightless were required to stay in their quarters and tie themselves down. Most, however, thought it was pretty cool to have this break from gravity, and if not assigned to a task, they acted like kids. At the sound of the final alarm, people moved toward the deck or chairs and waited for the engines to kick in and force everything down, though at one-third the force they had experienced getting to this point. With fifteen thousand people on board, it wasn't surprising that some didn't pay attention, at least for this first turn, and they fell to the deck or whatever was below them.

Sickbay was overwhelmed for a few days with broken bones and sometimes worse, depending upon what the nonconformers had fallen upon.

After that first turn back in 2068, Admiral Nimitz had called his senior staff together for a little celebration. All the ships had made the turn with apparently no major incidents, and he was elated. Everyone was congratulatory except Marvin Swartz, Vice Admiral of Operations, who remained rather quiet while tossing down wine. "Marvin!" exclaimed the admiral, "What is your problem? This is supposed to be a celebration!"

"Well," started the VAO, "I suppose it is, but the turn wasn't flawless. I was going to submit a report after I got the details."

Nimitz said with a lighthearted smile, "You and your operations engineers always have some kind of problem. What is it this time?"

Everyone except Marvin chuckled, but the mood in the room suddenly became more sedate.

"Oh," said Marvin, "it's nothing we can't handle. Your message to Fleet Command on Earth that all went well is all they need to know. However, Starship *India* had a devil of time diverting the plasma stream on engine number four. They're running a diagnosis to see if they can figure out why. And Starship *China* lost a bow thruster and had to use a shuttle to complete the turn. Both of these incidents seem minor. But this is our first of many more turns, and the operating engineers are expressing universal concern."

Nimitz said, "You have the best engineering minds on your crews that mankind has ever assembled in one place. I'm sure you and the operating engineers will work it all out."

As he said this, he remembered that the engineers had been required to sign a code of confidentiality that excluded everyone outside the operations group, including him. He had wondered about that but assumed that Marvin would tell him if there were any serious issues. After all, he was the admiral responsible for the success of this mission. Why would anyone keep important information from him? They wouldn't, of course. Would they?

If the admiral had known the answers to his questions in 2068, perhaps history would have recorded something different.

Instead, the answers would be reveled seven years later to someone else.

Chapter 16
Disaster

By 2075, seven years after the first turn, Sherman Hamer, the Finn, had successfully transferred from one ship to another over the years, so he had now been in all except the Starship *South America*. It proved handy, being fluent in every language, though he seldom demonstrated his ability. English had been established as the universal language on the ships long before the fleet launch, and it was used for all formal communications. But being the bartender and knowing the local language in a bar where people might want to have private conversations allowed the Finn to pick up the most useful information.

For one thing, he had learned that the fleet was no longer in communication with Earth. The "news from home" was being fabricated to maintain morale. This had been going on now since 2071. According to what the Finn had picked up, the senior staff attributed this lack of contact to the distance they had traveled combined with the untested communications system relying too heavily on Earth's sun's sunspots igniting the plasma field around the planet. There was no major concern in the highest ranks, but the attitude was, "Why get people concerned needlessly?" After all, the best minds the Earth had had to offer were on board the ships, and once the Gate was set into operation, the best of all types of communication would be established.

As for him personally, he had not received any communications from his team's habitat on Earth through his hidden communication equipment. He guessed things couldn't be that bad or someone would tell him. If things were bad, the rest of his team and maybe other teams would be removed from stasis to gather more information and generate a plan. For now, he would simply learn all that he could while being the best beer maker and the most understanding barkeep he could. *Still a pretty good job*, he thought.

Though it was not a secret, he had learned that the designated fleet flagship would now be the Starship *India*, as it was her turn in the rotation. Admiral Nimitz and Marvin Swartz, the VAO, were on board with their respective staffs. The VAAS, Ada Sylva, would be shuttled over from the Starship *United States* with the soccer team when the fleet maneuver was settled in.

Each of the fleet turnarounds had difficulties of one type or another. And after each turnaround, the operating engineers became increasingly agitated. The scientific staff was modifying the turnaround schedule to be more in line with the planned arrival at EE and they now deemed it was time for a turnaround. The fleet would be going from the approximate 0.5 g deceleration to the 1.5 g acceleration. In general, people felt better about this as it meant they would be heading to their destination faster even though in the end, it really made little difference. It just felt better.

Of course, all the crews were given adequate notice, and the battening-down process was completed without incident. There had been plenty of practice. But then, things really fell apart. Starship *India*, which had been having regular problems with engine number four, couldn't get it stabilized enough to redirect the plasma. It went out of control, and the crew had to jettison the engine. That was the first of all the engines to be jettisoned, but as each ship had two spares, it was initially understood that this was more of an inconvenience at this point in the journey rather than a significant problem. However, that wasn't the end of things. When engine five, one of the spares, was rotated into place and made operational for the first time, the hybrid fusion/fission-plasma reaction went critical almost immediately. This engine was also jettisoned, but before Starship *India* could get a safe distance away, the engine exploded. The ship was critically damaged with many hull breaches.

Admiral Nimitz, Vice Admiral Swartz, and ship's Captain Nero were all killed in the initial blast, along with many others, and even more died due to hull breaches. Key survivors included Chief Operating Engineer Karesh and four of her engineers as they had been fortunate enough to be in the main control room on the lee side of the blast.

Starship *India* was just beginning the acceleration mode and was at 0.3 g at the time of the blast. The engineers determined that it was better to keep the remaining engines running rather than shut them down as these engines seemed to be stable. But the ship had to be abandoned. In the immediate chaos that followed, it wasn't clear who was in charge. The Starship *India* CASO assumed command of the ship but with full reliance on the chief engineer.

Back in the *United States*, Ada Sylva understood that now she was the most senior person in the fleet and by default was now in charge. "Oh my God," was all she had time to say before giving orders. Addressing the remaining ships' captains by radio, she said, "We have just suffered a serious accident with the *India*. According to the *India*'s CASO and chief engineer, the ship is somewhat stable but has been seriously damaged. Admiral Nimitz, Vice Admiral Swartz, and Captain Nero are all dead. As the VAAS, I have assumed the position of admiral per protocol. At this point, we don't know how many have died or the extent of injuries, but the numbers appear to be high. The forward *India* shuttle bay appears intact. All shuttlecraft are to start evacuating *India* immediately, but we must be cautious. No more than two shuttles are to dock with *India* at any time. The other shuttles are to wait a safe distance for their turn. *India* crewmembers will be brought back to each shuttle's home ship and tended there. I will provide more information as soon as I get it." With that, she ordered the Starship *United States*' captain to the admiral's briefing room along with the ship's CASO. She asked her husband, Jesus, to come as well.

Ada Sylva went to the briefing room and found a half-empty bottle of whiskey. *Pretty soon, but not yet*, she thought. *This is going to be a long day.* She then told the steward, "I want you to get whatever you think we'll need to keep us going for the next twenty-four hours and set it up right here." And as the steward left, Ada found herself alone. She wept out loud, saying, "It was just a matter of time. It was just a matter of time."

Ada was sixty-four years old, but, just as her parents always had, she looked about fifteen years younger. Like her dad, she was tall at nearly six feet. Fair skinned, fair-haired, and genuinely attractive, she had no difficulty in finding suitors, though she never had much time to look. Ada had gotten her passion for science from her parents—her mom, a research engineer, and her dad, a biochemist. She had pursued her education toward a PhD in astrophysics, obtaining it at the age of twenty-one.

Her parents had met when they were in school at the University of Alaska. While they had worked a good portion of their professional careers in Massachusetts, they had moved back to Alaska in 2050, along with her brother, Karl, and his family to get away from the crushing population. Ada had stayed behind, working for MIT's Lincoln Labs in Lexington, Massachusetts. Her family had a Portuguese-American background, and because of that, she had always gone to the Feast of the Blessed Sacrament in New Bedford, eating her annual piece of beef cooked over an open fire. This was pretty much a blue-collar affair, so Ada had always tried to act casual. But she certainly didn't look Portuguese.

It was at one these feasts that she had literally run into Jesus Sylva, a first-generation Portuguese-American and a medical doctor. Ada and Jesus had each thought themselves of a higher class than the other, but Jesus liked what he saw and somehow, while they tried to wipe the Madeira wine off of each other after the collision, Jesus asked for Ada's phone number. Ada somewhat reluctantly gave this short, stocky, but incredibly handsome, man her business card. *A business card? That's a first*, he had thought. Later, when he'd actually looked at it, he had been shocked to see that Ada was much more than he had first thought. In short order, she had learned that he was much more than *she* thought. The respect they had for each other's intelligence soon blossomed into true love, and in 2033, they had married. In 2035, they'd brought a set of twins into the world, a boy they named Richard after her grandfather, and Dawn, named after his grandmother.

By 2057, Ada Sylva had risen to senior scientist at Lincoln Labs and was asked if she would consider being a part of the interstellar space program. She did, and she got so involved that when the crews were being put together, she was asked to be the Vice Admiral of Academics and Science. She accepted on the condition that her family agreed to go. Jesus, Richard, and Dawn were all well qualified in their own right and enthusiastically said yes. She had been honored to be given the post of VAAS, but now, suddenly, at sixty-four years of age, she was in charge of some ninety thousand lives hurtling through space.

The Starship *United States* lounge was empty, but the Finn knew that would change as the first responders to the *India* and the *India*'s crew came aboard. The shuttlecraft would become the triage area, and the Finn knew from the well-rehearsed disaster plan that the less-than-critically wounded would be sent to the lounge until they were called for treatment. They would want something to take their minds off the tragedy. First, it would be hot tea and coffee, followed later by something stronger, even for the strictest observers of religion. He would be prepared and at the same time to learn what he could about what had caused the disaster. He already had a pretty good idea about that, however.

In the admiral's briefing room, Ada Sylva, the new admiral of the fleet, was trying to calm herself down. Her exterior would have put the Sea of Tranquility to shame, but that only masked her internal angst. Jesus was the first to enter the room. He asked, "Are you OK?"

"What do you think?" returned Ada with a hint of desperation.

"You'll be fine," said her husband. "You are the most qualified person in the fleet, and you know what you have to do."

"Thanks, honey. I don't think I believe you, but it makes me feel better."

The captain of the *United States* and the ship's chief academic and science officer showed up. Ada directed them to get cups of coffee and to sit down at the table. She, in turn, refilled her own cup. "OK," started Ada, "how is the evacuation going? Do we know the extent of the injuries and the number of people who have died so far?"

"We only have estimates so far," said Jesus. "We think about three thousand were killed in the initial blast and maybe another two thousand with hull breaches. We won't know about the injuries until everyone is off the *India*. Unless you need me here right now, I need to get back down to sick bay."

"Oh, I'm sorry. Of course you do. Keep me posted on any new information," said Ada as Jesus left the room. Turning to the ship's captain and CASO, Ada stated the obvious. "There is a lot to be coordinated over the next couple of days, and I need to appoint new vice admirals to take care of it. Who do you think should have those jobs?"

"Umm…" said the captain, "…shouldn't there be a selection process? I mean, I wouldn't know!"

Ada replied, "In the best of circumstances, I would interview all the senior members of each crew and then decide. And maybe later on, that's exactly what I'll do. But for now, Richard, I'm appointing you as interim VAAS, taking my place, and Dawn, I'm appointing you as interim VAO. You are both qualified, and I can't screw around right now."

"Mom," said Dawn with a rapidly rising voice, "I like the idea that you think we're the best you have, but appointing your kids to these jobs is going to be a political nightmare for you. Not just because we're your kids, but because we're all from the same ship!"

"We don't have time for politics. And whoever said this was a democracy?" was Ada's terse retort. "This is what I need right now. Get this done, and then we'll worry about politics. Dawn, I need a plan to salvage whatever we can from the *India*, with everything Gate related as the second priority. That includes construction equipment. The Gate is useless if we can't install it. I know we have redundancy spread around the fleet, but I don't want to lose anything that is still useful. Oh, pick someone you trust to take over as captain 'on an interim basis.'" Ada held her hands in the air, making quotation-mark gestures with her fingers.

"All right," said Dawn, "but what's the first priority?"

"What do you think?" answered the admiral. "For you, it is to determine what went wrong." Turning to Richard, Ada said, "We need to know how many died and how many are being treated. We need to know which ships have evacuees, by name and job description. That is your first priority. Dawn will want to interview the operating engineers, so when you can, have them brought to the *United States*. Now go. You know what to do. And report back here at—let's see, eighteen hundred hours."

When Ada, the new admiral, was alone again, she asked the steward to come in. "Felix," she said, "I need to get an opinion on something that might have an effect on everyone in the fleet. Who would be the best person to ask?"

The steward's response was exactly what she expected. "Well, ma'am, I would think one of the counselors."

To which Ada responded, "No, not a counselor. They deal with individuals, with individual issues. I'm looking for someone who really has the pulse of the crew."

Searching for the right answer, Felix said, "You mean, like a bartender? People tell bartenders things they'd never tell anyone else."

"Perfect! And who would be the best one for me to talk to?

It took Felix no time at all to answer, "Probably Sherman Hamer, the Finn. He's been on nearly every ship, and everyone is so relaxed around this guy, they tell him everything. He has this way about him."

Ada pressed on, "Are you talking from personal experience?"

"Maybe," said the steward. "Just maybe. Shall I ask him to come up?"

"Please do," said Ada, "right away." And Felix left the room.

Ada knew about the Finn. Everyone did. In fact, he had served her a beer or two over the years, even on other ships. Still, when he flowed into the admiral's briefing room, Ada couldn't help but be awed by this seemingly gentle giant with long, almost white-blond hair, and—well, everything about him seemed perfect.

"You called for me, ma'am?" said the Finn, not sure why a bartender would be summoned to the admiral's briefing room at a time like this. "Did I do something wrong?"

"Oh no," said Ada. "Admiral Nimitz and Vice Admiral Swartz were both killed in the *India* accident. I have assumed the position of admiral, and I need to reestablish command positions. I need an opinion on what the fallout from my appointments of the new vice admirals will be. I think you are in a unique position to advise me. Please have a seat."

The Fin thought, *I hope this doesn't mean she's on to me.* But as he sat down, he said, "I'm not sure I'm the best person. But what's the issue?"

Wasting no time, the admiral said, "The VAAS that I have appointed on an interim basis is a forty-year-old male with a PhD in astrophysics. He has been a CASO since before the fleet was launched. But most important, I trust this person completely. Nothing would be held back. The VAO that I have appointed on an interim basis is a forty-year-old female. She has a PhD in mechanical engineering and has been a ship's captain from the beginning. I also trust this person completely. I believe both of these people have proven themselves to be good leaders, and they are respected by the crew."

"Excuse me, ma'am, but you seem to be describing your children. Is that correct?"

"Yes," said Ada, "that's exactly who I'm talking about."

Wow, thought the Finn. He considered the issue for some time and then said, "Under the circumstances, I think this will be fine. You are correct that they are both respected, not just here, but by their peers on the other ships as well. You have named them as interim, so they will have an opportunity to prove themselves in these new roles before you make any final appointments. The loss of the *India* will have everyone on edge, and they will be looking for firm leadership. Whether right or wrong, you must demonstrate that you will take responsibility and make corrections along with the authority that you now have. Responsibility and authority have to go together. These appointments will raise a few eyebrows, but with some thought, those individuals will see that you had little choice at the moment.

"You know, Admiral, we bartenders do more than tend bar. We have our own network for sharing information. If you would like, I can pass along pertinent items to my fellow bartenders, who in turn could pass some along to nervous patrons. It might help."

"Yes," said Ada. "If you are comfortable doing that, I would appreciate it, but only if you are a hundred percent comfortable. Are you?"

"Thank you for asking, but I am. You have my full support." And the Finn stood up, saying, "Will there be anything else?"

"Not right now," said Ada. "You are excused. But I may call upon you in the future. Thank you."

And as the Finn left the room, the admiral suddenly realized that she felt a new calm that she hadn't before this bartender had entered the room. She had felt the effect before when he'd served her in the lounge. Beyond his physical appearance, there was just something else about this guy, something special that put her at ease, and she suspected there was this same effect on everyone else that he met.

Enjoying this new feeling of calm, the admiral put through an announcement to the captains and CASOs of the remaining starships, essentially telling them of the interim appointments and what their immediate tasks were. Any and all information that would help them gain control of the situation needed to be provided. In her directives, she added, "The mission of the fleet, while certainly damaged, has not been compromised. We all knew something like this could occur, but it is still devastating. We will assess the full extent of the damage and reevaluate our operations as we move forward. In the short term, our greatest priority and concern are for those who have been injured while grieving for those who have given their lives for this most noble of human enterprises. It is our duty to move forward so that their sacrifice will not have been in vain. We will learn from this, gaining strength from this tragedy. Surviving members of the Starship *India* will soon be on the remaining ships. Everyone must do what they can to comfort one another, but foremost the survivors of the *India* as we integrate them into the crews. I expect to have a detailed plan in place within the next twenty-four hours. Please reassure your crews that the newly formed admiral's staff is doing all that it can. End of message."

At 1800 hours, the new VAO and VAAS returned to the admiral's briefing room. Richard was the first to speak. "We're still moving people from the *India*, so I don't have an accurate number, but it looks like two thousand nine hundred and seven were killed by the immediate blast, and twenty-one hundred were killed by hull breaches. About a third of the crew has died so far, and there will certainly be more from those with serious injuries. Those who have survived are being shuttled to the other ships. The *Russia* is the closest to the *India*, so they will likely end up with more *India* crew members, but we can sort that out later. The most seriously injured are being taken off first. Again, these are very rough numbers, but triage reports from the shuttlecraft indicate about twenty-three hundred have serious injuries and an equal amount have moderate injuries. About one-third of the crew seems to have been shaken up, but beyond that, they seem to be physically OK. I estimate about twenty-four hours to get the rest of the crew off the *India*. After that, it will take us some time to shuffle people around and get the *India* crew integrated.

"You know, Mom, I'm just talking numbers here, but we're really talking about people, and people on all the ships are going to be upset for some time."

Quietly, Ada said, "Let's get something understood right away. When we're in the admiral's briefing room or on the bridge or anywhere where there is anyone around beyond family, you are to address me as 'ma'am' or Admiral, but not Mom. We must maintain some sense of decorum. OK? Dawn, what have you got?"

"Well, *Admiral*," Dawn emphasized, "as we already suspected, it appears we must leave the ship behind. I wish there was some way we could take the one spare engine, but we don't have time for that right now. The heavy construction equipment seems to be relatively unscathed. I guess there is a reason they call it that. We will pick a few pieces to be moved to the remaining ships, but to be honest, we already have additional redundancy and not a lot of extra space for the equipment and supplies. The fuel reserve is gone. The garden decks were compromised, so no chickens survived. The honeybees have taken up residence all over the ship, more so than here, so they'll be left behind. There are a few canaries and dogs that we'll save. We need to do a more detailed search of the ship. Because of the hull breaches, we think there are survivors who can't make it to the shuttle bay, so we're going to have to take some time to search."

"How much time are you going to need?" asked Ada.

"I'll need a week," was the response.

Looking at Richard, Ada asked, "Can our scientists give us that much time before compromising our trajectory? I'm guessing we can stay at this 0.3 g level for at least the week."

The new VAAS said, "I'm not sure, but I'll find out."

"OK, we seem to be as under control as we can be for now. As soon as possible, I want the *India*'s operating engineers in this room," said the admiral. And after a pause, she asked, "What do you two know about the bartender they call the Finn?"

Richard said, "Well, I understand he is a little different, but he makes a fantastic beer. Oh, and he makes other stuff we're not supposed to know about, but no one cares. Why?"

"Dawn," said Ada, "get someone to find out more about this guy. There is something about him that I feel could be useful, but I don't know what it is. If there is nothing else right now, you are dismissed."

Chapter 17
Now What?

Within days of the Starship *India* disaster, the remaining members of its crew were safely aboard the surviving ships with the injured being cared for. Within two weeks, salvage of everything useful had been completed, and the fleet was underway once again, leaving the damaged hulk behind and temporarily still under 0.3 g acceleration. After some debate, the *India* was set to self-destruct once the rest of the fleet was a safe distance away. Logic indicated that the ship could have been simply left as is with no harm done, but it seemed prudent to "make it go away."

Admiral Ada Sylva was in her briefing room on the Starship *United States* along with the two interim vice admirals, the *United States'* new captain, and the new CASO. The captains and CASOs of the other ships were there too, but via videoconferencing. "So," started the admiral, "what is our status? Let's start with human side of things, and then we'll shift over to operational issues. I'd like this to be a free flow of information, so please let's not be shy in asking questions or providing more information. We just experienced a serious blow to our mission, and we don't have the luxury of pretending it didn't happen. We don't want this to happen again. Vice Admiral Sylva, you start."

The admiral's son, Richard Sylva, the current VAAO, started as directed. "Well, ma'am, there are 3,112 missing and presumed dead from the *India*. There were 2,752 injured, and of those, 1,177 were considered critical. *Russia* ended up with about twenty-five percent of the survivors, as it was the closest to the *India*. The rest are pretty much evenly distributed among the other four ships. I see no reason to move people around right now with the exception of some family units that need to be reunited. There is more than enough space for the survivors on the ships, and quarters are being assigned as we speak. As the survivors are able, they will be assigned duties to help get them acclimated to their new shipmates but also to keep them from dwelling on the disaster. Each one will be seeing counselors and the CASO on each ship. The CASO from the *India* is in sickbay, and when he is better, he will be going from ship to ship to meet with each survivor. I'm not sure what more we can do right now. Oh, and I have asked the scientists to recalculate the acceleration/deceleration cycles to get us back on schedule. We don't appear to have any major issues there."

Ada asked, "Do you have the name of each person and his or her position on the *India*? Some ships might need a hand in a particular area."

"Yes," added the Starship *South America*'s captain. "I could use some help in engineering. I seem to have a lot of illness in that department."

Richard responded, "You know, Captain, not many of the engineering staff survived the blast, and they will need to be interviewed, but once that is complete, we can discuss your request."

Ada next turned to her daughter, Dawn Cohen, the interim VAO, and asked, "What have you got?"

Dawn took a deep breath and said, "When the fleet as a whole was being designed, it was understood deep down that we would probably lose a ship. I don't believe anyone actually expected a disaster like this, even though we trained for it. No one wanted to believe it, and everyone should realize there is no guarantee it won't happen again. That being said, we have recovered much of the heavy construction equipment and anything else we could get our hands on and transferred it to the other ships. I don't want to leave anything behind if I can help it. There are no general stores between here and EE. We did lose all the construction-equipment fuel that was on board the *India*, but it appears we're still OK.

"I have had a short interview with one of the surviving engineers, but he seems reluctant to talk. He reminded me that his work was classified, but I reminded him that I'm the VAO and I'm now in charge of operations. I got a similar response from our own chief engineer, so I have a problem trying to sort this out. I haven't had a chance to interview the *India*'s chief engineer. She seems to be suffering from some sort of mental breakdown."

The *British Commonwealth* captain said, "I have been trying to find out what the big secret is for some time now and have gotten nowhere." The other captains nodding their heads murmured agreement.

"I have an idea," said Ada. "Dawn, please stay after the briefing." And then she addressed the other captains and CASOs. "How are things on your ships?"

In turn, each person indicated that things were as under control as they could be and morale was as good as could be expected for now. Ada thanked everyone and ended the meeting.

As everyone except Dawn was leaving, Ada asked Richard to send in Felix, the admiral's steward. When he came in, Ada said, "Felix, please have that bartender they call the Finn come up here. I'd like to see him right away. Oh, and have him bring along a case of his best strong beer and maybe a little something extra I'm not supposed to know about. Also, Felix, please have the galley send up some food for about ten people—something special—in about an hour."

"Yes, ma'am," said the steward as he left.

Dawn said, "What have you got up your sleeve?"

Ada said with a smile, "I have an idea. Get our chief engineer and any *India* engineers that are on board and bring them here. You have twenty minutes."

"OK," said a puzzled Dawn, and she left.

Within fifteen minutes, the Finn entered the room and said, "You sent for me, ma'am?"

"Yes. Your first name is Sherman, right? May I call you that?" said Ada, suddenly feeling that now-familiar refreshing calm coming over her. "Please have a seat. Others will be joining us soon. You had indicated that the engineers on all the ships were a very uptight group. Did you ever press them as to why?"

The Finn said, "Somewhat. There is something about the engines that scares them."

"When the others join us," said Ada, "I'd like you to sit at the other end of the table. Have your beer and glasses on the side table next to you. I'm going to use that as an excuse to get the engineers that are coming to sit near you. You don't need to say anything unless I ask you to. Are you OK with that?"

"Yes, ma'am," said Sherman, who, not being dense, had a pretty good idea what the admiral was plotting.

"Oh, and nothing you hear in here today is to leave the room, got it?" added Ada.

The Finn, now thinking of what his real mission might be and not wanting to lie, answered with a laugh, saying, "Oh, I might transmit everything I hear out into space, but I wouldn't say anything to anyone on board any of the ships."

"Fair enough," said Ada, not realizing that he actually meant what he'd said.

Just as Ada said that, Dawn and four engineers entered the room—the *United States* chief engineer, his second-in-command, a light-brown-skinned man with multiple bandages and an arm in a sling, and a light-brown-skinned woman who appeared not to have been hurt. As each entered, they all were surprised to see the Finn sitting at the table.

Ada said, "Please, come in. Do you all know Sherman? He makes the best beer in the fleet. He has brought along some of his famous Trappist beer for us to sample. I'd like everyone to feel comfortable, so if you'd like a beer, Sherman will take care of you. Just try to relax a little. In about a half hour, the galley will be sending up some food for us. This is not a formal inquiry. No one needs that added stress right now. I was hoping we might just share what we know about the accident as a preventative measure for the rest of the fleet."

Ada took the first beer and sat at the other end of the table from Sherman. Dawn took the second beer and sat midway down the table. The woman engineer politely said she didn't drink, but the other three eagerly accepted beer and, as predicted, sat near the Finn and the rest of the cold beverages. As they sat down, each one appeared to become much less tense than when he had first arrived.

Ada began by asking the two *India* engineers if they had families and whether they had survived the disaster. As it turned out, the *India* engineers were husband and wife and had no other family members with them. Neither of them had been the chief engineer. They felt they were among the lucky ones. After some more small talk, Ada asked them if they could explain what had happened on the *India*. At that, much of their apparent calmness started to fade, and they said almost in unison, "It was an accident."

Ada winced at that and said, "Everyone in this room except Sherman has full clearance on every aspect of this mission. Some of us may be new to our positions, but we now have the clearance based on rank, and we need to know what happened. Sherman, our bartender here, actually knows more about the issues facing the engineers than your admiral and VAO. Sherman has been on nearly every ship, and he tells me that the engineering staff is always uptight. We know there is something you want to share, so please do it, and do it now."

The nondrinking woman engineer cracked first, much to Ada's surprise, and blurted out, "You're right. I can't hold back any longer. The engineers were all sworn to secrecy because, quite frankly, these engines are all time bombs waiting to go off."

"Yeah," said the *United States* chief engineer, who also happened to be sitting right next to Sherman. "Sherman, can I have another beer, please?" And once that was in his now-shaking hand, he studied the bottle and without looking up said, "We were told that these engines were thoroughly tested and reliable, but because they were new, people might get concerned if they knew how they worked, so the engines and any work done on them was to be considered classified. We were not to discuss our work with anyone outside of engineering. Not even our spouses. When we left Earth's orbit, we found that the plasma jet was reasonably stable when operating at a steady state, but the fission/fusion power source needed constant attention. I'm talking constant, just as if you were in a car race doing two hundred miles an hour and you needed to keep the car on the track. It is exhausting. When we make a turn, the steady state of the plasma changes, which in turn changes the fission/fusion dynamics. It is all hands on deck to maintain some semblance of stability during each turn."

He poured the beer into his glass, took a big swig, and returned to staring at the bottle, continuing with, "The chief engineers were all alarmed and asked the United Nations Stellar Commission for guidance. We thought they should abort the mission. We were told in no uncertain terms that this would be considered treason and if we returned, not only would we face the consequences, so would our extended families back on Earth.

Besides, they said, 'This is expected behavior of the engines until they are broken in. After everything is settled in, there will be next to nothing for the engineering staff to do.' But they lied. There has to be an engineer at each engine around the clock, making constant adjustments. It is exhausting and stressful work. One mistake, and an engine could blow—which it did on *India*."

The injured engineer took another beer but said nothing. His wife, adding to the story, said, "We took all the precautions on *India*, but each turnaround adds another level of intensity as the plasma field is adjusted for the changed thrust. We'd already been having trouble with engine number four so weren't terribly surprised when it started to go critical and we had to jettison the engine. We then rotated engine number five in to take the place of engine four. That part went reasonably well, but the engine needed a cold start. The critical masses of the fission/fusion reactions and the interrelationship between them simply went critical within a matter of minutes, with no chance to do anything except jettison that engine as well and hope for the best. The rest, you know about."

Ada turned to the *United States* chief engineer, who was on his third brew, and asked, "Was this common knowledge of all the engineers?"

"Yes," was the reply, "and whenever former VAO, Marvin Swartz, said anything to mission control, we got the same answer— that 'Earth is depending upon you. You can't turn back.' That, plus the threat of retribution, kept us quiet. Besides, why panic everyone else? After a while, I guess they got tired of listening to us, because after 2071, they never responded to any new requests for information."

"Hmm," said Ada, "That's because we seem to have passed the range of effective communication a few years ago."

The woman engineer, looking puzzled, asked, "Well, what about all the news we've been getting?"

"All made up," said Ada, adding, "every bit of it."

At that, some mouths fell open, but the *United States* engineers both had clenched jaws and shaken their heads, saying, "Well, now what?"

"That," said the admiral, "is a very good question. We're about eight years out, with about twenty years more to go to reach our destination. There are a lot of unknowns about it, but that is as true now as it was when we left Earth. As we get closer to EE, the astronomers on board will start to learn more about our choices. If we turn back, our mission will be considered a failure. When people signed up for this mission, everyone knew there were risks. While no one said it, I believe we had in the back of our minds that many, perhaps all of us, wouldn't make it. We have everything we need to build the Gate, and even if we lose another ship with everything on board, we still have more than enough materials and equipment to complete the mission. Now, however, we have two pieces of information we didn't have before. Well, really one, but the other is relevant.

"The new piece of information is that our state-of-the-art engines are not as wonderful as we had been led to believe. Related to that is the fact that we seem to be out of contact range with Earth, so we are on our own. And that means our engineers can't get support from mission control to potentially correct engine design flaws. Maybe we can do it ourselves if more people are involved.

"Now, I'm just thinking out loud here, so if any of you have any ideas, I'd like to hear them. This is brainstorming, so that means there are no bad ideas. Let's get all our thoughts out there, and then we can discard the ones that seem to make no sense."

With that challenge tossed out, Felix interrupted the meeting, saying that the galley had sent up the food as requested. As it was being laid out on the sideboard, the admiral said to the galley staff, "That looks great, thank you very much." And then, turning to Sherman, who had in fact kept quiet as requested, she said, "Sherman, I think we need another round. And, by chance, did you bring up some enhancements?"

The Finn smiled, gave everyone except the woman engineer from *India* another cold beer, and placed a bottle of Canadian Club whiskey on the table, saying, "I know this is against the rules, but I brought a few bottles on board in my personal gear, thinking it might be nice to have when we arrived at EE. But, well, here it is."

As they tried to enjoy their meal, Dawn said, "We need to get more people involved."

"Eventually," said Ada. She added, "But first we have to have some idea of what to present. I'd like all the officers of all the ships to present their thoughts, and when they are done, we can open things up. Even though we are not operating in a democracy, I think people should at least have a say. By the way, there seem to be too many secrets—one about the engines and another about communications with Earth. Maybe more are out there. It has to stop. No more secrets. Everyone needs to know everything."

As Ada said that, Schem-Hampha-Rae, known as Sherman Hamer, aka the Finn, aka the bartender, thought, *Well, I think I'll keep my secrets to myself for a while longer.*

The *India*'s female engineer said, "Many of us on *India* thought that if we could get the ships' scientific staff involved as part of an official engineering-review committee, we might be able to correct some design flaws ourselves."

The *United States* chief engineer said, "I suppose it doesn't have to be all or nothing. That is, some ships could continue on to EE, and one or two could turn back with those who don't want to continue."

His assistant said, "We never carefully studied the idea of transferring an engine from one ship to another. We didn't have time when we left *India* behind. I think we could make the transfer, and if one ship finds itself with only three engines, it would give us another layer of backup."

And so it went for the next hour and a half. The only breaks were to refill plates and beer glasses and for brief trips to the admiral's head. The Finn had offered to record the suggestions on a board, but Ada did it herself, keeping everyone else at the table, close to him. As the admiral had suspected, the longer people were in the presence of the Finn, the more at ease they seem to become. There was just something about this guy. She had felt it the first time she had been in his company at the bar, and now she saw it on a somewhat larger scale. When the ideas seemed to stop flowing, the admiral excused everyone except him.

The Finn said, "Ma'am, I'm not sure why you had me here. It seemed inappropriate. I'm just a bartender."

The admiral stared at him for a couple of seconds and, slightly squinting her eyes, she said, "Sherman, I don't know what you are, but I do know you are a lot more than a bartender. You may act like everyone else, but you don't look like everybody else, and people sure as hell don't act themselves when they are around you. There's more to you than you let on, isn't there?"

So, Schem thought, *at some point, I'm going to have to say something. But not now*. Out loud, he said, "I am no one special," thereby defying the admiral's directive of full disclosure by everyone.

The admiral waited a long second to see if the Finn would add anything more and then realizing that nothing else was forthcoming on the subject, said, "Fine. Maybe you'll confide in me later. But for now, Mr. Bartender, what are your thoughts after sitting in on this today?"

At this, Schem said, "I think you are going about this the right way. The crews don't know you in your new role, and they will want to see how you handle things. Of course, you realize, you know more than most of them. That said, I agree that you should remove this cloak of secrecy that was placed over the engines and probably the Earth communications issue as well."

When Sherman left, Ada sat in silence. She considered her thinking to open things up. It had been a good decision. She would put everything out there for everyone to ponder, including turning around and going home; first, to the most senior staff, then layer by layer, down to every last person in the fleet. She would allow ten days for open discussion before putting a simple question on a ballot; go back to Earth or continue to EE. She wondered and discussed with her family what would happen if one ship voted differently from the rest. Would she honor that? What if the equivalent of one ship's crew decided to turn back? Would she allow crews to be transferred and that ship to turn back? That, she knew, would not be a good plan.

In the end, the vote was overwhelmingly in favor of staying on course. Of the nearly eighty-five thousand people left in the five starships, only 135 voted to turn back. In a separate poll, every member of the operating engineering staff voted to continue the mission. They said that removing the cloak of secrecy allowed them to share the angst they all felt. As a group, they now felt overwhelmed with the celebrity status that seemed to have been placed on them. In the ships' lounges, people would "buy" them beers—no one actually bought anything—but there was this new feeling of sharing. They were even more surprised when people volunteered to help maintain the engines, though few were even close to being qualified. As hoped, some members of the research units offered help in an attempt to get the engines to operate as promised, or at least closer to it.

Once things were settled, Ada sent a message to mission control back on Earth in the hopes it would eventually receive it. And as she hit "send," she quietly prayed for all future events to be minor.

Chapter 18
Gabe-Re-El's First Encounter

While Kem-U-El and his cousin Ere-Mi-El had headed east and Na-Ki-Ir and Ara-Ri-El had headed south to see what they could learn, Gabe-Re-El, being alone, had decided to take a different approach to the survey and stay in the northern latitudes. He had been in contact with other teams around the planet and knew they were scouting around as well. Not all teams had been activated. It would become clearer later on why that was so, but enough teams were out and about to know that things on Earth weren't all that good and something needed to be done to get things back on course.

Following normal protocol, Gabe put on his antigravity pack and let the multipiece panels expand out on each side of him, their seven feet and two inches of length matching his height. The golden glow of the protective shield surrounded him, and he took off across the Bering Strait toward Russia. He first wanted to see that area before spending more time in Alaska and Canada.

Going at maximum speed, Gabe first went down the coast for half the day. Turning back, he went inland fifty to a hundred miles before finishing the flight back at the habitat. His intentions had been to land and talk to some of the inhabitants. He hadn't stopped, because he found no one. Instead, all Gabe had found were villages abandoned years ago. He saw plenty of wildlife but no people. This was very disturbing.

Back at the habitat, Gabe pondered what he had seen, or more accurately, what he had not seen, and considered what he would do next. He suspected that there were people somewhere not too far away. He just had to find them. He would be winging it, literally and figuratively, with a plan outside of exact protocol formulating in his mind. For now, he had the habitat robotics serve up a healthy portion of fish stew and a carafe of that excellent wine they had located.

Gabe went to bed early with a head that was perhaps a little foggy. Combined with the long day's sights, he was left with an uneasy night of sleep. He had learned to like strong coffee many years ago from the locals in South America, so when morning came, he tried to counter the poor night's sleep with a really strong brew. After a few cups of coffee and a light breakfast of six eggs, a pound of bacon, and a half loaf of bread, he was ready to go, though a random thought crossed his mind as he wondered whose idea it had been to do away with gluten in the bread. It had tasted like a bad idea to him, and he informed the robots not to use that stuff again.

This day, he left the cloaking fog and headed southeast. As he flew over the water, he saw a sailboat below, along with some playful sea otters and whales. The sight lifted his spirits. *There are people*, he thought. He wasn't sure but thought maybe he'd gone undetected by those on the boat. Off to the side, he saw Homer, Alaska, and it looked like it had an actual community. There were some clouds today, so Gabe decided to use them to his advantage. He would definitely be breaking away from standard procedures, and the clouds would help. He wouldn't stray too far, though. Just a little. He usually worried more about protocol than the rest of the team, especially Ara, and he knew it, but as the team leader, he was supposed to set the standard. But sometimes a less than standard approach was called for, and today might be one of those times.

He got as close as he could to Homer while in the clouds before descending. As he came out of the clouds, the community spread out in front of him. It seemed active, but the way the structures were laid out before him made him both smile and cringe. Many buildings had been built into the sides of hills and looked like they could withstand the worst possible attacks from weather—or whatever. Curiously, many had large watercraft attached. Had they washed up on shore, or had they been brought there? He saw no really large boats at the dock or anchored, and the boats he did see appeared to be old sailing craft or rowing skiffs.

As he came in closer, one structure with one of the large boats attached caught his eye with some lettering on it. The rather large boat was called *Change Order*. He might have been out of touch for some time, but he knew what a change order was, and he also knew what *Original Contract* on the dinghy hanging from the davits meant. The names looked like something Ara would come up with. For the first time since emerging from stasis, Gabe laughed.

He was about to move on when he noticed someone on the bridge of *Change Order*, and this person, a woman, was staring directly at him. That's when a plan formed.

Gabe headed toward the boat, and as he got closer, he lifted one leg slightly, bending it at the knee. He lifted both hands to shoulder level, palms up. These motions controlled the pack, and Gabe gently landed on the boat's foredeck. Upon touchdown, his antigravity pack pulled in its panels, and the golden glow around him was extinguished.

Kim Sue Bickmeier was taking a couple of hours from her activities to go to her favorite place to read and relax. She had had a difficult morning with one of the electricians, Jerry, who had experienced an anxiety attack. She wasn't a doctor, but no one else in town had any medical training either, so Kim Sue, taking a lesson from one of her books, had spent some time with Jerry to talk him down and give him some home remedy she had cooked up. She didn't know if the remedy actually did anything or not, but Jerry had taken it, and he'd felt better. *Power of suggestion,* she had thought.

Kim Sue was now reading the third of the Harry Potter books by J. K. Rowling and wondering if there was any such thing like the magic described in it. The books seemed like they had been written for kids, but still, they provided a mental escape for her. The bad guys in this book had just performed some black magic on the good guys, and Kim Sue was looking up from her reading, pondering the results of these spells. The clouds above seemed to have a hint of what she had read about clouds playing a role in the plot. Clouds, after all, were good places for wizards and witches to hide from nonwizards and other witches.

As she looked at the clouds, she thought she might be losing her grip on the here and now. Had she somehow gotten herself so into the story so far that reality and the story line were now blurred together? Could it be true…was she really seeing this winged creature dressed all in white and surrounded by a golden glow descending from the clouds? She stared at it with her mouth open as it got closer and closer, gliding gracefully down to the deck just in front of the yacht's bridge. Terror raced through her, and she thought, *My God, I've finally lost my mind.* She was still holding the book; she glanced at it and threw it down, wringing her hands before looking up again and seeing the massive figure one deck below.

For a moment, Gabe and Kim Sue stared at each other. Then, Gabe smiled broadly and gave a slight bow toward her. Her mind raced. Her husband, son, and grandson were all at sea. She wasn't sure where Maria was. Kim Sue wheeled around, looking in every direction. She saw no one else. She felt more alone then she ever had in her entire life. And then she fainted.

Gabe saw her collapse below the bridge windows and assumed that she had fainted. He hoped that was what had happened, anyway, and nothing more serious. Still, he said out loud, "Oh, this isn't good—and definitely not part of the plan." He raced up to the bridge and found this petite woman crumpled into a heap on the deck. He scooped her up and laid her gently down on the cushioned bench seat at the back of the bridge. Her pulse seemed fine. He noticed a glass of water that Kim Sue must have been using, grabbed a towel he saw hanging on the helm, soaked it, and placed on her forehead. He then pulled up a chair near her, sat down, and waited.

A few minutes later, Kim Sue started to come around. As she did, Gabe gently held her hand and said in a very quiet voice, "Fear not, lovely lady. I am not here to hurt you or anyone else."

Kim Sue, opening her eyes, saw this huge man nearly three times her size, with long, silver-blond hair and dressed all in white. But now, with him this close and actually holding her hand, she was no longer afraid. *Strange*, she thought. *Everything about this tells me I should be afraid, but I'm not. I feel joyful!* With no trace of concern, she asked, "Am I hallucinating? Are you real?"

Gabe answered the only way he could. "No, you are not hallucinating. My name is Gabe-Re-El. You may call me Gabe. And I am here only seeking knowledge."

Kim Sue said, "So, I did see you descend from the sky?"

"You did," answered Gabe. "A simple machine attached to my back allowed me to do so."

"Where did you come from?" asked Kim Sue.

"In due time, lovely lady. For now, that is not important. But I will say that I am not from around here."

Kim Sue, regaining her faculties, said, "Really! You could have fooled me!" and they both smiled at this obvious observation. "My name is Kim Sue Bickmeier, but you may call me Kim Sue."

"Thank you, Kim Sue. It is pleasure to meet you, though I do regret that our initial encounter caused you concern. Are you feeling better now?"

"Yes," said Kim Sue as she removed the towel and sat up, with Gabe still holding her hand. "I am fine now." And she meant it. In fact, she couldn't recall the last time she had felt this calm and reassured, all the while thinking, *Why am I not scared?*

Gabe, to avoid an awkward silence, and not completely untruthfully, said, "I am from a volunteer research organization that is evaluating living conditions in various parts of the world. I have been assigned to Alaska and Canada. I am just getting started. If you would allow me, I'd like to get a better understanding of social changes that might have occurred in the past decade or so from the perspective of the people actually living in various communities. This information will be assimilated with information gathered by other volunteers and then will be shared with government officials for possible policy modifications. I am not allowed to tell you what I have learned thus far, though at a later date, recommendations may be shared with the community. I know this is lot to be dumped on you after my rude appearance, but is this something you'd be willing to participate in? If not, I will be on my way."

Kim Sue, was still a bit taken aback by what had happened to her in less than an hour. But at the same time she was enjoying the calm that had settled over her and said, "Yes, but let's have a cup of tea first. Come with me to the boat's galley." And they both stood and went down the steps to the galley with Gabe towering over the small Kim Sue and ducking as he went through the openings.

Gabe couldn't actually stand straight up at all, as the deck-to-deck spacing was considerably less than his height, but he did manage to get comfortable sitting down. As Kim Sue prepared some tea, she said, "You might want to think about a different set of clothes if you're going to be in this part of the country for very long. There are a number of things about you that don't exactly fit in, but the clothing you have on certainly doesn't help your cause any."

Gabe considered that and said, "I suppose you are correct. This is a standard-issue uniform, and, while it is most comfortable, I guess I never considered that in this part of the world, it might not be acceptable."

Kim Sue said, "Maybe you might fit in near the equator, if you weren't so big."

Gabe said, "Everyone in my family is big. I can't help that. But I guess I could change my wardrobe if I could find something that fit."

"Yessss," said Kim Sue very slowly. "That could be a problem. I'll think about it." All the while, she was really thinking. *Are you nuts? You don't know anything about this guy, and you're worried about his clothes?*

With hot mugs of tea in front of them and sitting across from each other at the galley table, Gabe started by saying, "Do you live here alone?"

"Oh no," said Kim Sue. My husband, son, and grandson are off fishing today. I'm not sure where my daughter-in-law, Maria, is at the moment."

Over the next three hours, Gabe asked questions, with each new one requiring a more complex answer. Kim Sue poured out everything she knew. At the same time, she realized this was exactly what her grandson wanted to know, but in Len's case she had found it difficult to share. *Why?* she thought. *I can't seem to help myself with this stranger.*

Kim Sue told Gabe about the death-flu pandemic, the interstellar space fleet, and how new social orders had come about. The time flew by until Kim Sue realized she was getting tired. "Let's go for a walk. I need to move."

As they went up on deck, they saw Maria hanging laundry out on a line to dry with her back to *Change Order*. "Maria," said Kim Sue, "I'd like you to meet someone. This is Gabe."

Maria turned around, still holding a wet shirt. She saw Gabe and dropped the shirt, with her mouth wide open.

"Hello, Maria. Kim Sue has told me lot about you. It is nice to meet you," Said Gabe.

Maria nearly yelled at Kim Sue, "Where did he come from?"

Kim Sue, without thinking, said, "Oh, he just flew in. He's a nice guy. He should stay for dinner and meet our guys."

Maria couldn't believe what she was seeing and hearing from Kim Sue. She was acting like this sort of thing happened every day. But as Kim Sue and Gabe descended the gangway toward Maria, Maria relaxed more and more with each step Gabe made and then said, "Of course! I'll set another place at the table."

Gabe helped Maria finish hanging the laundry, and the three of them strolled around Homer. Gabe was introduced to many surprised citizens as his guides explained how everything fit together in their community. While they walked, Gabe said, "I haven't seen the school."

"Oh," said Maria, "We don't have a school here. There aren't any kids. My son is the youngest in town, and he's twenty-five."

This fact hadn't come out in his questioning, and it took him by surprise. Gabe said, "So, where are they?"

"Where are who?" asked Maria.

"The children."

"There aren't any here. No one in Homer has had a child in decades. Just haven't," said Maria.

Wow! thought Gabe. *Maybe this wasn't the best place for me to start my survey after all.*

Around 5:30 p.m., Kim Sue said, "It looks like the boys are coming in," as they could see the *Elusive*'s mainsail and jib wing and wing, heading for the dock. She looked at Gabe and continued, "We'll go help them tie up and see what they caught."

Don was at the helm with his dad and son, enjoying a stress-free ride. "So," said Karl, as he usually did when he was about to tell a joke. "This pirate walks into a bar and orders a drink. The bartender says, 'So, where have you been? You look terrible.' The pirate says, 'I feel fine!' 'Well, what about the peg leg?' 'Oh,' says the pirate, 'I was in a sea battle, and a cannonball blew me leg off, but I feel fine!' 'Well, what about your hand?' says the bartender. 'Oh,' says the pirate, 'I was in this sword fight, and me hand got cut off, so I fitted meself with a hook. But I feel fine—really!' 'Uh-huh,' says the bartender. 'Well, what about the eye patch?' 'Oh,' says the pirate, 'I was out on deck, and a flock of birds flew over, and one of 'em crapped in me eye.' 'That put your eye out?' asks the bartender. 'No,' says the pirate, 'first day with the hook!'"

"Really, Grandpa? Where do you get these gems?" groaned Len, not expecting an answer.

Don smiled at Len's reaction, but he was cut short as he looked some distance toward the dock and said, "What the—!"

Karl and Len both stood up and, looking toward the dock, saw Maria and Kim Sue on each side of very large person dressed in all white.

Len asked no one in particular, "Who's that?"

Don answered the only way he could. "I have no idea."

Karl stared for a minute and said quietly, "Interesting."

Kim Sue and Maria were all smiles as *Elusive* came toward the dock. First, the crew rolled up the jib and, just at the right moment, let the mainsail luff as they coasted up to the dock. Len tossed a line toward the trio on the dock, expecting Maria to grab it, but Gabe took it and pulled the boat in so hard, it nearly knocked Karl off his feet. As the boat was being secured, Maria said, "This is Gabe. Gabe, this is my father-in-law, Karl, my husband, Don, and my son, Len."

Gabe said, "Very nice to meet you."

The boat crew wasn't sure what to say, but while this was unusual at the highest level, they all felt as though it was all just fine.

Maria said, "How was fishing today?"

"Not bad," said Len eagerly. "Dad decided not to waste time with Augustine Island, and we went straight for the halibut and cod. That weird fog just hangs around the island."

And as the fish box built into the cockpit was opened, Gabe and the women saw one halibut weighing at least 150 pounds, with Don saying, "That should tide the townsfolk over for a bit, with some left over for the winter."

A ship's davit mounted on the dock was used to hoist the fish ashore as town residents came down for their share of the fish. A pair of seals moved up to the dock and a few gulls landed, hoping to get shares themselves. Len started cutting the fish while Karl and

Don washed down the boat and put their fishing gear away. Karl couldn't help but notice that as people came down to the dock, none of them seemed to pay any attention to the huge stranger. In fact, they all seemed to treat him as if he had been part of the community for years. "Interesting," said Karl to himself.

Kim Sue told the men that Gabe had been invited for dinner, so they needed to move things along, but Maria interrupted that decree by saying, "Let's have a community dinner tonight at the meeting hall. Everybody bring something. We haven't done that for a long time!"

Karl thought, *Where did that come from?* but what he heard from the people who had come down for their fish was, "Yeah! Let's do it!"

By seven thirty that night, the hall was filled with people. Tables along one wall were covered with the favorite meals of each household. For obvious reasons, there were numerous fish dishes, but there were also moose-meat pies and pork dishes. There were dozens of creative vegetable dishes and desserts. On a separate table, the town brewer had set up kegs of beer. Everyone seemed to be in a party mood.

There was no head table exactly, but the table that Gabe and the Bickmeiers had claimed as their own was soon treated as one. Everyone, whether a good cook or not, brought plate after plate of food to Gabe, who proceeded to eat everything placed in front of him, washing it down with mug after mug of some fantastic beer. *After all*, he thought, *I haven't had anything to eat since breakfast.*

Only Karl seemed to notice how much food this stranger was packing away. He didn't care exactly. He was feeling pretty good himself after a couple of pints of the local brew. It was good to have a spontaneous party! Still, Karl had to ask Gabe, "Man, how can you eat so much?"

Gabe said, "I'm sorry, I don't mean to be piggish, but everything tastes so good, and to be honest, it's been a while since I ate last." By his standards, he supposed that to be true.

After they had eaten, a few people grabbed some instruments and started playing, and before long, people were dancing, laughing, and generally having a good time. *Interesting*, thought Karl.

Because it was summer, the sun was still out when 11:00 p.m. rolled around, but folks started drifting home. Kim Sue asked Gabe if he had a place to sleep. Gabe said he didn't but asked if he could sleep on the deck of *Change Order*. He said, "I've been cooped up for some time and wouldn't mind sleeping out under the stars, if that's OK with you."

"Sure," said Kim Sue. "I'll bring you some blankets and a pillow."

"You are too kind," said Gabe as they headed back to the Bickmeier home.

All the Bickmeiers, and for that matter, everyone in Homer, had the best night's sleep they could ever remember. Even Gabe slept well, falling asleep while staring up into the sky, looking at the stars when the sun dipped briefly below the horizon.

As they were in bed about to doze off, Maria said to Don, "Do you think this Gabe and what we saw the other night are related?"

"I'm guessing yes," said Don, "but how? I couldn't say. I think my dad could easily summarize this day in one word."

"Yeah!" said Maria. "Interesting."

Chapter 19
Benevolent Dictators

On July 16, Karl Bickmeier was up early, as he was most days, almost always before everyone else. During the growing season, he liked to spend time alone out in the garden, seeing how things were doing, pulling a few weeds, looking to see what nasty critter or bug Mother Nature had sent to attack his crop, and maybe pick a veggie or two. But mostly, he just wanted to be alone for a little while to think about life in general and to say a few quiet words of thanks for his family and the good life he had been fortunate to have for the seventy-two years he had been around. So many had died during the death flu pandemic, yet his immediate family had come through it unharmed. He thought of his sister, Ada, and her family hurtling through space and prayed they were fine. It couldn't hurt!

Karl hadn't been in the garden for very long when he felt a presence. Turning around, he saw Gabe there just watching him. At that, Gabe said, "Can we talk?"

Karl said, "Certainly. What's on your mind?"

Gabe said, "As I have said, I'm on a fact-finding mission. I have learned a lot from your wife and have truly enjoyed the few hours I've spent here in Homer, but I need to learn more. You appear to be more objective around me than most people. That could be useful in my mission, so I was wondering if you'd accompany me for a while as I travel; probably not too far. I'd very much like to have someone around to help me sort things out."

"Interesting," said Karl. "Let's have some breakfast and talk it over with the family. I'm not a kid anymore, so I'm not sure about a big adventure, but it might be nice to do something different for a change."

"Fair enough," said Gabe, "let's talk over breakfast."

Karl said, "After what you ate last night, are you even hungry?"

"I have a high metabolism," said Gabe, "but a light breakfast might be nice."

Gabe really tried to watch himself at breakfast, but Maria and Kim Sue made it hard with eggs, bacon, buttermilk pancakes with blueberries, fresh-squeezed vegetable juice, and strong coffee. He asked, "Where do you get your coffee?"

"Oh," said Don, "we may be isolated out here, but we do make trips to Anchorage for supplies when we need to. We're not completely off the grid. There are a lot of trees growing coffee, and there are settlements in South America like ours. Commerce is not even close to what it was before 2071, but it does exist. The biggest issues are variety and how long one might have to wait for something. Planning ahead is critical."

Changing the subject, Gabe asked Karl, "Have you considered my request?"

"What request is that?" asked Kim Sue.

Karl answered, "Gabe here would like me to accompany him as he continues his 'fact-finding mission,'"—he made quotation marks in the air—"as he calls it." Chuckling, he added, "I actually think he plans to eat every community he visits out of their food supplies. What do you think?"

Don said with a smile, "I think Gabe has to keep moving just to find enough to eat. I think he is part cicada."

"You know, son, you make a good point. Maybe I should go just to document how much he can consume," said Karl.

With this banter, everyone was smiling and looking at Gabe who was pretending he wasn't the focus of the attention.

When Gabe said nothing, Karl got more serious and asked, "What do you think about my going with him? It would just be a few days."

"I want to go," said Len as he looked at his dad.

Don, caught off guard, thought for a moment and said, "Well, I suppose I can get one of the guys in town to go fishing with me." Then continuing the food consumption theme said, "If you do go, you better get to the dinning room table before Gabe so you don't starve."

Kim Sue spoke up. "OK, enough with food humor already." Then went on with, "I suppose you guys could go as long as it isn't all summer, but not until we get this guy into clothes that might let him blend in a little better."

"OK," said Karl to Gabe. "It looks like they want to get rid of me for a few days. I'll do it, but only if Len comes along. This might do him a world of good. Where are you planning to go?"

"I'm not sure where I should go," said Gabe, wondering if he should respond to the food topic. Deciding to stay quiet on that, he said, "I think I'd like to try to meet the governor. How does one get to Juneau from here?"

Karl said, "Juneau! Your organization doesn't know much of anything, does it? The governor isn't in Juneau. That was always a strange place for a state capital, with no roads into it. Everyone had to either fly in or take a boat. Because it was so isolated, it fared well with the death flu, but when the dust settled and the military took control of federal and state offices, they moved the capital to Anchorage. They didn't care about any state rules prohibiting it. I doubt if there is anyone left who actually cares."

Kim Sue, the only one who had seen Gabe fly and had no plans to mention it, asked, "Are you going to use standard transportation or something else?"

"How did you get here in the first place?" asked Don, but he didn't get an answer.

"Is there a vehicle we can use?" asked Gabe, glancing at Kim Sue with a facial expression imploring confidentiality.

"I have a car!" Karl said with a touch of excitement. "I've got a beauty that takes these terrible roads like nobody's business, and it's high time it went on an adventure."

"Oh, geez," said Len. "Are you serious? Maybe I don't want to go now."

Looking around, all Gabe saw were smiling faces except Len's, so he asked, "What am I missing?"

"You'll see," said Len. "You'll need to sit in the back seat, though. You won't fit in the front."

"OK, I guess," said a puzzeled Gabe. "We'll leave first thing in the morning, if that's all right with everyone."

Gabe was still curious about the ride but let it go. Instead he asked, "Can I assist with fishing today?"

Don said, "It's a bit late in the day to go out, and your outfit would look wonderful covered with fish guts…"

"Is there a favorite spot nearby?"

"Well, yeah, but it's been a dry hole for weeks," said Don.

"Let's give it a shot, if you don't mind. I'd like to go out on the water," said Gabe and, in spite of Don's skepticism, they agreed and set out.

By midafternoon, they returned to Homer, the boat loaded with cod, huge halibut, salmon, and even some striped bass. Don had never had a day like this, and Gabe didn't have a spot on him. Back at the dock, Karl looked at the catch and said to himself, "Interesting."

At the evening meal, Kim Sue proudly presented Gabe with two flannel shirts and a pair of pants that looked more than sturdy. As she handed them to him, she said, "Everyone in town looked into their closets, and we found enough shirts that looked similar that we could take them apart and make some that should fit. Same thing with the pants. But you'll have to stick with the sandals. We couldn't guess the size, and even if we did, I don't know if we could make anything that quickly."

"This is very special," said Gabe honestly. "Thank you. I'd like to make a donation to the town, if you'd let me. Just a token of my appreciation." And he produced two gold coins out of what seemed to be thin air.

"Are you kidding me?" said Maria. "Are these real gold?"

"Yes," said a concerned Gabe. "Is that a problem?"

"Oh no!" said Maria. "Not a problem at all. Thank you."

Gabe was used to people who wanted to help, yet the clothes were exceptional, and he was touched. That night when he tried on his new clothes, they fit perfectly.

On July 17, Karl, Len, and Gabe headed out early for Anchorage. Kim Sue and Maria prepared a basket of food, Karl and Len each had a small bag of essentials, and Gabe had his strange-looking backpack plus a small package holding his spare new shirt and his regular clothes.

Gabe was surprised when he saw the 1914 Model T Ford touring car and nearly blundered when he said, "I remember when Henry Ford wanted to build luxury cars but was convinced that it would be better for people in general if he built a car everyone could afford."

Karl stared at Gabe and asked, "You remember?"

Catching himself, Gabe said, "From history books."

Karl said, "You know that tidbit but don't know where the capital of Alaska is? Interesting."

In fact, Gabe more than remembered Henry Ford's attention to cars for the masses. Gabe was the one who had suggested it to him. Technology had been moving at a rapid pace back then, and the use of horseless carriages meant that the pollution in the cities would be reduced when the stench of horse manure disappeared. Of course, that corrective measure wasn't supposed to mushroom into a complete change in culture, creating other problems later on. "Unintended consequences," as they say.

So they cranked up the ancient Ford and climbed in, with the luggage rack on the running board full of bags and spare fuel and the back seat full of Gabe.

Karl said, "This was my granddad's car. He restored it and made it better for driving. That was back about 2015 or so. I was just a little kid but loved to get in this thing when we lived in Massachusetts and go for short rides. When I earned my BS in mechanical engineering, he gave it to me with the promise that I'd take him on drives once in a while. I drove it some early on, and we used it when I got married to Kim Sue. Then it sat for a few years, but when we moved to Alaska in 2050, there was no way the old Ford was staying behind. I've had to make a few modifications to make it happy running on straight ethanol, and I have to start it on the magneto now as it is far too expensive to get a battery, but it is still very reliable. Maybe a bit slow on a good road, but there aren't many of those these days. Cars made around the beginning of this century were built for smooth roads and are so complex that there are very few people who can keep them running, even if they could find or afford the parts. But you probably know all that."

Gabe hadn't known all that, even if he didn't say so. He did ask about fuel and was told that there were a couple of refineries left that made gasoline, diesel fuel, jet fuel, and other products, but at least in the United States, these were now overseen by the government, and it was often difficult to gain access to the products for civilian use.

The trip to Anchorage was going to be a long one, so it gave Gabe ample opportunity to learn more about society in general and the Bickmeiers specifically. Karl told him that he had received his Bachelor of Science and master's degrees in mechanical engineering, plus a second master's—in electrical engineering—all from MIT. He hadn't seen a need for a PhD and noted that if he had earned one, he'd have been writing grant requests all the time and really hadn't wanted to do that.

Karl's sister had gotten her PhD, was married with two kids, twins, and they were all on the interstellar space mission. Karl missed them and wondered if he would ever see them again. He hadn't heard anything from them since 2071, when the death flu hit. He assumed that those on the ships had been protected from the pandemic but was worried that there might not be anyone left on Earth who could complete its portion of the mission. He simply didn't know. But maybe this adventure with Gabe would shed some light on that subject for him.

Gabe was surprised and more than a little curious when Karl mentioned his sister and the space mission, but decided to let that go for now. Gabe did, however, express a desire to know about the government structure, and while Karl thought that it was interesting that Gabe seemed to know almost nothing about anything current, he tried to fill him in. The death flu had been so contagious and spread so fast, any place where there had been concentrations of people and someone might be infected, nearly everyone had perished. That had had a profound impact on political power as most career politicians had succumbed. In spite of what people might say about politicians, this had created a large vacuum filled in a number of different ways around the globe, but in the United States, military organizations had been, in many cases, able to isolate themselves from the death flu. The Joint Chiefs of Staff had reorganized, and with their organizational structure relatively intact, though weakened, they had taken over and established a form of martial law. It hadn't been a military coup; they had only filled a vacuum. There was currently a four-star general elected by the joint chiefs who had taken over as president. Even today, the top dog called himself president even though he wore a military uniform for almost every public appearance and was, in fact, the commander in chief.

From there, there were really only two government branches now set up: the traditional military branch and the government branch. The government branch assigned military governors to the various states. In Alaska, there was an air-force colonel in charge. Under her authority were the so-called state police, along with what were left of the old bureaucratic functions.

Karl told Gabe, "Of course, the number of states has changed. The territory of Alaska alone stands unchanged, but there were some new boundary lines established, with parts of Canada joining in and parts of Mexico, New Mexico, Arizona, and California becoming a new state of North Mexico. People of Mexican descent mostly populated those regions anyway.

"Government isn't anything like it was in the old days, but it does work. When something needs to get done, it might take some time, but it does get done. Television and radio stations all shut down because, as for-profit enterprises, they needed funds to operate. Few businesses or customers of those businesses meant no profits. So the government took over the stations with the strongest signals, hired the operators and broadcasters who had survived the pandemic, and they now broadcast news three times a day via radio. We don't have TV around here. Maybe they do in the south. The news might be biased, but then it was in the old days as well, depending upon which station you listened to.

"So, from my perspective, the system works. As long as people pay attention to the rules, they are left alone, and if something is needed, it seems to come about. I'd call this a benevolent dictatorship."

Around midday, they had made it to Moose Pass and the cutoff to Seward. They stopped for a much-needed break from the ride and set out a lunch. Gabe said, "The pass seems aptly named as there seem to be moose everywhere."

"Yeah," said Karl. "They're everywhere like squirrels, only bigger."

Len had been quiet all morning, listening to his grandfather's stories, but at this squirrel comment, he groaned, bringing Gabe's attention toward him. "Len," started Gabe, "there's quite a contrast between what you and your grandfather experienced up to about the age you are now. Is that opportunity something you miss?"

"I don't know," said Len. "I mean, my grandparents have taught me a lot. And the people in Homer have each taught me something. I don't know how you can compare my education with an education someone else might have received, but I think I could hold my own, certainly from a hands-on, technical point of view. What I think I'm missing is social studies. No one is inclined to fill me in on subjects like the pandemic, climate-condition changes, and why I don't see any other young people. I get bits and pieces, but no one really wants to talk about these things."

Karl said, "I think Len can probably fix anything except electronics. We don't have much need for anything like that around here these days. And he is correct. Besides missing out on learning about social and environmental issues, he has missed out a lot by not having anyone around his age. Maybe we can fix that someday."

Gabe managed to ration himself food wise, limiting his meal to three cold pulled-pork sandwiches made with thick slabs of homemade bread, a half gallon of iced tea, and large piece of cake left over from the community party. Karl sarcastically asked Gabe, "So, not hungry today? You might fade away if you're not careful."

Not really picking up on the sarcasm, Gabe answered with, "No, this will be fine. I'll have a big meal this evening when we get to Anchorage. We will get there today, won't we?"

"We should," said Karl. "I'm not sure Anchorage has enough food for a big meal to satisfy you. Unbelievable. Len, you drive for a while." And they loaded up and drove off.

Late that evening, they arrived on the outskirts of Anchorage. There were a number of old, abandoned buildings they could have used, but they chose a bed-and-breakfast that the

Bickmeiers stayed in from time to time. Gabe opted to sleep out on the back porch under the stars, which worked out well as there were no beds big enough for him anyway. Before heading out for a dinner, Karl took the innkeeper aside and warned her that his traveling companion could pack food away like no one he had ever seen. "Be prepared," he warned, "and we'll cover the extra cost."

Before turning in, they went to a local diner. As usual, Gabe managed to eat for at least two people. He didn't stand out as much as when he wore his standard-issue uniform, but he was still noticed because of his size and long, silver-blond hair, though currently tied back, it wasn't his most striking feature.

In spite of Karl's warning, the innkeeper wasn't nearly as prepared for breakfast as she'd thought she would be. Not a crumb was left when they finished eating. Since the trio planned to stay that night as well, she vowed to have enough the next day.

Following breakfast, they cranked up the old Ford and headed for the capitol building on the other side of town. It was actually in the corner of the Richardson Military Reservation. Karl figured that spot had been selected for efficiency. Unlike the military operations, the capital building had no fence around it. Certainly, the architecture was nothing to write home about, but it didn't look uninviting either.

As they drove up, the honor guards had them stop as the trio entered the parking lot. But the guards only wanted to look at the car before letting them proceed. Gabe caught their attention as the car stopped, but nothing more.

When Karl parked the car, he said to Gabe and Len, "I wouldn't be surprised if we have to make an appointment. The governor probably has a full plate. But let's find out."

A master sergeant at the reception desk confirmed that the governor was in and did have a full agenda. It didn't look like they would get past the receptionist until Gabe started talking with him. With each passing moment, the sergeant became less and less convinced that the governor couldn't see them until finally, he said, "Let me see if you can have a moment with her."

The governor colonel was sitting at her desk when the trio entered her office. She was in full-dress air-force uniform and had a pile of papers in front of her. She was older than Gabe expected, and she was visibly annoyed with the unscheduled interruption. Still, she stood up, introduced herself as Colonel Sheffield, shook hands, and offered everyone a chair. When she shook Gabe's hand, Karl seemed to notice annoyance and tension melt away. In a very polite voice, she asked, "What can I do for you?"

Gabe explained his mission, and for the next two hours, questions and answers were exchanged. Much of the information they obtained confirmed what Karl had said, but with more detail. The way government was now organized; senior officers didn't retire with comfortable pensions after twenty years of service. They stayed on as there were so few new recruits coming along behind them to take their places. When government positions became available, older, senior officers were transferred to them from military operations, the exception being the president, who was selected by the Joint Chiefs of Staff.

Support staff was selected the same way. The receptionist, for example, had been in the service many years but instead of retiring had been assigned this desk job. They usually chose support staff from the same military branch as the governor's, with governors usually selected based on a state's geography. Heavy maritime states might have a governor who was either a navy captain or rear admiral. An air-force colonel had been assigned to Alaska because of the need for aircraft to cover the state and the protective bombers and fighter planes based there.

Colonel Sheffield had a close working relationship with the military side of the operation and had a shared concern over Korea. Because North Korea had remained isolated from the rest of the world, very few North Koreans had succumbed to the death flu. This had left them in a strong military position, and they had used it to their advantage, annexing South Korea and becoming an even bigger worldwide threat. Korea had never attacked the United States directly, but the constant threat meant the United States military had to stay vigilant. Korea could flex its muscle at any time.

No new aircraft were being built, but older equipment was being constantly repaired using parts from "donor" equipment. It didn't really create a shortage, as the number of staff within all branches of the military was smaller because of the death flu and lack of new recruits. Since no other country was developing any new technology, the United States still had the most formidable military force.

This was the first time Karl had seen information flowing from the authorities so freely, so he took advantage and asked about the interstellar space fleet. Was there any word from it?

The governor looked at Karl gravely and said, "I wish I knew more, but quite simply, I can say it doesn't look good. Everyone on the United Nations Space Commission died during the pandemic. I have no details, but it appears the technical support staff also died or disappeared. They had moved, or started to move, the communication center out of Houston as the ocean waters threatened to flood it. They intended to setup a redundant system up at Poker Flats north of Fairbanks, but from what I understand, it wasn't completed. I have no idea how far they got.

"The Gate was functioning before the pandemic hit, connecting the colonies in our solar system. Actually, because of the Gate, the pandemic spread to the colonies, and at least the party line is that no one survived. Beyond that, I have not heard a thing. What's your interest?"

Karl, trying to remain composed, said, "My sister and her family shipped out with the fleet. We have not heard anything from it since 2071. Is anyone doing anything to reestablish the space command?"

The governor said sympathetically, "As far I know, few people in authority are doing anything to get the program back up and running. It isn't that they don't care; it just isn't a priority for them. Part of the problem is, of course, the need for international cooperation to get things back together organizationally. Remember, this initiative was global. I'm sorry. I wish I could tell you more. Though I think we should assume your family is fine until we know for sure."

That night, when he thought no one was around, Karl went to his knees and prayed. Not saying a word, Gabe watched and listened from the shadows.

The next day after breakfast, Gabe said thanks to Len and Karl and said he would be moving on. He didn't tell them, but he was going to Poker Flats to see what condition the communications center might be in.

Len asked, "Will we see you again?"

And Gabe responded simply with "There's a strong possibility."

Karl and Len then cranked up the old Ford and headed back to Homer.

Len said, "I like that guy, but what a difference in the Ford with him not weighing us down. It felt like we were driving uphill the whole trip. Thanks for letting me come along. It was interesting, to say the least."

Karl said, "Yes. Interesting."

Chapter 20
Poker Flats

After leaving Karl and Len Bickmeier, Gabe found a quiet spot and changed into his standard-issue clothing, bundling his new clothes into the antigravity pack. He then put on the pack and took off for Poker Flats where the redundant communication center for the space fleet was supposed to be set up. He wasn't sure why, but something told him Poker Flats needed to be better understood before a plan could be formulated.

Gabe flew following the road, as he saw no one who would spot him. When he got to Fairbanks, he skirted around the edge of the once-thriving community. It certainly wasn't thriving now. There were piles of supplies that been delivered for one purpose or another, but they looked like they had been there for years and had remained untouched. He noticed only a few people walking around the streets.

The once-proud university appeared abandoned, as was true also of the nearby air-force base. *How sad*, thought Gabe. *It would be little wonder if Poker Flats were abandoned.* Poker Flats had been the University of Alaska's rocket-launch facility. The only university-owned facility of its type, it had originally been designed to help study the aurora borealis. It seemed logical to Gabe that it would make a good backup communications center. It was away from high-population areas and potentially easy to make secure. Had they in fact done so? He would take a look.

When he arrived, he was disappointed in what he saw. Three Redstone rockets from a bygone era were each sitting on one of the four launch pads. They looked like they had been there for some time and were in poor condition. At the fourth pad, a rocket was lying on its side.

Gabe landed and, not seeing anyone around, walked through the unlocked door into the control bunker. With a sinking feeling, he saw crates stacked high, each with the words "United Nations Stellar Commission: Caution Sensitive Equipment" on it. Everything was covered with thick dust. There was no sign anyone had vandalized or looted anything. *Even so*, Gabe thought, *it's a good thing this is the backup facility to Houston.* As he continued to look around, it became clear that no one had even been there in many years. Outside were abandoned trucks and a crude mass grave. On a piece of discarded metal was a list of the names of people who had been buried there. The last person alive must have simply walked away. Hopefully, he or she had survived.

There's nothing to see here, thought Gabe. When he left Poker Flats, he glided over the only road in and out of the facility. It was in horrendous shape. Along with the world's new focus, it was easy to see why no one would have come back.

Gabe had plenty of time to process what he had learned thus far. He started to understand why his people had been awakened. In many respects, the world was in a better place than it had been in centuries, though it had been at the expense of the human population. He supposed something had to give with its rapid technological advancements. Sometimes though, slow and steady is the best course so things don't get out of control. Gabe's mind then progressed to thoughts of the future. *Where is humanity going from here? What about the space fleet, and what about Schem?* He hadn't been sent out with the fleet without something for him to do. It seemed like the options for Schem would have been limited, but were they? Certainly, he wouldn't have been sent off without any hope of rejuvenation. Or would he? That was a thought that Gabe did not want to consider.

He felt a sense of depression he hadn't experienced in centuries. He knew his people would be depending upon him for guidance. He had to snap out of it and come up with a game plan before consulting the Boss. He'd often thought that the Boss manipulated his and his team's actions. There were always too many coincidences. Still, he was always reminded, "Don't bring me a problem without a possible solution."

That last thought didn't help. Good grief!

Chapter 21

Results

By August 1, Gabe and the other members of the group except for Schem-Hampha-Rae were back at the habitat in Augustine Island, with Naki and Ara the last ones to return. Little was discussed prior to everyone being assembled, as Gabe thought it was important for his team to hear the results uniformly and firsthand. With other teams activated around the globe, it wasn't initially clear which team was to take the lead, so he took the time while waiting to confer with these other teams and it became obvious which group that would be. Gabe would also share that with his team after a hearty meal and a good night's rest.

On August 2, the five earthbound members of Gabe's team met in the galley for breakfast. The robotics had done their usual fine job of collecting fresh food and preparing it for the group. Eggs, ham steaks, waffles with real maple syrup, coffee, grapefruit, toast, and jam was a good start for the morning. While finishing up, Gabe started the meeting. "We started our surveys with some basic information already known. It is the nondata facts that we need to understand. So, starting with what we knew already, what are the facts?"

Naki said, "It is obvious the world's population was growing beyond the Earth's capacity to accommodate it. You'd think that people would have been a bit more intelligent about it, but the world's political and religious leaders, avoiding political blunders, never made the hard choices to reduce population growth until it was too late, or almost too late. So, instead of facing the issue head on, it appears that officials elected to distract the general population with this scheme of someday moving huge numbers of people to another planet."

Ara added, "I'm not sure when, but a transporter of some kind was invented that allowed people to instantaneously move from one place to another. They call it a Gate. The catch was that you needed a Gate on both ends. They were playing with it inside the solar system, but to work between star systems, a Gate would have to be built at the other location. So they sent off this fleet of ships with everything they needed to build that Gate. This is—or was—a huge endeavor."

Gabe interrupted saying, "Schem was brought out of stasis long before the rest of us and led to go with the fleet. Out of all the teams, he was the only one brought out at the time. I admit, I don't always understand the workings of the systems or the Boss, but this is right up there with many of the great mysteries we've dealt with over the years."

Naki asked, "Have you tried to reach him?"

"You mean Schem? No. I'll try to reach him later," said Gabe.

"So," Naki said, "on the way back, one of our stops was at Earth's Gate installation. I'm not sure what to make of it exactly. As far as we could tell, it is all there, and it is well protected, but there doesn't seem to be anyone around who knows how to operate it."

"Just as bad," said Ara, "the interstellar command and communications center in Houston doesn't seem to be operational. It could be, I suppose, but the chances of it being flooded out seems high. The place also has the similar issue of no one knowing how it is supposed to work, but in any case, it appears to be damaged through neglect beyond a simple repair. There was apparently a move to set up a backup system when Houston was facing flooding waters from the Gulf. Naki and I have no information on the status of this so-called backup facility."

Gabe cut in. "It appears they were in the midst of moving the vital equipment to Alaska as a safer option to Houston. I actually went to the site already and found it abandoned, with crates of parts just sitting there."

Naki said, "As far as anyone we met knows, there have been no communications with the interstellar space fleet since the death flu hit in 2071. Up until then, it appears the fleet was functioning as planned. That is truly amazing, if you ask me. It will be interesting to hear from Schem."

"So, the death flu hit in 2071," said Ere, almost as a passing thought. "Why did our habitat wait so long to bring us out of stasis?"

Gabe answered, "I think I know why. The Earth's population being reduced by the death flu might have been considered a natural adjustment, like many events in the past—other plagues and major wars, for example. However, the real concern, as in the past, is when things start to go too far in the wrong direction. Nuclear holocaust, for example, is not acceptable and requires intervention. Excessive pollution is not acceptable. In this case, the issue is the continued drop in the population. Globally, there just don't seem to be traditional family values that include children. It seems that even the children who are born are more like accidents rather than planned. I met one young man who seems to fall into that category. If this keeps up, humankind will simply die off. I believe it is that trend that finally activated our teams. I don't know how Schem fits into this theory, so there is probably more for us to discover."

Ere said, "I think Kem and I met an example of failed family thinking. The fellow we met—well, actually, we never actually met him, but we spoke to him—is a real loner. I think it has been years since he actually saw anyone in the flesh, and he doesn't seem to care. Unless you're really clever, it is pretty hard to make kids all by yourself, and while this guy seems really clever, that is not what he's interested in. Oh, and by the way, Kem and I discovered that we've been enjoying this guy's wine. How is that for a coincidence?"

"That is very interesting," said a surprised Gabe, "but let's stay on topic. What else have we learned?"

Kem said, "The death flu really forced a lot of changes. Territorial lines have been redrawn, and at least the United States government is administered by the military. They control everything that is important while still protecting the nation's population from foreign aggression. Equipment is maintained as best as it can by taking parts from machines that are no longer used. It's a great recycling program, but a lot of work. Korea seems to be the biggest threat."

"Yes," agreed Gabe. "I talked with the governor of Alaska. She confirmed that the military is in charge. The younger members of the military are filling the more traditional military roles, though 'younger' is starting to be a relative term. Older members are put in traditional political and bureaucratic government roles. They did this to fill a void, and I got the impression they wouldn't mind going back to the old ways if it were possible. National boundary lines have changed in most areas. Some minor, some major. Kurdistan is now a recognized country and seems to be the only stable force in that part of the world. The Kurds occupy all the lands they consider theirs and have drawn some pretty tough lines around themselves while allowing all the others in the region to continue to fight and kill each other off. They suffered like everyone else during the pandemic, but their strong sense of wanting a peaceful religious country has served them well. But that is just an example."

Kem said, "We didn't get into this very heavily, but it appears that the feared 'global warming' or, more correctly, climate change, really did occur. Traditional coastal areas are flooded. We saw some pretty interesting efforts to protect Boston from rising waters. Fluctuations in the weather are much more severe than predicted, with storms that are apparently unbelievable. In the North Atlantic regions, there is a new mini–ice age starting. Storm after storm is dumping snow in Greenland and other northern lands for nine months of the year. It doesn't seem like it will take long, relatively speaking, before glaciers start moving again. That should prove interesting."

Gabe said, "I did have a virtual conference with the other team leaders. They confirm that what we have been seeing is true on a global basis. With the exception of Korea, most populations continue to decrease. The common theme for everything we've been skirting around is that very few seem to care about anything beyond the immediate future. Or, if they do care, they are waiting for someone to tell them what to do. In the meantime, people are doing what they are comfortable doing and not much more. Living life, but not planning for the future."

All agreed that it seemed to be what they had witnessed.

Gabe said, "I think it's time I talk to Schem, assuming he is still alive."

That last comment startled everyone as they had never considered the possibility that someone in their team might actually die. They sat speechless as Gabe headed for the communications room.

Gabe knew that there had not been any official communications with the space fleet since 2071. It was now 2085, and there must be some part of Schem that wondered why he had not heard from anyone in his team.

While it had still worked, the UNSC's communications technology had had a time lag between messages that increased with the distance between the fleet and Earth. Gabe's system operated very differently. He would send a message and wait for a response, assuming Schem was not near his portable unit. There was no time delay when both parties were "dialed in." Their system required only pure thought that operated outside the human realm of understood physics. Pure thought meant there could be no distraction so the communicators needed to create a necessary meditative state in order for the system to work. In the communications room, Gabe closed the soundproof door behind him and placed the thought translator on his head. To the uninitiated, the thought translator looked a lot like an old rag mop. Once on, the "rag" transmitters fell down around his head a full 360 degrees. There were no cables or any other ancillary equipment. Once it was in place, Gabe lay down on a bed with the lights turned off and the door sealed. Ventilation was completely silent in the room and perfectly regulated. There was nothing to distract him from his thoughts.

It was here that Gabe's training in the thought translator came in. He was a level-four user, the highest level that could be obtained, and it was reserved for group leaders. Schem was a level-three user, which was more than adequate with a level four at the other end. No one else in the group was above a level two, and Gabe wondered if that was why Schem had been the one brought out of stasis initially. Had something, somewhere determined that this type of communication would be required? Probably.

Gabe relaxed and let his thoughts take over. He then steered them toward Schem. Gabe pictured Schem out in space, and after several minutes, he focused in on Schem's thought transmitter. The good news was that it was intact. It had not been destroyed or damaged. But, as Gabe had suspected, it was unattended. He would leave a message and try to establish contact in twenty-four hours. Protocol required Schem to check his device once a day, but after all this time with no communications, protocol might not be the highest priority for him. Gabe could only hope that things would fall back into place for his wayward team member.

It seemed like only a few minutes had passed, but in fact, Gabe had been in the communications room for nearly an hour and a half. That's what concentration can do. He left the room knowing he would return the next day.

Chapter 22
The Fix

It had been decided long before the interstellar space fleet was launched that official time on the ships would be adjusted to match the date and time on Earth. So, even though the passing of time on the ships was different relative to Earth time, work schedules were set according to the official time. It helped maintain a psychological link to home. So, the actual date on Earth of August 3, 2085, was the official date for the space fleet. This helped get people reestablish some sense of normalcy after the *India* disaster.

To further aid in the sense of normalcy, the admiral and the vice admirals maintained the tradition of transferring the flag from ship to ship, but with one modification. One vice admiral would remain on a different ship just in case. No one wanted to take the chance of losing all three of the highest-ranking officers in another accident. There was also one other more or less subtle change. The Finn was no longer a bartender. He was now special counsel to the admiral. Initially, there had been a number of raised eyebrows over this promotion, but in his role as special counsel, he would meet anyone who had a concern over his position at a ships' bar, and within minutes, all questions relative to the promotion would simply fade away. There was just something about this guy that made people feel so comfortable that they would simply mellow out. The admiral had seen this happen more than once, and wanting to take advantage of whatever was happening, made sure that the Finn was never far away. Of course, in this new formal position, he was usually addressed as Sherman Hamer, his adopted shipboard alias, or simply as Counselor. Even Schem was now getting confused on what he called himself these days.

This month, the admiral and VAAS were quartered on the Starship *British Commonwealth*. A lot had changed in the last ten years, some good and some very troubling. The good news was that the engineers had become free to discuss the problems with the engines and open up a dialogue. With this opportunity, the scientists on board the ships acted like kids in a candy store with an opportunity to explore the faults in the engines, specifically the fission/fusion reactions. Where the engineers wanted everything to function as planned, the scientists, on the other hand, looked at the problem as a challenge and almost didn't care about the consequences of the engines not functioning properly. Theories were put forward and batted around. Scientists would propose one thing, and the engineers would find the flaws in the theory.

Back in October 2079, the admiral's flag had been moved to the Starship *China*. Along with the admiral, the VAAS, and special counselor to the admiral, Sherman Hamer was in residence. The counselor was usually free to wander the ships when the flag was transferred, except that he was required for most meetings in the admiral's quarters. Schem took this opportunity to better understand what was going on within each ship and periodically offer some advice. There was usually nothing significant needed in the greater scheme of things, just helpful support with personal issues. Curiously, this often led the recipient of the advice to find the ship's chapel for some quiet time of reflection.

During the second week of October, Schem was in his favorite place, the ship's lounge, having one of his not-so-light snacks. The ship's chief machinist mate, Fung Lee, asked if he could join Schem, and of course Schem, in perfect Mandarin, invited him to a table. A couple of fresh pints of a cloned Tsingtao beer were shared while Schem finished his snack. When he was done eating, the machinist mate started talking about the engines. "I'm only a machinist mate," Lee said, "but I have an idea. I'm not having much success getting our engineers and scientists to listen to me, but can I show you what I have in mind?"

"Sure," said Schem, "but you realize I'm not a scientist or an engineer."

It was true that he wasn't an engineer or scientist as most people knew him, but his knowledge was far above what anyone would suspect. Schem had known what a fix could look like, but team rules only allowed him to encourage leadership, not lead. This was potentially the opportunity he had been hoping for, and he eagerly viewed the drawings showing the new piece and how it could be retrofitted to the engines. It was elegantly simple, yet nearly perfect in concept and in design. Schem was thrilled and said, "Well, I don't know if it will work, but you need to show it to the right people. How can I help?"

Lee continued, "There is another piece to this fix that I think should be looked at, but the details on how it would work are beyond me. This would require a lot of higher math. The biggest danger from the engines and plasma fields is when they are essentially shut down and then turned back on each time we make a turn. Why do we do that? Why not simply make a huge one-eighty-degree turn with the ships while adjusting the propulsion without shutting them down? The momentum would still keep us moving in the right direction, sort of like a controlled skid. I got the idea watching some of the old movies where a guy races his car down the street and then turns the steering wheel hard, turning the car around, and while driving backward, he starts shooting at the bad guys.

"If you take these two ideas to the admiral or vice admiral of operations to see what they think without mentioning where you got them, they might like it. If they don't, I don't want to be ridiculed. Make something up about how you got this plan, but don't tell them it came from a machinist. I don't care who gets the credit if it works. If no one thinks it will work, at least they won't laugh at me. And, well, I'd feel a lot safer if it does work. After all, I'm on this ship, too."

"OK," said Schem, "I'll see what I can do. In the meantime, let's raise a glass to ideas, and you can tell me how things are going for you other than this." Lee, now feeling somewhat relieved with someone taking him seriously, spent the next hour talking about his expanding family and his job. This was as important to Schem as seeing the potential fix to the engine issues, because it reinforced a new concern he was having about the ships' population.

At 0800 hours the next morning, Sherman Hamer, special counselor to the admiral, met with her for breakfast in her quarters. Schem helped himself to a hefty plate of food and some strong tea. Ada said, "Sherman, I don't know how you can pack away so much food and never seem to get fat. You must work out a lot to stay in shape."

Sherman didn't tell Ada that he had already had a full breakfast in the mess hall before coming to the briefing room. Having breakfast with the admiral on a regular basis allowed him some relief from hiding his appetite. He felt a little guilty needing to eat so much, but as no one was going hungry because of him, he felt only a little guilty, not a lot. Instead, he said, finishing with a laugh, "I have a high metabolism, and you keep me pretty busy, you know."

Ada looked at Schem with her increased use of squinting eyes and said simply, "Not that busy."

"I have something to show you," said Schem, quickly changing the subject as he pulled out Lee's plans.

"What's this?" asked Ada. "Are you now a designer of some sort?"

"No," said Schem. "I'll be perfectly honest. The chief machinist mate, Fung Lee, came up with what he thinks is a fix for the engines. He asked me not to mention the source of this potential fix because the *China* engineers and scientists won't even look at it, and he's afraid others won't either if they knew the source. You know, 'How can a simple machinist come up with a fix when our great minds can't?' So he asked me to show this to you and maybe the VAO for an opinion. What do you think?"

Ada answered, "Sherman, I have no idea if this would work. Richard transferred to the *China* with me, and Dawn is back on the *British Commonwealth*, but they are due to trade places in a couple of days. I think Dawn is much more qualified to evaluate this than I am. Send her a copy of the plans, and we'll discuss them when she gets here. I'm not happy that this has not gone through any chain of command. I hope this isn't setting some sort of precedent. On the other hand, I'm more than a little troubled that *China*'s engineers and scientists are so impressed with their own so-called genius that they can't be bothered to consider an idea that someone else might have. What else is going on?"

"Well, there is more," said Sherman. "Everyone knows it, but I suspect the obvious was so obvious that no one could see it. It appears our Mr. Lee had an epiphany while watching some old movies. Instead of shutting down the engines when we turn, he is suggesting we keep the engines on and go into a giant skid, turning the ships around while the engines are still running. Reduce the output to the 0.5 g as we go into the deceleration leg. With our speed, the skid would be huge to avoid crushing everyone, but that would be up to our scientists to calculate."

The admiral raised her eyebrows and said, "Well, it isn't like we don't have enough space to make the turn. Hmm. It would also mean that we wouldn't experience any times of zero gravity. That has never been a hundred percent smooth in implementation. On the other hand, depending upon which way the ships turned, we might have a hefty centrifugal force to deal with pushing us down or making us feel like we're walking up and down a hill if we turn on our side. Interesting idea, though. The number crunchers will have a field day figuring out how big a turn and recalculating direction and arrival time." She added with a laugh, "It's about time these geeks had something worthwhile to do!"

The admiral and the admiral's special counselor spent the next half hour talking about the "weather." In Schem's presence, Ada calmed herself before facing another trying day.

During the next week, the VAO, Dawn Cohen, studied the proposed fix with engineers on the *British Commonwealth*. Dawn didn't tell them the source of the fix, and some assumed that she was the designer, even though she continually deflected the credit. During the last week of October, all the engineers and scientists from all the ships were invited to review the proposed fix. The *China* engineers and scientists thought the plan looked familiar, but since they had never actually studied it when Fung Lee presented it, they never put two and two together, probably showing their real level of genius. All agreed that the fix was simple. In fact, it was such a simple solution that for the next two months, the scientists and engineers tried to prove that it wouldn't work. But, try as they might, they finally concluded that the modification should work, and it was implemented—first on one engine, then the rest.

In the meantime, the VAAS, Richard Sylva, introduced the concept of a skidding turn to the astrophysicists. Just as his sister had done with the possible simple fix to the engines, Richard kept the source of this concept to himself until the scientists were well into accepting it and were busy with their calculations. They thought the concept was fascinating.

On December 24, 2079, Admiral Ada Sylva identified the chief machinist mate on the Starship *China*, Fung Lee, as the source of the design and the skid-turn concept. Some engineers and scientists were mortified. Others were so involved with the result that the reaction was more along the lines of "Yeah, yeah, whatever." They didn't care. In the end, Fung Lee was honored. The admiral called the fix and concept Christmas gifts that he had brought. Some children took the Christmas spirit a bit further, noting that Fung Lee was in fact rather round and also sported a white beard. The beard was a bit thin by Santa Claus standards, but it didn't stop Fung Lee from getting nicknamed Saint Nick Lee. He accepted the title in good humor even though he was a practicing Hindu.

Schem was more than pleased with the result. Obviously, he was pleased that a fix for the engines had been achieved, but he was even more pleased with the date of the announcement bringing a new attention toward the meaning of Christmas. Everyone seemed to feel the Christmas spirit, even those non-Christians who would call the feeling something else. Schem didn't care. This was the happiest he had felt in a very, very long time.

The unfortunate part of the fix was that it hadn't come sooner. As had been suggested in 2075, the ships' engineers had looked at the possibility of moving engines from one ship to another as an additional backup to the two spare engines carried by each ship. They decided that it could be done and eventually learned that they would have to do exactly that. Before the modification and new turning protocol could be implemented, more engines went critical and had to be jettisoned. While no serious damage was done to the five remaining ships, engine inventory was taking a beating. The Starship *United States* had lost an engine, so with one spare rotated into place, it had one spare left. The Starship *South America*, however, had lost three engines by 2077. The fleet stopped acceleration for two and a half weeks while one spare engine from the Starship *Russia* was removed and reinstalled on the *South America*. The installation was successful, but it was a nightmare for engineering to keep engines from going critical during the shutdown. With the two-and-a-half-week schedule change, the scientists had to once again do some serious recalculations of the acceleration/deceleration schedule. Once the ships got moving again, everyone breathed a sigh of relief with gravity being reinstated. Canaries, chickens, dogs, and bees floating around for two and a half weeks had created all kinds of havoc.

By 2085, a new crisis was appearing on the ships. Each had been designed to accommodate eighteen thousand people with an initial complement of fifteen thousand. The extra space had been designed in for flexibility in the ships' populations. That, of course, had been somewhat taken up when the ship *India* was destroyed. And from a planning standpoint, this had worked out fine. However, planners had expected people to die and children to be born on a one-to-one ratio with some margin of error. By 2085, death rates were far lower than expected as people stayed healthy. The average life expectancy was much higher than on Earth. At the same time couples, both formal and informal, were producing more children than expected. It was probably a combination of feeling free of the population-control measures implemented on Earth before they had left and not enough to keep the mind occupied. In any case, the result was that the ships were getting crowded.

Just like on Earth before the ships had been launched, rules were being put in place on the ships to reduce the birth rate, first voluntarily, then as a matter of law. Still, children were being conceived, and no one wanted to take harsher measures. Instead, the admiral's special counselor, Sherman Hamer, was sent out to preach and to meet with young-couple groups and ask that they use birth-control measures. His presence seemed to make an impact, and the birth rate dropped.

This population fix took a decade to solve, with the total population on the five ships stabilizing at around 100,000. This was about 10,000 over the 90,000-design capacity of the five ships. It was crowed but still manageable.

So, while not everything on board the space fleet was perfect, all key issues had been addressed. At least on the ships, humankind was back on course.

Chapter 23
No Longer Alone

It was after one of those particularly long days of talking to people that the admiral's counselor quit for the day. It was August 3, 2085. He had been off duty for an hour, had his fifth meal, and was back in his quarters. He tried to check his clandestine communication device every day, but after eighteen years on the ships, he had started to wonder if the habitat had made a mistake, and he became a little lax. Had he been brought out of stasis and led to the starships by mistake? Would he make it back for rejuvenation before it was too late for him? Well, he was here, and he had certainly tried to make the best of the situation.

Today, however, he did check and was surprised to see a faint, red glow indicating a message. The message had to be short, based on system design, so all it said was, "Gabe-Re-El, August 4, 1400 hours, Greenwich Mean Time." Schem was overwhelmed, and for the first time in centuries, he wept, thankful his team members couldn't see him, and at the same time, thankful he wasn't alone anymore. He almost didn't care what Gabe had to say. He now could share and maybe find out what was going on.

On August 4, 2085, a few minutes before 1400 hours Greenwich Mean Time, Schem was in his quarters. He secured the door, used whatever he could find to seal out any light and sound, placed the communicator on his head, and lay down on his bed. Schem was not at the same level of training with the device as Gabe, but he was good. He put himself into a trancelike state and waited. Precisely at 1400 hours, Schem heard Gabe's thoughts.

For over an hour, Schem and Gabe shared what they knew. Gabe wasn't too surprised to learn about state of the interstellar space fleet and still didn't completely understand why Schem was there in the first place. Schem, of course, wasn't certain why he was there either.

For Schem's part, he was shocked to learn about Earth's pandemic, the state of global climate change, and the continued loss in human population. While it hadn't been clear why Schem had been brought out of stasis, it was certainly clear why the rest of his team and the other teams on Earth had been activated. A new course for humankind was once again required, perhaps as significant as the one he and his team had witnessed over two thousand years earlier. This was a lot to comprehend.

Before the session ended, Schem asked, "What shall I do? Shall I inform the admiral?"

Gabe answered, "I'm not sure yet. How would you explain how you learned about Earth if you don't tell her everything?"

Schem said, "The admiral already has suspicions of me. I suspect that if I just tell her everything, it might only confirm her suspicions, and we can move on from there. At some point, I have to tell her something as the entire fleet assumes that communications with Earth will be reestablished once the Gate is installed and activated. If Earth's Gate isn't ready to send or receive, the ships' crews will need to be prepared."

Gabe said, "Let me have some time to consider Earth's communications systems and Gate status. I hesitate to bring this up right now, but how much do they know about their destination, Epsilon Eridani?"

Schem answered, "Well, they have their eyes on one planet, EE b, that they think is best suited for human occupation, but they also know they have to explore a little and may have to pick an alternative planet. There's a lot of work to set up the Gate, and they don't want to rush into anything, especially after the amount of time it will take to get there. Plus, their resources will not allow a false start."

Gabe said, "Do they know the planet is inhabited?"

Schem, somewhat shocked, said, "I'm sure they don't. I didn't know! Are they friendly?"

Gabe answered, "I'm not sure."

With this latest bombshell, Schem and Gabe terminated their communication, agreeing to be in touch again in three days at the same hour.

Schem pulled himself out of his trance, sat up, removed his headgear, and sat for the longest time with eyes closed, his hands together, and his head bowed, contemplating the exchange. He had thought he would be happy to be no longer alone. He was, but he was also filled with despair. He was on a spaceship heading for a planet where the inhabitants might not want these aliens preparing their planet for a massive invasion of humans. And, on Earth, few cared about the space fleet and certainly were in no condition to support it. What a mess.

Back on Earth, Gabe was also sitting with his eyes closed, hands clasped, and head bowed. He also had a lot to consider.

Chapter 24
Gabe-Re-El's Dilemma

On August 5, 2085, Kem-U-El, Ere-Mi-El, Na-Ki-Ir, and Ara-Ri-El were still waiting in the habitat's galley, waiting for word from Gabe-Re-El. Gabe had been in the communications room for twenty-six hours. Since he was in there with nothing to eat, they all figured he would have to come out soon. Just the thought of Gabe not eating was enough for the rest of the team to order up a meal, which they were enjoying when Gabe emerged at about 1600 hours. Without a word, he sat down at the table and joined in the mealtime. Everyone else at the table looked at Gabe, waiting for some word. Anything. But no one wanted to be the first to speak.

After Gabe inhaled some food and a fresh-brewed cup of coffee, he finally noticed that everyone had stopped eating and that they were staring at him. Somewhat perplexed by this, he nearly whispered, "What?"

Kem took the lead and asked, "Well, what happened? Did you communicate with Schem? Is he OK? What's he doing, for heaven's sake?"

Gabe said, "'For heaven's sake' seems appropriate. He is, in fact, with the interstellar space fleet, way out in the heavens. He is actually more than fine and has managed to work his charm from lowly bartender up to being the admiral's special counselor. They all think he is from Finland, and he has assumed the name of Sherman Hamer. He does think that at least the admiral isn't completely on board with the story, but she trusts him anyway. He was more than relieved to hear from us. He has been out there without any of his own kind for far longer than most of us ever experienced in the past. Making it even worse for him, he still isn't sure why he was brought out of stasis and led to the fleet in the first place.

"As far as the fleet is concerned, they lost one of the six ships to an explosion killing thousands. Apparently in their rush to get the fleet underway back in 2057, the people in charge hadn't provided enough time for adequate testing of the engines. And, as seems to be typical, the decision-makers weren't going on the mission so were a bit cavalier about potential engine problems. Anyway, the fleet seems to have come up with a fix, and they are still on their way to Epsilon Eridani. They believe they are no longer in communication with mission control because they are out of range. That might be true, but we happen to know there is more to the story, and now Schem knows.

"Schem tells me that they have a couple of new problems coming up. One, I think, you're going to find very interesting. It is a hundred and eighty degrees from what we're seeing here on Earth. While the human population continues to decrease at an alarming rate here, there seems to be a baby boom in the fleet. That's combined with the fact that people are living longer on the ships than expected—a lot longer, as it turns out. The upper echelon has had some success getting this under control, but the ships are overcrowded. Curious."

Gabe stopped to sip his coffee, and Ara quipped, "So, no big deal, huh?"

"Right," said Gabe sarcastically. Then, at least recognizing the attempted humor, he added, "Schem is having a wonderful time."

"OK chief, what's next?" asked Ere.

Gabe's only response was, "Excellent question," leaving the rest of the team in suspense. A few more sips of coffee and a large cinnamon bun later, Gabe looked around at the team and said, "I don't have an answer yet. I'm going to have to get some guidance from headquarters. We are the team given the lead on this because it appears all the major components needed from the space fleet standpoint are in our area. The other teams will follow our lead, so we have to be careful. The last time we had an all-out intervention, people misunderstood much of what they saw and heard. As it turned out, the misinterpretation actually worked to our advantage, but we can't always count on that. These days, people are more skeptical and don't take things at face value. If we are going to guide a change in the course of human history on a large scale again, we need to be reasonably certain we know what we're doing.

"As I see it, we have few options. We could do nothing and just monitor the situation, but I don't think that is why we were all brought out of stasis. We could go out in front of everyone on a grand scale and tell everybody what to do. I think the population, as a whole, would likely tell us where to go, so I wouldn't recommend it.

"We can do what we've usually done in the past and select a few people to whom we would reveal ourselves to some extent, but we'd have to be careful that we pick people who wouldn't get too carried away and take a large segment of the population in a wrong direction. The selected ones would need to be individuals who have a level of respect and are leaders. This is a basic model that headquarters has endorsed in the past, but with mixed results based on each individual's understanding of the message when presented."

"Yes," agreed Kem, "it hasn't always worked. You end up with factions that go off in different directions and are distrustful of the others. Christianity, Islam, Hinduism, Judaism, and many more all started with a common theme. Then people started misinterpreting certain points, and then these larger groups started to fracture even more. Some of this happened because of self-promotion by the so-called elders and some out of pure jealousy. After thousands of years with no consistent clarification it was bound to happen, I suppose, especially with many languages and limited ability to record facts. Maybe this time, we can insist that the teams have a more comprehensive theme. If each team simply gives out only a basic concept, you know those listening will interpret it differently. And I suggest we need to use a carrot-and-stick approach with those selected so they stay on theme. If we don't, you know we're going to end up with people placing themselves above the rest and then taking care of themselves first, with everyone else second. I know that is cynical, but it's what happens, isn't it? "

Ere asked, "Can't we just pick a few people and work quietly with them? I don't think we need to go crazy. Get them to focus on the details, and the big stuff will fall into line."

"Exactly," agreed Gabe. "That's why we need to be careful. If we go this route, we need to decide how many people we need to bring on board—many, a few, or one. We had a handful of individuals from the Allied nations during the World Wars, and that seemed to work."

"Yes," said Kem again, "but how many of us were brought out to deal with the situation? Only a few. In this case, it looks like members of several teams are waiting for direction. They weren't woken up if they were expected to be standing around watching us."

"I know, I know!" said Gabe. "A part of me wonders about all this effort that seems to be getting set up. After I talk with the Boss, maybe things will fall into place, but remember the rule: 'Don't bring me a problem unless you have a recommended solution.' That's my dilemma at the moment. I'm not sure what to recommend exactly.

"So here is my thinking: First, Schem is allowed to tell the admiral everything—well, not everything exactly, but everything related to humanity. Maybe later, he mentions the population on Epsilon Eridani. That may require a slightly different line of thought. I think the bottom line for the space fleet, however, is that they need to set up the Gate, otherwise the fleet crews, including Schem, are going to be stranded out in space someplace completely isolated from Earth.

"We have already made some contacts during our surveys. Most of them seem to be operating at a higher-than-average intelligence level. I'm guessing we might have been guided to these people, and maybe they are the ones we want to try to influence."

Ara interrupted, "Influence? To do what exactly?"

"Ara, let me finish this thought, please," said Gabe as a gentle rebuff. "I think we have two issues. One is the Earth's human population continuing to decrease. While this has given the planet's flora and fauna a chance to recover from human overpopulation, this is an overcorrection still in process that needs to be brought back to some balance. I don't know where the balance is, but headquarters will not be pleased if the human population dies off completely."

With everyone nodding in agreement, Gabe continued, "The second issue on the surface seems less important, but I'm beginning to think that it is integral to the first issue. Schem was guided to the interstellar space fleet for a reason. Maybe it wasn't clear at the time, but as I'm thinking out loud here, the fleet has the exact opposite problem, with an exploding population. I think that cultural childbearing experience needs to be brought back to Earth on the same international scale that sent the fleet off in the first place."

This time, Kem interrupted. "Sure, but that is small potatoes compared to the situation here on Earth."

Ara said, "Since when are we talking about vegetables?"

Gabe, trying to get control back, said, "Are you two done?" With no answer, Gabe continued. "Maybe they would simply be the stimulation needed here. You know, like planting seeds. If half of the space fleet contingent were to exchange with the population here on Earth, it might be the catalyst needed to get things back on course." Staring at Ara, Gabe finished with, "Any serious thoughts?"

Kem asked, "When you were talking with Schem, did he think the intellectual level on the ships was suffering?"

Gabe said, "Not at all. They seem to be playing off each other on each ship, and each ship's crew is competing with the others for intellectual breakthroughs. The children are given the best education possible, and while physical activity is encouraged, it is still limited, meaning that they have more time for studies. They have kids as young as fourteen with the equivalent of an engineering degree. I thought it was funny that one of the problems they have is keeping the kids away from the heavy construction equipment they need for the Gate. Just like here, the really young kids are fascinated with equipment. They have pictures of dinosaurs, and the monster excavating equipment is a mechanical representation to them. They play on the operating simulators with games of precision that they make up. It will be interesting when they actually get to play in soil."

Naki had been sitting off to the side, listening. He finally added to the conversation. "We seem to be focusing on the population issue and the potential of bringing the crews of the space fleet back to Earth, or at least some of them. What about the Gate back here on Earth and the lack of communications between here and there? Seems to me, we have to get that solved first. Wouldn't that be the details Ere was suggesting?"

Kem asked, "Are you suggesting we fix the Gate? You know we aren't allowed to do that."

Naki said, "No, I'm not suggesting we do it, but it appears everyone familiar with the operation of the thing is dead. Seems to me, a little guidance isn't going to cut it. There is no one left to guide. We need to recruit and push and take care of those details, not guide."

Gabe added, "Maybe we'll get clarification when I contact headquarters."

"When are you doing that?" asked Kem.

"Right after I finish my dinner," said Gabe, and without another word, he polished off a sizeable pile of waffles and departed the galley for the communication room, leaving the rest of the team to wait for his return.

Two hours later, he returned in a much more decisive mood that when he had left.

Chapter 25
Nearly Coming Clean

Schem-Hampha-Rae had been placed in a similar position before, but that didn't make it any easier to deal with. On August 7, Gabe-Re-El had been back in touch with him, relaying instructions from headquarters. "Schem, the Boss has decided that time is a factor here on Earth, but it is less important at the moment for you and the space fleet. We have some immediate actions we must take care of on a global basis. You have some time to be subtler in your assignment because, quite frankly, the space fleet will probably continue on its current course but with some corrections in the ultimate goal. You are to prepare everyone for this change without creating a panic."

Schem, demonstrating some frustration in the exchange, asked, "And what is that supposed to mean?"

Gabe answered, "Come on, Schem, you've been down this road a dozen times at least. You need to guide people toward a solution without giving away who you are and without laying out a specific solution. Make them think it was all their idea."

"You know," said Schem, "you're telling me to guide the fleet toward an answer, but I don't know what the question is. You want to give me a hint?"

Schem couldn't see Gabe, but he had a distinct vision of him with a wise-guy smile on his face when he said, "Hey, I can't do all the thinking for you!" But after a pause, he continued, "Look, we're going to try and get the communications system here working again so the fleet can get Earth news. We know their system has a huge built-in delay between transmission and reception, so I'll have to let you know what information is sent so you'll be prepared on your end. You'll need to make sure the fleet system still works and is staffed. Not having any communication from Earth in such a long time with the assumption that they are out of range might mean they have shut the system down. Do you know the status?"

"No, I guess I don't, but I'll find out," said Schem.

Gabe continued, "The universal belief is that the fleet should continue on its mission, though the end result is going to look a lot different from the original plan. One thing to keep in mind is that turning the fleet around is not going to work at this late date. The Gate needs to be set up so people can move back and forth between the worlds."

"And so I can get back to Earth!" interrupted Schem.

"Yes, that too," said Gabe with not a whole lot of conviction in his voice, bringing a sudden knot to Schem's stomach. Gabe went on, "At some point in the future, the fleet's crews will need to be prepared mentally that they will be alien invaders on a planet that likely will not feel kindly toward newcomers digging it up."

Schem asked, "Do we know much about the indigenous population?"

"Headquarters is supposed to forward information from the archives," said Gabe. "When I get something useful, I'll send it along, but don't expect to hear from me for a little while. We have a lot to get done here on Earth, so I expect to be away from the habitat."

"Anything else?" asked Schem.

"Nope, that's it for now. Good luck." And Gabe ended the transmission.

Schem removed his communicator device, put his cabin back to its normal operation, and sat. These sessions were always draining, and he had a lot to think about—not because Gabe had given him a lot to consider but because Gabe hadn't given him a lot to do. This was less than satisfying. He had half expected Gabe to tell him to confess everything he knew to the admiral. Wouldn't that make for an interesting conversation. He could just blurt out "Hey, Ada, my real name is Schem-Hampha-Rae, but my friends all call me Schem. I made up all that stuff about being a bartender and that I'm a Finlander. I was sent here to guide you down a new path. I can't tell you where I came from, who my boss is, or how I know what's been happening on Earth, but you and the hundred thousand or so others here in the fleet should trust me and everything I say." Oh, yeah, that would work.

So, Schem's first priority was to determine the status of the mission-control communication systems on each ship. How many were in working order and staffed. Only one was needed, but at least one was essential.

If Schem was supposed to keep things under his hat—if he wore a hat—he would have to be subtle in his inquiries. He would think about that for a few days, but in the meantime, he had an extremely important personal mission that would not be delayed any longer. He was hungry.

Schem went to the galley and ordered up a picnic lunch for two. When asked who the lucky gal was, Schem just smiled and winked. He then stopped by the lounge and struck up a conversation with the bartenders about the Trappist beer brewing and learned that the bartenders and brew masters missed the magic touch that Schem, or Sherman, the bartender, had had on the brew. As simple as the expression was, it made Schem feel a bit better as he helped himself to a full growler of beer and two glasses. Usually, a full growler was discouraged in order to hold down drunkenness, but Sherman had connections, and besides, he was obviously setting up a picnic for two.

With his picnic lunch and beer, Schem went to the recreation deck. The former soccer field was not in use at the moment, and there were only a few people taking advantage of the quiet space. A few birds were singing away, and some free-range honeybees were visiting some flowers. The bees had set up an unauthorized hive in the stands, but no one would care until it got to be a little too large. Until then, it added to the Earthly feel of the man-made space park. It was here that Schem needed to be. He picked a secluded bench and laid out his lunch. There was no lucky gal. The picnic for two and two beer glasses were simply a way for Schem to have a decent lunch. It was hard to satisfy his appetite.

After a half sandwich and a glass of beer, he could start to focus on his real purpose for being here. He had felt so relieved when Gabe had opened communications with him a few days earlier. He wasn't going to be alone any longer. But the truth was, he was still alone. While it seemed that everyone in the fleet felt they could share their lives with Sherman Hamer, the reciprocal wasn't true for him. Schem had to deal with his loneliness among people by setting himself apart from time to time, meditate, and think through his future actions. He reminded himself that he needed a plan, even if it changed a couple of times. Not a very profound observation, but accurate, and one his team members made more often than they liked.

This quiet time away from everyone was his chance to consider a plan or at least outline one. In spite of what Gabe had told him, Schem went back to his thought of telling the admiral everything that he knew. While headquarters maintained that the prescribed course of action was always the correct one, the wisdom of this was at least suspect based on some of the outcomes of the past. Could it be that headquarters was far enough removed from the field of play that the directions it provided needed to be tweaked a bit? Maybe he should tell the admiral something, if not everything.

Schem took his time finishing his meal, including the last of the beer in the growler. He was deep in thought when a beautiful dark-skinned woman came by, sat on the bench next to Schem, and without saying a word, unbuttoned the top of her uniform, threw her arms around him, and started kissing him madly. Schem woke with a start, thinking out loud, "What the heck was that all about?" He hadn't had any thoughts or dreams remotely like that in—well, ever, as far as he could remember.

He looked around. The food was gone, and the growler was empty. There was no beautiful woman. He had finished everything before falling asleep. He guessed the stress was finally getting to him. Also, he realized, not being in stasis and rejuvenation might be getting to him as he aged. "I'm thinking too much," said Schem to himself. "Time to do something, anything, even if it might be wrong. I'm going to see the admiral." And, with new determination, he headed off.

So, on August 9, Schem found himself with Ada Sylva, the admiral; her husband, Doctor Jesus Sylva; her daughter, Dawn Cohen, the vice admiral of operations; and via a communication link, the admiral's son and Dawn's twin, Richard Sylva, the vice admiral of academics and science. *Keep it all in the family*, thought Schem.

Schem, in his role as Sherman, the admiral's special counselor, had asked for the meeting. A bit unorthodox, but as the special counselor, he could get away with it. Though Sherman often had breakfast meetings with the admiral, today he had asked if the others could join in as well. He said he had some disturbing news that he needed to share and had decided that the family should all be brought in. He didn't specifically invite the spouses of Richard and Dawn, but he decided they could be told because Richard and Dawn were probably willing to share. After all, eventually, everyone in the fleet would get at least part of the story. Schem had also decided to wear his standard team uniform. He himself wasn't sure why. Maybe subconsciously, he thought it would give more credibility to what he had to say.

Everyone was assembled and picking at their meals when Schem entered the admiral's conference room. Unlike most days, Schem asked the steward to leave and to close the door when he left. Also, quite unlike Schem's routine, he skipped the breakfast cart, poured a mug of coffee, and stood in front of the assembled group in his billowing white tunic, white pants, gold sash, and sandals. His long hair was hanging loose and not tied back as had become customary for him.

Ada, with her eyes wide, said, "What's with the outfit? That isn't exactly the professional appearance I expect from my special counselor."

"I'm sorry, ma'am," said Schem, "but this is my customary clothing when I'm on official business."

Ada's eyes narrowed and in a quiet, slightly irritated, voice, she said, "This is not what I expect when you are on official business for me, so what other kind of official business could it be? I'm still the one giving orders, aren't I?"

This brought smiles to everyone's face, including Schem's, but before the admiral could say anything more, he said, "Let me explain. I have a lot to share, and while it may be somewhat disturbing, I have no other way do this but to simply give it to you all at once. Please bear with me.

"I was sent to join the interstellar fleet by an authority not associated with the Space Commission. I had no specific orders except to monitor activities and at some point report back to my associates."

Dawn interrupted saying, "What for? Are you telling us you are a spy for somebody? Like the secret police or something?"

"No, no!" said Schem. "Nothing like that. I'm a member of a benevolent society that is not allowed to interfere with your mission. If I can be of assistance by listening to people and providing some encouragement from time to time, that is what I do. I have been doing exactly that since I signed on board as a bartender and then as the admiral's special counselor. I have had no contact with any of my associates since leaving Earth up until a few days ago."

Dawn said rather forcefully, "What are you talking about? There are more spies in the fleet?"

"No," said Schem. "I am alone here. The associates I'm talking about are on Earth."

In spite of Schem's usual calming effect on everyone, Ada was getting increasingly annoyed and said, "Are you on drugs? No one has heard anything from Earth in years. You know that as well as anyone, so what makes you think you have heard something from Earth?"

Schem paused, sat down, and took a sip of coffee. With all eyes staring at him, Schem said, "Ma'am, you have always suspected that there is more to me than I was willing to let on. You were correct. When I came on board, I brought with me a special communications device. It operates with an advanced technology that will only work for those who are specially trained. It has been completely inactive until a couple of days ago, when I was told some troubling news."

Dawn said, "You don't expect us to believe that you were able to smuggle on board, and transfer from ship to ship, a communications system that can communicate with Earth when our state-of-the-art system can't? It would have to be huge. This is one incredible story you're spinning."

"I know," said Schem. "I was actually told not to tell you about the communications system I have, but I had no other way of telling you that I have heard from Earth. In fact, there is nothing technically wrong with the fleet's communications system. It does work, and when used, messages are transmitted. It takes a long time for the messages to travel to Earth, but they are being received."

This time, Richard piped up, asking, "Then if you know so much, how come we're not getting any messages? Answer me that!"

Schem grimaced and said, "No one is listening. There is no one left in mission control. They are all dead."

Ada pushed in a rather loud voice, "What are you talking about? What do you mean, 'they are all dead'? How can that be?"

Schem said, "I know this is a lot to swallow, and it gets worse. You can choose to ignore everything I have to say, but here is the short version. In 2071, a vicious form of flu broke out. It killed nearly everyone it came in contact with, and it spread rapidly, with no cure. In fact, it was dubbed the death flu. It was particularly deadly where there were concentrations of people, like mission control. Once one person was infected and brought it unknowingly to others, they in turn became infected within hours and died shortly thereafter. The last message you received was cryptic, wasn't it? The facility manager sent it. He had been away from the facility, had not been infected, and sent the message when he returned. When he showed up at mission control, all he found was death. He was not familiar with the equipment and tried to tell you what had happened, but you only received the part of the message that said 'You are on your own.'"

Jesus Sylva, turning to his wife, said, "Putting on my MD hat, there had been speculation that at some point, the Earth's human population size would reach a tipping point and collapse. Technology was keeping the inevitable at bay. This space mission was supposed to provide the relief needed, but I suppose it could have been a little late. What I'm saying is that Sherman's story could be true. At least on that point, anyway."

Schem said, "I suppose I might as well tell you now, I'm not Finnish, and my name isn't Sherman Hamer. My real name is Schem-Hampha-Rae. I usually go by Schem, but if you don't mind, I'd still prefer to be called Sherman Hamer."

"Anything more you're holding back?" said Ada, now shaking her head in disbelief.

"No," was the simple but not exactly accurate answer.

"I'm not saying I'm accepting all this, but assuming I do, what is the status of the Earth Gate?" asked Dawn.

Schem said, "My associates tell me that it is set up and guarded. But—and this is a big but—it is only assumed to be functional. There is no one left currently who knows how to make it operate. It is rather complicated. I can only surmise that the only ones knowledgeable enough to operate it are here in the fleet."

"Great, just great," said Richard. "And the only way to get the operators back to Earth is through the Gate that no one can operate. Is that what I'm hearing?"

"OK, that's enough!" said Ada very abruptly. "Everyone leave, except Jesus and Sherman—or whatever your name is."

Chapter 26
The Admiral's Reaction

The admiral, with a strange mixture of calm, frustration, and sense of incongruity, sat staring at Sherman Hamer. Ada's husband, Jesus, became increasingly unsure of what he should do for his wife to break the tension. Minutes passed, and then more passed. After Sherman had unloaded his information, he'd positioned himself at the end of the admiral's conference-room table and remained motionless, with his hands folded on the tabletop, waiting for Ada's reaction.

After what could have passed for an eternity, Ada said, "So, Mr. Hamer, as I'm processing all this so-called news from Earth, I should be concluding that we, and I mean the entire fleet, are screwed! We can get to EE, but then what? To plagiarize an old expression, we will have won the battle but lost the war. We will have completed the mission to EE, but to no avail. Earth can't help us, and we can't help Earth. Is that what you are telling us, condensed down to a nutshell?"

"I don't want to sound impertinent, and I beg you to not take it that way when I say that I only provided facts—facts that I learned only a short time before I told them to you. I cannot interpret the facts or devise a way out of this, but I assure you, I am more than willing to help if I can. The only difference between yesterday and today is that you know some facts that you didn't know yesterday. Isn't that better than blindly moving forward with false assumptions? Also, keep in mind that I am not immune to the situation. I have no escape from it other than what you and your officers decide. Everyone in the fleet is in this together."

Ada said, "This is all very unbelievable, and I'm pretty sure your getup doesn't add to the credibility of what you've said." Then, after another few minutes, she added, "But I suppose we might continue to hope and maybe pray for the best, but let's plan for the worst. You have certainly laid out a scenario that I suppose could be even worse, but it is bad enough. Sooo. Let's assume for a moment that I don't actually believe what you are saying. We also lose nothing by assuming that what you have said is correct. We'll go with that. You know, trust is a fragile thing. I trust that you are looking out for our collective best interests. Please don't prove me wrong."

"Bless you, Admiral," was all Sherman had to say.

With that seemingly settled for now, Jesus Sylva, MD, wanted more details about the death flu and asked about the mortality rate. Had the flu recurred? How fast was the population decreasing, and why? And so on. Finally, did Sherman know about any family members' survival?

Sherman answered as best he could and concluded saying, "I'm sorry Dr. Sylva, but I have no details about any individual's survival." Uncharacteristically, Sherman wept openly as he said this—not just for those closest to the couple in the room, but for all humanity and for himself, as Schem-Hampha-Rae. Emotions he didn't know he had suddenly overwhelmed him, and he couldn't hold back.

In a role reversal, Ada tried to counsel the counselor. "These years must have been difficult for you. Be assured, we have built a relationship over these years that will only get stronger as we work through this. Please take a break with some time off."

Sherman looked a bit shorter than his six feet eight inches at this point, leaving the admiral's conference room and heading toward his quarters. He had not eaten for some time and had not felt like eating at the breakfast meeting, but now his stomach was demanding satisfaction, so he detoured to the mess hall. He also had not slept for some time, thinking about the meeting. Now that it was over, he would in fact take some time off and have a restful nap.

Back in the admiral's conference room, Ada said to her husband, "What do you think?"

Jesus responded, "Well, I think you hit it right on the head. What Sherman offered up is very disturbing, and it may not be true. Or some of it might be true. In any case, we have nothing to lose if we can develop a plan that mitigates the potential issues. We will still continue to EE no matter what. Or am I assuming too much here?"

Ada said, "No, I think we need to continue on. Turning back now will get us nowhere. What would we do if we returned the fleet to Earth? Let's get the kids back in here."

"You know, dear," said Jesus, "they are not kids anymore. Both are very grown up and are vice admirals. Did you forget?"

"Well, dear," said Ada, dripping with sarcasm, "they will always be kids to me no matter how old they are. But if it makes you feel better, would you be so kind as to have Vice Admiral Cohen return to the conference room? I will reestablish video communications with Vice Admiral Sylva."

"As you command, Admiral."

Ada just shook her head, and Jesus left to get Dawn. When the VAO returned to the table and the video link with Richard was reestablished, both were very animated. Richard blurted out, "So, do you believe Sherman?"

"Maybe," said Ada, "but let's talk about it. I see no good reason to turn back at this late date. It would do no good. On the other hand, if we can't reconnect with Earth once we reach EE, we will be on our own on a planet that could support us or not. Research indicates that we could survive there. That's why we're going there in the first place. We just might be alone starting a new civilization, and maybe that's not so bad."

Dawn said, "Good. Richard and I were talking, and we think we have an idea."

Jesus looked curious, but Ada said, "Go on."

"Well," said Richard, "It wasn't rocket science."

Jesus, shaking his head, said, "Nice that you can crack jokes at a time like this."

Richard continued, "Well, I could have said 'brain surgery.' But listen. Sherman—we're still calling him that, right? Anyway, Sherman said he can communicate with Earth. We have the expertise in the fleet to get the Earth Gate up and running, but we are here, and the Gate is there. What if we could find people on Earth who were technically capable and then we challenged them to get the thing up and running? We could guide them through the steps needed to get the Gate functional, and at the same time, maybe we could get Earth's communications system working as well. I mean, we have five ships with five communication arrays, while Sherman has only one. If that should fail, it sure would be nice for us to continue to communicate with Earth."

"It is a start," agreed Ada. "Richard, we have Gate experts scattered around the fleet. We probably need them all, but I don't want to run the risk of having them all in one place. I want you to meet with all of them individually and then set up a system where they can stay on their assigned ships while providing the technical input we need through one team leader. In fact, maybe that's you. The Earth Gate should certainly be more ready than the one we have to build on EE, so unless we have idiots on the other end, they should be able to get it working for us in plenty of time. After all, when we reach EE, we will still have at least a year's worth of work."

"Yes, ma'am," said Richard in his most formal way of addressing the admiral.

Turning to Dawn, Ada said, "I want you to consider what kind of people need to be recruited on Earth. We have to assume the worst and that no one familiar with the communications and Gate design is still around. The plans are probably available, so maybe we don't need a scientist exactly. Give it some thought. We obviously will have to rely on Sherman, and yes, we will continue to call him by that name as he requested. Anyway, we hopefully will have the aid of Sherman's associates on Earth to find the right people and get them up to speed. There have to be a few intelligent people on Earth that escaped the death flu."

"Yes, ma'am," said Dawn, mimicking her brother.

"Death flu!" Ada said, "What an ominous name. I can't imagine what it must be like back there with ninety percent of the population wiped out." Then after a pause Ada added, "This doesn't give me a good feeling about my brother and his family." Then after another pause, she said, "I told Sherman to take some time off. You don't need to know why. See what you two can come up with between now and the end of the week. I see no reason to panic, so take it slow. You may tell whomever you talk to what we're trying to do and why, but ask them not to spread any rumors. I will address the fleet, telling everyone everything we know, once we confirm our plan. I will talk to Sherman and see if he can add anything to it. For lack of a better name, let's call this Operation Earth Gate." Then, looking at Jesus, Ada added, "Dear, I think it might be a good idea if you checked on our friend Sherman. It appears he will be very critical to Operation Earth Gate, at least until we have our communications back. Maybe give him a once-over. We can't afford to have him getting ill."

"Certainly, dear—I mean, yes, Admiral," answered Jesus.

Dawn shook her head and said, "You know, there is a certain decorum that must be followed by senior officers of the fleet, or the rank-and-file members will question your authority. One could even argue that this fraternization between you two borders on sexual harassment."

"You know, Vice Admiral of Operations, you sometimes make me wonder if I made a poor choice in promoting you," said Ada. With a smile, she added, "OK, everyone leave. I have other issues that need my attention." When everyone had gone, Ada called in the steward and said, "Felix, I know it isn't even ten hundred hours yet, but please find me a Bloody Mary in a tall glass."

"Yes, ma'am," said Felix, "and mum's the word. Tough morning?"

"Something like that. You'll know soon enough."

Chapter 27
Recruitments

By August 7, 2085, it had been Naki's suggestion of recruitment that won the day. The plan, though simple, required somewhat complex implementation. The idea was to first reestablish the communications link with the space fleet. Once that not-so-simple task had been completed, they were then to get the Earth Gate functioning. The Gate work would be done by people recruited on Earth, with technical guidance from the scientists on the ships. A little clandestine communications between Gabe and Schem would be required to get things started.

On August 10, Gabe and his team learned that the leadership on the space fleet had developed the same line of thinking. It would fit nicely with the general mandate of nudging a solution rather than producing one.

It was agreed that the other teams around the globe would focus their energies on two tasks. One was to eventually reestablish the UNSC. This would require a great deal of interaction with global leaders. It would not be an easy task, for while there was at least a stable government structure in the United States, it was an anomaly. Anarchy was still the norm in many areas of the world. Fighting in the Middle East and Africa continued, but as those regions weren't part of the UNSC in the first place, it really had no effect on the plan.

In other regions where there had been UNSC participation, governments weren't always stable. Every two-bit dictator wannabe would gain support and start a fight. Fortunately, with a population that was generally increasing in age with few young recruits coming along, fighting bands remained small. Still, it certainly wasn't conducive for harmonious agreement on something like the UNSC. Getting things back in order meant there had to be some consolidation of power among key population centers. This was going to be a huge task, and the teams would have to start immediately to identify and then recruit leaders—not just people who would be in charge but true leaders whom people would respect and follow. Some would likely be religious leaders that could unite people under a banner spanning more than just ethnic and geographical boundaries. It had been done before; it would have to happen again. However, finding and recruiting these leaders meant the other teams would have their work cut out for them.

In conjunction with stable governments being reestablished, the second task was to get people thinking about the future and lead them toward the day when the space-fleet population might remix with the remaining Earth population. Of course Earth's population was much larger than that of the fleet. Plus the average age on Earth was much older and it appeared to be weaker intellectually, so introducing the fleet crew back into Earth's society had to be well thought out. For many, the space fleet was nothing more than a passing thought, if they thought about it at all. Apathy was the standard. Gabe, his team, and the other teams all thought this would be less of a challenge once new global leadership was in place. Stability alone would get many to focus away from the here and now and toward a brighter day. The reality of people returning to Earth from such an adventure should certainly generate a renewed sense of optimism. Maybe.

On the North American continent, recruitment would look different. There was already a stable government. While it was true that the age of the population in North America was in sync with that in the rest of the world, it seemed that an apathetic mind-set was somewhat less of an issue. Recruitment was thought to be easier here. First to go toward reestablishing the communications link with the space fleet and then making sure that the Gate was operational. The fact that both the communication centers in Houston and Poker Flats as well as the Gate itself were in the United States certainly factored in.

"Easy beans," quipped Ara.

There was no question that the US government needed to get on board. By default, the United States could take the lead or simply take over the project. Who would object to something like that when there was little interest from other governments? It was only necessary to get the US government on board enough to allow this all to happen. Recruiting people without any authorization or support to allow any work would be impossible and against the core values of the team.

Gabe decided on a multiple-front assault on the problem. He would take on the political problem while the rest of the team focused on the technical side. But he also had a thought—or was once again led to one—of how to potentially jump-start the technical side. "Naki, you and Ara should come with me and meet the Bickmeier family. I think we have some talent there. They also have a vested interest in the project. Kem and Ere, what do you think about the guy you met in the East?"

"Well, first off, we never actually met the guy. He never came out of his house. But based on the technology he seemed to be employing, he is certainly a person of interest," Kem said.

"OK, then," said Gabe. "Tomorrow, I'll bring the other teams up to date and get them started. The day after, we'll head out first thing in the morning. We have a plan! I'm starting to feel very optimistic? How about breaking out some of that merlot." So, out came the merlot, and a banquet of sorts was prepared.

On August 11, Kem and Ere headed back to the state of New Maritime to reestablish contact with Abel Fisher. Gabe, Naki, and Ara made the short trip over to Homer. Gabe had learned enough about the Bickmeier family to believe that the men were probably off fishing and Kim Sue was probably alone in her boat-bridge sanctuary, either reading, meditating, or preparing some words for a Sunday service. With this belief in mind, the three team members glided in for a landing on the boat's foredeck. His guess was correct, and no one saw them except Kim Sue. She was a bit less startled this time with the visions coming toward her but was more than curious, maybe even concerned, that there were now three visions, not just one. Kim Sue went down to greet the three and, shaking Gabe's hand, she said, "How many more of you are there?"

Reassuringly, Gabe said with a smile but not really answering, "Don't worry, Kim Sue, these are my associates Naki and Ara. I won't be staying very long, but I'd like your husband, son, and grandson to meet Naki and Ara and discuss a possible project with them. I think it is something they would be interested in pursuing. If they agree and I'm successful with my part of the plan, there is a good chance that your family will be able to communicate with your other family members in the space fleet. Do you think they would be interested?"

"Are you kidding? They would certainly be interested," Kim Sue said, but she added, "Now, I don't believe you're joking, but how do you think you can make that happen?"

"I can't," said Gabe honestly. "All I—that is, we—can do is set things in motion. A great deal of cooperation and effort on the part of many will be required."

"Well," said Kim Sue, "this day is certainly starting to appear to be an interesting one. Maria is baking some bread. Shall we have a cup of coffee and have a slice? Do your friends have the same appetite you do?"

Naki said, "It is nice to meet you. We had breakfast not too long ago, but coffee and a slice of freshly baked bread would be welcome." And they headed to the main part of the house. Truthfully, he was hoping for more than a slice of bread.

As they entered, Kim Sue said to Maria, "We have guests."

Turning around, Maria looked up to see three very large people all dressed in white. She had got somewhat comfortable with Gabe, but three of them made her cringe at the thought of potentially feeding them. *Oh, well*, she thought, *It is what it is. I hope the guys have a good haul today.*

By midafternoon, the sails of *Elusive* were dropped and the boat eased up to the dock. Kim Sue and Maria were waiting for the men as usual, but so were Gabe, Naki, and Ara. Karl looked at the three large figures and mumbled, "Interesting."

More people came down to the dock, and while most were happy to see Gabe again, they were somewhat puzzled with two more the size of Gabe all dressed in white. Greetings were made all around. The catch, a good one for the day, was divided up.

It was a beautiful day, so the Bickmeiers and the new arrivals went back to the Bickmeier home and sat out on the back deck of the yacht. Up until now, only pleasantries had been exchanged, but Kim Sue brought things around to the topic of the day by informing the men that Gabe had a plan to open communications with the space fleet.

"Interesting," said Karl. "How do you think that is going to happen?"

"I won't mince words," said Gabe. "I'd like you men to consider going to Poker Flats to get the communications system up and running."

"Huh! Just like that?" said Don. "Now, why didn't we think of that before? Are you crazy? What makes you think we can just march up to Poker Flats and get the system operating? We know absolutely nothing about it. Besides, how do we even get there?"

Gabe said calmly, "I don't think it was pure coincidence that I met you. I can't explain why or how, but the fact you have close relatives on the ships has somehow led me to your door, or more correctly, your deck. I think everything will fall into place with a little faith. I'm leaving shortly to see the governor and try to move up the chain of command with the goal of getting some assistance from the government. Assuming I can do that, you three, along with Naki and Ara, can hopefully evaluate what might be needed. Naki and Ara will go along to coordinate through me for whatever resources might be needed. They have no technical skills at all, but they know how to find human resources. If you are interested, they will stay here with you, or in town anyway, so collectively, you might determine what you might need initially. I have it on good faith that all the needed communication equipment is in Poker Flats. It just needs to be put together."

"Right," said Ara, "just some assembly required. You know, insert part *A* into part *B* with only a screwdriver. Maybe a metric adjustable wrench."

At least Don thought this was amusing. Karl, deep in consideration of what Gabe had said, thought, *Interesting.*

Poor Len didn't know what to say. After years of pretty much the same routine, Gabe had taken them on an adventure of sorts, only to return now with a plan that was more than exciting. Len couldn't believe it. He said, "I'm in."

"Not so fast, buckaroo," said Don. "This is a family decision. How long do you think we might be away?"

Gabe said, "For this communications array, I can only guess that it will take at least a year." Left unsaid was anything about the Gate itself.

After a pause allowing everything to sink in, Karl said, "You get us permission to go and arrange for transportation, and we'll take a look. Then we'll decide if we're in or not. I don't want to break anything so that someone couldn't make it work later. That said, I would do anything to talk to my sister again."

Karl looked at the family, and they nodded in agreement.

"Fair enough," said Gabe, and off he went. He knew the Bickmeiers were in. When he was out of sight, he activated his antigravity pack and headed for Anchorage. When he landed, again out of sight, he changed into the clothes that the people of Homer had made him, and he walked into town. He made arrangements for lodging and meals at the B&B where he, Karl, and Len had stayed before, but this time, the owner of the B&B felt she should head to the grocery store and stock up.

There was phone service in Anchorage, so Gabe called the governor's office and was able to get an appointment with Colonel Sheffield for the next day. With the conversation he had in mind, he thought it best not to just barge in as he had done the last time.

At 9:30 a.m., August 11, Gabe was once again sitting in front of Colonel Sheffield. Remembering their earlier conversation, she asked what Gabe had learned on his fact-finding mission, and he disclosed the essentials. He had made it to Poker Flats only to find unopened crates piled high and the place completely abandoned. He had seen a mass grave that was likely of the staff that was on-site when the flu hit. He had no idea who had buried the dead. Nothing else had looked disturbed.

Gabe went on to say that he thought he had identified people who could get the communications system functioning, but he would need authorization. He would also require some transportation, preferably by air, at least initially. The road from Fairbanks to Poker Flats was in such terrible condition that it was essential to at least get the rockslides cleared and the road graded. Finally, Gabe assumed that something in the crates would be either broken or missing, so he hoped he could get assistance in locating replacement components.

Colonel Sheffield listened and made notes. Occasionally, she shook her head and rolled her eyes. When Gabe appeared to be finished, the Colonel said, "I can make some of this happen, but only if we have authorization from the president. If he agrees to this, I can help. But you realize this equipment falls under the UNSC's control and not that of the president. By the way, how did you get to Poker Flats?"

"I hiked," was the less than satisfactory answer he provided before saying, "I understand the political part, but look at the facts for a moment. There is currently no UNSC. Everyone who was appointed to the commission is dead. Very few here on Earth give a hoot about the space fleet or the people on board the ships. Assuming they are even still alive, someone should care enough to at least confirm it. The two command centers are both in the United States. The one in Houston seems to be heavily damaged, leaving only the one in Poker Flats having a chance to be functional. The Gate is also in the United States. Since everything is here and there is no one around to object, I think the president has every right—no, let me rephrase that—an obligation to get things working. My associates and I are willing to coordinate efforts at no cost to the government. I'm only asking for permission and a few resources to make it happen.

"Furthermore, I have identified some technical skills in people who have a vested interest in reconnection with the fleet. You met them. Karl Bickmeier and his grandson, Len, were here with me on my last visit. Karl's sister is among the fleet's crew, along with her husband and children. Karl is both a mechanical engineer and an electrical engineer. Len is a mechanical whiz kid. I don't think they can do it alone, but it is a great start, if you ask me."

Though Gabe's presence had a calming effect on the colonel, she had been in the military a long time and was well disciplined in proper procedures and understanding levels of authority. As a governor, she did have access to the president but wasn't about to go off half-cocked based on Gabe's proposal. Instead, she said, "Well, Mr.—by the way, what is your last name?"

"El," said Gabe-Re-El. "My last name is El."

"Well then, Mr. El, you have enough of an argument that I would be willing to talk to the president to see what we might be able to do. Twice a year, the governors meet with the president as a group. We each have a meeting with him beforehand so he can determine what our nation's priorities might be. This, and the meetings with the Joint Chiefs of Staff, is how the government operates now. There is no House of Representatives or Senate anymore. I will be flying to Washington next week." Concluding, Colonel Sheffield said while standing up and not allowing a response, "You should come with me. The sergeant will be in contact with you with details. Just let him know where you are staying. Thank you for coming in."

Gabe left, quite frankly, somewhat surprised at how well it had gone. He had always been good at persuasion, but it usually took a little more effort for something this big. *I'll take it*, he thought and went back to the B&B after stopping at a nice-looking pub for a meal and adult beverage.

While Gabe was meeting with Colonel Sheffield, Kem and Ere had reached the tree line at Abel Fisher's home. As they had done the first time, they flew in and furled their antigravity panels. They thought that Abel would be monitoring them. They were correct, and a booming voice came out over loudspeakers. "You're back. Can I borrow one of those packs?"

Kem said in a most sarcastic tone, "Yes, we're back. It nice to see you, as well."

Of course, Kem and Ere couldn't see Abel any more than they could the first time, so they didn't know that Abel was wearing clothes. He had, in fact, worn them since their first visit. Abel didn't know why, but somehow, he now felt more comfortable dressed. Not so anyone would notice if they saw these clothes hanging from his frail body, but Abel felt a physical difference in his body as well. He now spent less time in bed, and though it was exhausting at first, he had gradually built up a little stamina. He thought he liked it.

There was another, even more profound, change in Abel. After the last visit from Kem and Ere, Abel had contacted Megan. In her usual less than subtle manner, she had wanted to know if Abel wanted some video sex and in the same breath said, "Oh, you're wearing clothes. That's different. And you shaved! Sexy!"

The response was not one she ever would have expected when he said, "Can we talk? By the way, can you put on some clothes?"

Megan had suddenly left the screen and returned wearing a bathrobe, seemingly quite embarrassed. "What's going on?"

In his usual straightforward tone, he'd asked, "Are you a real person or just a computer-generated image?"

Megan suddenly ended the video link but reestablished it about an hour later. With a frosty tone, she had said, "Yes, I'm a real person you jerk. You mean to tell me that we've been playing sex games all this time, and you didn't know? Or care?"

"Right," said Abel, "but now I do." And for the next two hours, Abel and Megan talked.

Some of Abel's thinking had changed since that first visit from Kem and Ere. *What is going to happen with this visit?* he thought.

Abel repeated his question to Kem and Ere. "Am I going to be able to borrow one of those flying things?"

This time, Ere spoke up. "Remember we said we might let you borrow one if you did us a favor? We are here to trade a favor for a favor. If you can help us, we will let you borrow one of the flying packs for a month."

"What's the favor?" asked Abel.

Kem and Ere traded back and forth, telling Abel about the Gate and mission control. Abel knew of the space mission, but not the status of Earth's part of it. He never really thought about it. Besides, doing his FarmVille enterprises, repairing his fleet of robots and drones, reaping the benefits, and communicating with Megan, he had had little time or interest for anything else. Abel listened to Kem and Ere for some time with no apparent reaction observed by the pair until a procession of robots brought out a table, chairs, and a meal very much like the last one they had had there. It was then that Abel said, "You said you liked my merlot. You said you'd tell me about my missing barrel and the appearance of coins. So, tell me."

Ere sampled the latest offering and said, "This is a fine vintage. Where we come from, we have our own robot and drone fleet that scavenges for our group's needs. We are not poor, but we don't like to be any more open than we have to be. It was determined by one of our scout robots that your wine was superior. How it was acquired cannot be divulged, but as you noted, our robots always leave a payment that far exceeds the value of the product.”

“I am impressed and can relate to your objections to be out in the open. Continue with your story,” said Abel.

Ere and Kem continued with the story, concluding with Kem saying, “We would like you to accompany us to Alaska to assist with the installation of the Interstellar Mission Control Center. We have others who will be on the project, but we don’t anticipate many. Also, if you know of anyone who could be helpful, we can compensate. That is the favor we want in return for loaning you one of our flying units. You do not need to answer yet as there are issues that need to be worked out first. Will you at least consider?”

Abel said, “I will consider,” and then added, “if you have the technology to find and then take my wine from a secure facility undetected, what do you need me for?”

Ere said, “It is complicated, but all I can say is that we are not allowed. That is not a good answer, but it is the best I can do.”

The meal was finished, the robots removed all evidence of the dining experience, and Abel said one last word. “Good-bye.”

As Kem and Ere deployed their antigravity panels, Ere said to Kem, “That is one very strange guy. Do you think we have him?”

Kem replied, “I think so.”

Chapter 28
Mr. President

For the next week after the meeting with Colonel Sheffield, Gabe-Re-El spent his time meditating and mingling with the citizens of Anchorage. He had some fine meals and left the staff in the dining establishments with large smiles, as he always paid with silver or gold coins. Word traveled fast around town about this apparent eccentric millionaire.

It took Gabe some time to put his finger on it, but it was something he had noticed with the Bickmeiers, and it seemed to be a common trait of everyone else he met. Then it hit him. There was a general lack of energy in people. It was what someone might experience after a major adrenaline rush followed by complete relaxation. People in general followed their daily routines and had good times together, but there were no signs of energy. No one was in a hurry to do anything. No one pushed for a position of authority or power. Success had quietly been redefined as something much more personal. Perhaps that was why the military establishment could simply take over the running of the country. No one cared. In fact, Gabe detected the same attitude from Colonel Sheffield and her staff. They did what they had to do for the good of the country because that was how they were trained, but the colonel exhibited no desire to be anything more than governor of Alaska.

This general melancholy almost seemed like an extension of what an individual might exhibit when diagnosed with a serious disease and told that he or she had only months to live. After the news was accepted, few things seemed important beyond the moment while waiting for the end. Was the world's population subconsciously waiting for the end and just living for the moment? Gabe surmised that the population viewed the death-flu pandemic as that serious-disease diagnosis. Perhaps that could explain the dwindling population and general lack of interest in the interstellar space fleet mission. Of course, not everyone would be affected all the time, and some would obviously not be affected at all, but generally, it certainly appeared to be true. This really needed correction via a general energy boost toward a universal peacetime goal.

True to her word, the governor colonel made arrangements for Gabe to be picked up on August 18 one week after their meeting. A staff car, obviously rescued from some defunct car-rental company many years earlier, picked him up at 0500 hours and brought him to the airfield. The executive jet was ready for takeoff when Gabe climbed aboard. He had to stoop to get his seven feet two inches of height to his seat next to Colonel Sheffield, who was already buckled in. No words were immediately exchanged as the plane took off with two air-force officers in the cockpit and two staff members farther back in the cabin.

Once they were airborne, Colonel Sheffield said, "When the dust settled after the death flu, a lot of executive planes were simply abandoned. They are much more cost-effective to operate than the traditional military aircraft, so the military assumed ownership of a lot of them. Some are now used for spare parts, but there are so many. This is about a nine-hour flight with no stops, so make yourself comfortable. We'll have plenty of time to plan out our meeting with the president. In about an hour, we'll have breakfast."

Gabe didn't say anything about already having had breakfast. An additional small snack, by his standards, would certainly be welcome. Instead, he asked, "How does the president like to be addressed? General, President, or something else?"

The colonel said, "First off, while we're alone like this, you can address me by my first name: Linda. As for the president, he prefers the more civilian designation. President Grainger, to be exact. Do you have anything a bit more formal to wear than flannel shirts?"

Gabe thought, *Well I suppose I could put on my uniform, but that would be probably be a huge distraction.* Instead, he said, "Not really."

"OK, then," said Linda and with a slight smile. "I suppose typical Alaskan attire will have to do. The sandals really are a great complement to the wardrobe."

As promised, the trip was long. With Gabe's large frame confined in the small cabin, it seemed even longer. The flight was calm, with a clear sky. In eight and a half hours, Washington came into sight. Gabe had had an idea of what to expect but still was surprised with the extent of the fortifications around the central capital to keep the Atlantic Ocean from flooding the place. Prior to the pandemic and with the seas rising, the American Society of Civil Engineers had reduced options to two: build a new capital or fortify the city. With so much infrastructure in place above and below ground, the choice had been to build dikes along the Potomac and Anacostia rivers. Gabe thought, *This isn't exactly what the original planners of the city had in mind.*

A staff car was waiting for Governor Sheffield and Mr. El when the plane taxied into a hanger. From there they were taken to the Alaska office suite. Since there was no longer an elected Senate, each of the state governors had offices previously occupied by the senators and their staffs. Some of the space had been converted to bedrooms. This was considered much more efficient than renting rooms while also providing an opportunity for the governors to interact on a less formal basis. Each governor had a small staff in residence throughout the year.

Gabe was shown to his room. He was informed that Colonel Sheffield was always referred to as such while in Washington, and this day, she was to host an evening meal for six other governors. Most of them had served together when they had been in the active-military branch of government. Gabe was invited to this dinner, creating quite a stir. He was, after all, the largest person in the room, and with his clothing completely contrasting with the formal uniforms of the governors, he certainly stood out. A great deal of alcohol was consumed, and Governor Sheffield used the occasion to generate interest in Gabe's proposal to reactivate the Earth's Interstellar Mission Control and Gate. Support would be needed for the long run.

Governor Sheffield's appointment with the president was the next day at 1400 hours. At that exact minute, she and Gabe entered the Oval Office. President Grainger wasn't exactly a small man at six feet two inches and probably 220 pounds of what appeared to be pure muscle, defying his age, which Gabe guessed to be mid seventies. For meetings like this, uniforms were not usually worn. The president wore a traditional striped suit and tie. The governor wore a pantsuit. Gabe wore the Alaskan outfit he'd been given, though it had been cleaned.

The president was not accustomed to looking up at people, but with a foot of height difference, he did this time when he was introduced to Mr. El. Still, he didn't exhibit any reaction when gesturing for the governor and Gabe to have a seat. When the president sat down he got right to the point. "Usually, my conversations with the governors are related to their states' needs. I have only been told this is a national and probably international issue. Are we going to be attacked by North Korea across the Bering Strait or something?" He actually cracked a smile.

"I hope not," said the governor. "I'll let Mr. El give you his story."

Gabe started, and as the story unfolded, the president seemed to get more and more interested. Gabe told him that he was a member of a society dedicated to recording events as an archive for future historians. They were self-supporting and therefore required no funding assistance. This, in turn, allowed them to remain completely unbiased. The death flu had affected them, so it had taken some time to regain the organizational strength necessary to continue their mission to record events. Recently, they had learned that the interstellar space mission seemed to be have been collectively ignored with the death of most, if not all, of the mission control staff on Earth. Gabe's society wished to attempt to reestablish communications with the space fleet. Since the original mission control, the backup one, and the Gate itself were within the boundaries of the United States; the country could and should take the opportunity to do something. Gabe's society would identify the technical expertise necessary to get things operating, but some support would be needed from the government, probably from its military branch.

Gabe concluded with a warning. "Mr. President, we have about ten years to put this together. It may sound like a long time, but if we don't start now, the fleet, if it exists, will be stranded, and no one will ever know its fate."

President Grainger took this all in with polite interest. He sat back in his chair, interlaced his fingers, held his hands up to his face, and with his thumbs, started rubbing his lips. He said nothing for some time, making Gabe think he had failed.

Finally, the president picked up the phone and after dialing a number said, "Would you mind coming to my office? Thank you." He then said to the governor and Gabe, "I'm having the secretary of state come in to get his opinion." And within minutes, a rather senior-looking gentleman walked in.

Unlike the president, this man was short and completely out of shape. He certainly didn't look former active military, but Gabe was certain that he was.

The president repeated what Gabe had said almost word for word, demonstrating a remarkable, nearly total-recall capability. Gabe was impressed. What the president wanted to know was how the international community might view a unilateral effort on something that had been multinational in origin.

The secretary said that when the world leaders got together, they sometimes brought up the subject of the Space Commission, but all seem stymied as to what to do. Combined with the general sense of apathy, he was not aware of any initiative at all toward that enterprise. "Bottom line? If the president wants to do something, I think he should. Even in the unlikely case that another nation might find out, why would any complain? That said, we should place someone in charge of the operation that was part of the original mission-control group. That could support an argument for continuity."

"Hmm, good point," said the president. Then turning to Gabe, he asked, "Well, Mr. El, is there anyone we could put in such a position?"

The governor interrupted this thought with, "Sir, does that mean you are authorizing Mr. El's proposal?"

"Yes, I suppose so," said the president, "provided we make it appear as though we're only getting the project back on course rather than doing a restart."

Gabe remembered that Naki and Ara had spent some time with the facility manager in Houston, so he said, "President Grainger, I am aware of only one person who has been with the project from the beginning. There may be others, but this gentleman has never abandoned his post. He only escaped the death flu by a set of circumstances, and then he returned to Houston Control only to find everyone was dead. In fact, he sent the very last message out to the fleet before all went dark on this end. His name is John Carpenter, and he is the resident facility engineer or manager at Houston's mission control. He probably only has a basic understanding of the technical aspects of the communications systems and probably even less regarding the Gate, but he is on the payroll and, as I said, has remained steadfast in his dedication to the facility."

"That will have to do," said President Grainger. "I will have word sent to him." Then, smiling, he added, "Hmmm. I suppose he needs a new, lofty title: Interstellar Mission Control Chief of Operations." He laughed. "That doesn't make for a very good acronym, but it sounds impressive. Mr. El, you can work out the details. Governor Sheffield, you are to make whatever resources we can spare available to this effort. I feel good about this. Thank you for the initiative." He stood up, and it was clear that everyone was dismissed.

Gabe was used to being the one, or at least one of many, who could modify behavior and put pieces of a puzzle together. President Grainger was going one step further by taking the completed puzzle and initiating real action. Gabe now had authority and the makings of group that could make a huge difference. It didn't usually come together this easily. What are the chances of the same limited group of people whom he and his team had already met being the same ones being recruited to the end goal? Was a higher authority really directing things here? Well, maybe, but so what, as long as things were getting back on course.

As Gabe and Linda left the president's office, one of the governor's staff members met them and said, "Governor Sheffield, ma'am, we are grounded for a couple of days. A category-five hurricane has formed off the coast and is closing in fast. Your plane has been moved to an underground hangar, and everyone is preparing for the storm. It appears things will clear out the day after tomorrow, and we'll have a clear flight home."

"Great," said the governor. "That's the second one in two months."

"Is this normal?" asked Gabe.

Governor Sheffield looked at Gabe, furrowed her brow, and said with no expectation of a response, "In what sand pile have you been sticking your head? The East Coast gets hammered by these storms at least four or five times a year. At least this is only a category-five storm. Washington has seen two super storms this season, stretching the fortifications along the Potomac and Anacostia rivers to their limit. I wouldn't say it was routine, but it is certainly something people are used to. I can't believe your so-called survey work hasn't noted these events."

And with that, they returned to their quarters and waited out the storm with the rest of the governors. On August 20, they took off but not to Anchorage. They would go there after a detour to Houston to pick up John Carpenter.

Chapter 29
Team Building

By September 20, 2085, things were getting organized. The core of the mission-control team had been identified and was starting to come together. The governor, the three Bickmeier men, John Carpenter, and Gabe-Re-El and his team were assembled in Governor Sheffield's conference room in Anchorage. Gabe had made arrangements for clothing in Anchorage for the rest of his team so they wouldn't stand out quite as much as they would in their standard white uniforms. Gold and silver coins seemed to move the tailoring of custom sizes of pants, shirts, and even real shoes along at an amazing speed. However, even with the plaid shirts and jeans, the long hair, perfect complexions, and physical size could not be disguised. The five of them stood out wherever they were, especially when eating. They could each put a lumberjack to shame at any dining table.

The governor had made arrangements for the three Bickmeier men to fly by helicopter to Poker Flats so they could at least see what they might have to work with. Not surprisingly, they reported that it was impossible for them to determine how much work would be involved, but they agreed to give it a shot. At the same time, a crew with heavy equipment was dispatched to rebuild the Steese Highway from Fairbanks to Poker Flats. The road would be essential for equipment and accommodations of all types to be brought in. It was noted that the power lines were down and there was no evidence of any site power.

Kem and Ere had met two army sergeants named Falkner and Roberts when they had gone to the East Coast. These men were supply sergeants. That is, they had a list of things that technicians and mechanics needed to keep military hardware functioning. They traveled the country, obtaining parts so equipment could be repaired. Kem thought these two might be helpful, and they were added to the new team.

John Carpenter didn't know what to feel. For years, he had labored to keep mission control in Houston in some semblance of readiness, praying that someday, his final message to the interstellar fleet would be answered, reestablishing communications with the humanity hurtling through space to an uncertain fate. Quite unexpectedly, he was told that he had been promoted to Interstellar Mission Control Chief of Operations. *What a mouthful*, he thought while wondering what exactly he was supposed to do.

In fact, John had said, "Look, I appreciate the president even knowing I exist, but I'm an engineer, and I like things organized. I have no idea what I'm supposed to be doing, so I hope someone can tell me."

Governor Sheffield had smiled at this and said, "Not to worry, Mr. Carpenter. Things are happening rather quickly. The fact that you like things organized is going to be a huge factor as we move forward. You will meet with Mr. El and me at least once a week. You have an office down the hall from me to use when you are in town, so you and I can meet as needed, but at least once a week with the two of us. Per the president, you tell me what we need, and I'll do what I can to make it happen. Everyone recruited for this project reports to you. You will build the team needed to make this work. You have built teams before to run facilities, haven't you? Well, this is only slightly different. You'll be fine."

All John could muster for response was, "Oh boy!" And he looked down at his shoes, shaking his head back and forth slowly. Then, looking up at Gabe, he asked, "And what about you and your people?"

Ara jumped in saying, "Oh, we're the guys who will take all the credit if everything goes well. You know, pictures in all the publications and such. But we'll toss you under the bus if things fall apart."

As John stared at Ara, Gabe said, "Don't listen to him. He thinks he's funny. We'll be around for moral support, but we are not capable of physically helping out. We don't have the technical skills, and even if we did, our boss wouldn't let us. It's complicated."

Kem and Ere reported that Abel Fisher would be joining the team and that he had recruited a Megan Benoit from the south of France. They weren't sure how Abel knew her, but he claimed she had a great deal of computer-programming experience. Governor Sheffield wasn't too pleased at sending a plane to France to collect this Ms. Benoit, but it was being done. Abel would be coming to

Anchorage in a couple of weeks after he took care of some business. Kem and Ere both thought that Abel had demonstrated a high level of skill, but they had never actually met him face-to-face.

When Kem mentioned Abel Fisher, Karl looked up, suddenly saying, "Did you say Abel Fisher?"

"Yes," said Kem. "Do you know him?"

"I might know him," said Karl. "My mother's maiden name was Fisher. She had one brother who had a son named Logan, and Logan's son was named Abel. He was a teenager when we moved to Alaska, so he would be about your age, Don, if it is the same person. Interesting. Very interesting."

Ere said, "And your sister and her family are with the space fleet?"

"Yes," said Karl.

Ara said, "This is starting to get freaky. Is everyone involved related? How about you, John? You must be related somehow. At least adopted or something."

"I don't think so," said John, "but you know, they claim everyone is related if you go back a few generations. And then there is that Adam-and-Eve thing. But maybe we can ignore that for a minute and concentrate on the mission." And from there, John Carpenter, Interstellar Mission Control Chief of Operations, started stepping into his role as team builder. He felt more buoyant than he had in years. He now had a real task that he could feel passionate about. He could finally tie up a loose end—a loose end he believed he had created when he sent the final message to the space fleet. All he had to do was tell the fleet "You are no longer on your own."

He told everyone that he didn't want to wait for others to show up. He wanted to get to Poker Flats, open the boxes and crates, and start to lay things out. He had some idea of how things would look based on his years in Houston, so there was little reason to delay. Road reconstruction should be finished by the time the team could determine what else was needed. "We will need support staff, said John. "We need people to order food, cook, and clean up, for starters."

Ara said, "Well, since this looks like a family affair already, what about Karl's wife and daughter-in-law? They can cook; quite well, as a matter of fact. Plus, a little spiritual guidance from Kim Sue wouldn't hurt either as the site starts to get populated."

Karl looked at Ara and said, "Hmmm. Interesting."

Don said, "It is OK with me. We pawned off all our responsibilities before we left. The people of Homer view Kim Sue as their spiritual leader, but they are a good lot. I think it's OK with me, but isn't this now John's decision?"

"I think this is a great idea. Let's do it," said John.

"Really?" said Ara, "I was only joking."

"Gotcha," said Gabe. "You remind me of a stopped clock. Even it tells the correct time twice a day."

"Great," said Ara, "now I have to compete with you for a laugh?"

"You were never that funny to begin with," said Kem.

An increasingly energized John said, "OK, it is settled. This was a great Monday-morning start for a new adventure. Governor, can we get up to Poker Flats tomorrow with enough supplies to get started?"

So, on September 21, 2085, two military helicopters took off from Anchorage and headed to Poker Flats. On board were the three Bickmeier men, John Carpenter, Kem, and enough supplies for a week. Included were camping gear, portable heaters, and a small Honda generator to provide enough power to get started. Helicopters would refresh supplies for the next month until the Steese Highway was repaired, allowing heavy trucks to bring in large generators and more permanent housing. Even with climate change keeping the Poker Flats weather warmer than it had been a century ago, it would still get cold, and camping gear was not going to cut it.

A third helicopter flew to Homer. Kim Sue and Maria weren't immediately prepared to leave town. With no communication lines to Anchorage, they didn't know they had been drafted into the team until the helicopter landed and the air-force pilots told them. Kim Sue thought, *How things have changed since that Gabe-Re-El seemed to descend from the heavens on that Sunday back in July*. She wasn't sure if she was scared or simply excited about what she thought was happening around her. One thing was certain—her spirituality was stronger than ever.

Maria Bickmeier thought about her very early adventures leading her to Alaska and her husband. If not always calm, she was at least content to stay in Homer and had actually hoped that she would not have any more adventures. But when she was around that fellow Gabe and his buddies, the calm she felt was quite real, and she decided this adventure might just keep that feeling alive.

On September 23, the two women, with their pots and pans and everything else they thought they might need, boarded the helicopter and were flown to Poker Flats. While they had not been prepared for the harsh reality of the place, it wouldn't take long before they softened the living environment. Even though John was in charge of the operation, the women took charge of the rest, starting with the abandoned visitor-and-office building. By the end of the week, they had enough of it cleaned up that camping out was no longer required. They all camped inside the building, and the now fully functioning kitchen allowed for more satisfying meals, even if the place was still a bit chilly.

The men were happy that the women had arrived, and Kem was especially thankful for the cooking.

Kim Sue had decided that there would be no serious work on Sundays. Planning was OK, but work in the control room was off limits. John decided that discretion was the better part of valor, and if a happy team was contingent on a happy Kim Sue, so be it. On Sunday, September 30, Kim Sue and Maria had laid out a midmorning Sunday brunch. It was here that Kim Sue would take a few minutes to reflect on life in general and what might come later. Nothing heavy, but she felt surprisingly more inspired since Gabe's introduction into her life and now with Kem in their midst. On this day, she felt inspired to talk about Noah's ark, as it seemed to relate to those in the space fleet looking for that "dry land."

Around midday, a helicopter landed, and two more members of the team emerged. Abel Fisher and Megan Benoit met face-to-face in Anchorage for the first time that morning. They, of course, recognized each other from their many video meetings, but it was still extremely awkward for both of them. Personal interaction with real people was something the techy world had avoided. In Anchorage, they were ushered from their planes to a helicopter with their belongings, and it took off for Poker Flats. Not much beyond a hello was shared between the two.

When Abel, Megan, and a small robot emerged from the helicopter, it was a strange sight for the rugged people of the north. The sight of a five-foot-eight-inch man weighing about 115 pounds, obviously freezing in ill-fitting clothing, was only less shocking than the five-foot-one-inch, 85-pound woman standing next to him. In fact, no one was certain this wasn't a child. No two people could have looked more out of place. Still, they were greeted and invited in, with the robot adding just the right touch to this first encounter.

Once inside, Abel said, "Where's the equipment?"

John said, "Today is Sunday. We will catch you up on what we've been doing, but we'll go to the control room tomorrow. We'll spend today getting to know each other better."

"Why?" said Abel.

"How about because I said so?" said John as Kem decided to get closer to Abel.

Megan said nothing, looking completely overwhelmed by everything, but especially all these large people and most especially an extremely large Kem, who was nearly two feet taller and nearly two hundred pounds heavier. *My God*, she thought, even though she was a nonbeliever. *What have I been talked into? I traveled halfway around the world to this forbidding place, surrounded by giants.*

Neither Abel nor Megan were interested in eating anything, but they did accept cups of tea, and they all sat down. Kem sat next to Abel, who initially appeared to be quite uncomfortable but gradually seemed to be more at ease.

Karl asked bluntly, "Was your father, Logan Fisher, born in New Bedford?"

Abel was visibly surprised by this question but said, "Oh, you must have looked at some files."

"No," said Karl, "I'm pretty sure we're cousins. My mother was Laura Fisher before she got married, and she would have been your grandfather's sister. His name was—Matthew? If that is correct. I remember you as a teenager before we moved to Alaska."

"Are you for real?" asked Abel. "I thought all my relatives were dead. I do remember you a little. Is your sister still alive? Didn't she go on the space mission?"

"My sister, Ada, and her family did leave on the interstellar mission. Didn't you know we are here to reestablish communications with the space fleet? We are trusting that the fleet and its crew are still on course," said Karl, "but we don't know."

Abel guessed that deep down inside, he probably did know why he was there, but he had been so focused on the flying backpacks, he hadn't really thought about the actual mission. Reconnecting with his long-lost family might be an added bonus. Maybe. He wasn't sure he wanted that.

John said, "This family-reunion thing is getting ridiculous. Only Kem here, and I, seem to be outsiders, though I'm guessing Ms. Benoit isn't related either. Is she?"

Abel had thought he was in love with Megan before he'd actually met her but no longer knew what he felt. His thinking was getting very confused. It certainly wouldn't be good if they were related. But he could only muster, "I don't think so."

Maria asked, "Are you two an item?"

Megan finally spoke and said, "A what?"

Maria continued, "You know, an item—boyfriend, girlfriend? Engaged to be married?"

"No," said Abel, ending that round of getting to know each other. He didn't want Megan to know that maybe, just maybe, he had feelings for her. He wasn't sure.

"OK, then," said John, somewhat perplexed at the cold responses from the new team members. "How did you get recruited?"

Abel said, "This guy, Kem, said I could borrow one of their flying packs if I agreed to help out. I want to figure out how it works and make more. I want to fly."

Kem hadn't expected that to come out. Kim Sue, however, knew exactly what Abel was referring to though had never considered the concept of a machine being involved. Her consideration had been in a different direction altogether.

"Flying machine?" asked Don.

"Not important," said Abel, to Kem's relief. "Catch us up."

And they did. The team building was as done as it was going to get for now.

Chapter 30
Mission Control

It took nearly a year to get Poker Flats Mission Control functioning—or, at least, the belief that it was functioning. They wouldn't know for certain until they got a response back from the interstellar fleet. In some respects, the reconstruction was easy. Each of the crates had been clearly labeled, and many contained already-assembled components that could be plugged into each other. So, after everything was uncrated, John had the the various consoles and related components placed as he remembered their relative locations in Houston. Once that was completed, each subsystem was carefully checked for any obvious issues, such as frayed wires or corrosion.

Karl's background in mechanical and electrical engineering meant he was in charge of assemblies and electrification. Don and Len did a great deal of the actual component assembly in the control room. Megan's unique talent was put to good use as she was able to "see" how the individual circuits worked. It was actually a little unsettling to watch her open an access panel, place her hands, and loose touch with reality while she virtually traced circuits. Problem areas that human hands couldn't reach were repaired using Abel's neural connection with miniature robots and nanobots. The rest of the group watching Abel and Megan do their thing were both mesmerized and a little terrified.

Setting up the antennae was a whole different ball game. When the weather finally warmed up in May, the Army Corps of Engineers was called in for the assembly. The end result was easy to visualize, but it was huge and had to be completely assembled on-site. Its center looked like a huge cannon 30 feet in diameter and 213 feet in length. In the center of the barrel, projecting out an additional 55 feet was a shaft 13 inches in diameter. Around the barrel were lattice dishes. The one closest to the base was 135 feet in diameter. There were nine additional lattice dishes that reached the end of the barrel, each one slightly smaller than the one below. This apparatus was mounted on a turntable and hydraulic arm so it could be aimed up and down or all the way around, with the horizon establishing the only limits. Once it was completed, six engineers were left behind, joining the team to actually provide the support needed to aim the monstrosity.

Another problem the team ran into was in obtaining electric power. The system required twenty-four hundred volts of direct current (DC) that fed massive electric coils to generate the signal. Power could come from either DC generators or alternating current (AC) generators that then converted the power to DC. The army helped with this as well. As suspected, Sergeants Falkner and Roberts were needed. Gabe sent Ere-Mi-El to work with them as he had already befriended them. Both sergeants were happy to see Ere again and took great pleasure in locating what was needed and delivering it to Poker Flats. They made five grueling trips in total from the lower United States. Tucked away in the truck here and there on each trip were specialty items requested by Kim Sue and Maria to make life a little nicer.

The operational parameter for the antennae was to aim it so that the signal would intercept the fleet when it reached a calculated position. While it didn't have to be precise, the intercept tolerance had to be reasonable. Because the Earth revolved, there were only certain times of the day when the antennae could be aimed with any hope of the signal reaching the space fleet.

To aim the antennae, a mathematician with something of an astrophysics background was located and added to the team. Dr. Sheila Tanawa fit right into this strange group. She was an attractive South African. Somehow, the combination of her dark skin, wild hair, and colorful clothing seemed to work. She brought a crazy sense of humor, constantly expressing a misunderstanding or the wrong meaning for words and using double entendre. Anyone listening to her had to pay close attention. On the other hand, when she was asked a seriously complicated question, her eyes might roll up into her head as if the printed words of what to say were on the inside of her forehead. Then, looking straight at someone, she would give an answer, but often not the one expected. She was fun to be around, but if serious work was required, it was best to leave her in a room completely alone with no distractions. Her job was to try to determine where the antennae should be aimed when a signal was to be sent. For a starting point, John Carpenter was able to find the predicted course for the fleet. Outside of Kem, however, no one on the team knew that the fleet had modified its flight trajectory to accommodate the issues of engine failure and the fleet was not near the predicted location. Kem still hoped the fleet's position would be within an acceptable signal width.

Additional staff was brought in to maintain the facility and to be system operators. Once a message was sent, monitoring for a response would be 24-7 in case any incoming message had to be enhanced electronically in real time. With the delay between sending and receiving, no one wanted to take a chance that something might be missed.

During all of this, Abel actually developed some muscle tone and now tipped the scales at 130 pounds. Megan had filled out as well. Not that anyone noticed exactly with her new weight at ninety-seven pounds; except for Abel. He noticed, as he and Megan took up in real life where they had left off with their virtual lovemaking. Both concluded that this was much better once they got used to the actual touching and feeling, though Megan took it a step further, initiating activity nearly every time she and Abel were alone. Abel's stamina was a major beneficiary as she pushed his limits. He also decided that a little more meat on Megan's bones was an improvement over what he had previously thought to be the perfect body. Roundness in the right spots actually added a lot, he concluded!

At some point, Abel remembered the family Model T Ford and was very surprised to learn that Karl still had it and drove it from time to time. As Abel softened up over the winter, he had Karl promise him a ride in the old buggy.

On August 1, 2086, John Carpenter sent his second message to the interstellar fleet. It was far more complete than the first message he had sent fifteen years earlier. "This is John Carpenter, interstellar mission-control chief of operations, calling from Poker Flats Mission Control, transmitting to Admiral Nimitz of the interstellar fleet. Your home planet has suffered severely since your departure with climate change and a pandemic. It has taken us until now to reestablish a communications link. We collectively hope and pray that this message finds all are well within the fleet and the mission is still on track for completion. We are monitoring for a reply 24-7, and once we hear from you, we will provide complete information. We have calculated where the fleet should be based on the original plans. Please advise if this has changed so we may better calibrate any future transmissions. Until then, we stand by and look forward to a reply."

The message was sent no less than one hundred times, with the antennae aimed in a slightly different direction each time. If the fleet was off course, it was hoped that it wouldn't be so much that all the transmissions would miss. Beyond the time delay, distance was not a problem. Being outside the narrow beam of the transmission would be, however. When the final scheduled transmission was sent, Kem casually encouraged one more "for good measure" and suggested a direction.

Outside of Kem, no one in mission control knew that the fleet was waiting for the transmission. Gabe had used the habitat's communications to tell Schem what was going on back on Earth. It was during one of these sessions that Schem relayed the correct location of the fleet. That would be the only transmission received— the one "for good measure."

Because Admiral Sylva was in the loop on Schem's clandestine communications system, she knew that it would be a long time before she received the message via the fleet's communications systems. She decided to move things along and sent the return message as soon as Schem told her what it was going to say. *Won't they be surprised to hear from us this quickly?* she thought. *That will be our little secret, at least for now.*

Chapter 31

Back to the Gate

The Gate on Earth had worked well when it was being used for teleportation within the solar system. However, it had been operated by scientists and engineers functioning at such a level that your everyday genius would look at these people as super nerds and geeks. It had been said that the nerdiness permeated the air to such a degree that people could smell it when they entered the control room, though it might not have been nerdiness that people smelled. But while these people had operated at a higher intellectual plane, they also couldn't prepare operating and maintenance (O&M) manuals that anyone could follow, including them. True, they had put things down on paper, so to speak, but only because they had been told to. They were so into the technology they had created, they didn't want to waste time documenting with the thought that someone else might need to operate the systems. That wasn't very exciting. Besides, lower-life people simply wouldn't understand and were deemed unworthy, so why bother?

Unfortunately, with the death flu eliminating this exclusive club, it had left a piece of technology that no one on Earth could understand or operate. The official gatekeeper, Summer Snow, was a very intelligent woman, and she had spent many hours near the equipment trying to understand the technology or at least how to make it work. But she continually found herself feeling like the archeologists must have felt centuries ago when they had tried to understand how the pyramids were built in Egypt. The pyramids were obviously there, but how had they done it?

She had tried to focus on how to make it work using the analogy of driving a car: you can drive one without needing to understand what makes it work. She was just missing the operating manual. If she took the crap that the nerd herd had written down and compared that with what was in front of her, maybe, just maybe, she could figure out how the damned thing worked.

On the other hand, the interstellar space fleet had on board scientists and engineers who knew not only how to make it work but also the principles of its operation. They had been considered second tier to the operators on Earth, just as the operators of the other Gates in the solar system had been considered second tier. The difference, however, was that this second tier hurtling through space had had enough time on its hands to rewrite the O&M manuals and teach classes to a younger group of scientists and engineers. After all, they were the ones who would have to assemble a Gate before they could operate it. If that understanding could be instilled in a new group of Earth-based operators, then, in theory, teleportation would be established when the new Gate was built at EE light-years away.

Gabe's team knew all of this, and it had the means of transmitting verbal communications that could help a technically savvy person, or a team of them, and then create a good O&M manual on Earth. The fleet's admiralty staff obviously understood this, as well. The rub was that Gabe's team was only permitted to assist, especially if there was another way to allow this to happen. That path now existed, though it would be painfully slow.

Now that mission control was functioning, transmissions from the fleet back to Earth would allow an Earth-based team of technicians to gradually piece things together. Gabe decided that this was what would have to happen. There was plenty of time for this transfer of information to occur. The fleet was still a long way from EE, and once there, construction of the Gate, if unimpeded, would take at least a year. The one concession he did make was to allow communication assistance in order to cut the response time in half.

Na-Ki-Ir and Ara-Ri-El were the team members who had first visited the Gate in Ziebach County, South Dakota. While Kem and Ere had been assigned to guide the mission-control effort, Naki and Ara had been held back and were given the task of evaluating the general population's thoughts and feelings regarding the space fleet. Did people believe it existed in the first place, and did they think it was still on mission? Many had come to the conclusion that the space fleet was just a myth established by the governments to sidetrack collective awareness from Earth's real problems—a manufactured distraction turned to disillusionment about the Earth's future.

Members of other teams assisted Naki and Ara in their survey efforts. As an unintended consequence of these surveys, stories were beginning to circulate about glowing entities in white flying down to Earth and asking questions. It was especially noted how the encounters left people with a sense of calm excitement for the future. The fact that these strangers ate far more food than normal was noticed, but it was somehow never passed along to any degree. Much to Naki's annoyance, Ara would always try to start an introduction by saying, "Hi, we're from the government, and we're here to help you." Or, "Hi there. Seen anything unusual lately?" Naki would cut Ara off as soon as he could and would tell him to "knock it off," which only made Ara chuckle.

When mission control was functioning and the first message was received back from the fleet, there was cause for celebration, and the mission-control team acted accordingly. Big time.

A message would be sent from mission control, and Gabe would repeat the message to Schem over their clandestine system. Since their message was received instantaneously, the admiral would send a reply before the official message came in, cutting the response time in half. Outside of Gabe's team on Earth, only Dr. Sheila Tanawa realized that the message received had arrived in half the time expected. The fact that it repeated over and over absolutely baffled her. No calculation she did could ever account for it, and no one on Gabe's team would ever tell her why. It was to remain a mystery.

With communications now set, Governor Colonel Linda Sheffield, with a suggestion from Gabe-Re-El, decided to move the focus to the Gate itself. Many of the technical team reestablishing mission control would move to South Dakota, including all the Bickmeiers, Abel Fisher, and Megan Benoit. The space fleet wouldn't have the EE Gate functioning until at least 2096, yet all team members agreed to go. Gabe assigned Naki and Ara to provide support. John Carpenter and Dr. Sheila Tanawa would stay in Poker Flats as the director and chief scientist, respectively. Kem would also stay behind. Ere would continue to work with the supply sergeants and travel the country with them.

President Grainger had informed Summer Snow that support was coming. This had made her both excited and apprehensive—excited that there was renewed interest in the Gate, but apprehensive that she might get pushed aside by unknown scientists and engineers descending on her domain.

Naki and Ara didn't wait for the more traditional means of air travel provided by the military and instead found their way to South Dakota in their usual manner and wearing their traditional clothing. They planned their arrival to coincide with when they hoped there would be fresh breakfast sandwiches at the same roadside stand they had found before. When they walked over the ridge, the same couple that had served them before was there with the same cooler, but this time, there were a few folding chairs. When the Sioux couple saw Naki and Ara approaching, they walked over to greet them. Hoping for some gold coins, they wanted the outsiders to be well fed and, remembering all the details, they said, "It is good to see you again. Would you like one of each kind of sandwich? We now have chairs for you to use."

Ara looked at the chairs and decided that he'd rather stand than break them, but he said, "Yes, we look forward to your excellent sandwiches and some coffee please." And eat they did. Naki and Ara also hoped for the same lone horseman to show up on his way to work at the Gate, and he did, right on schedule, as the last of the sandwiches disappeared, including the one he had planned on eating.

The horseman said, "I did not expect to see you two again."

"You never know," said Ara with a broad smile. "Except this time, we really are sent by the federal government, and we really are here to help you. Would you mind escorting us to Summer Snow's office?" And off they went, with Naki shaking his head and remembering, *Even a stopped clock is correct twice a day, and so once again, Ara is correct.*

The Sioux couple thought that this time, they might not get paid, but after he had walked away a few feet, Naki stopped and said, "Oh, I'm sorry. Will this cover our breakfast?" And he handed over a couple of silver coins, to the delight of the couple.

Naki and Ara followed the horseman as they had the first time, through the security fences and guard dogs and up to the office. When asked if anything had changed since their first visit, the horseman thought for moment before saying, "Summer Snow seems to have a different demeanor. Still focused but with a quieter resolution in her actions. There are some other changes since the president notified us of a renewed interest in the Gate, but I'll let Summer fill you in."

When Naki and Ara entered the office, Summer Snow was studying plans scattered over a large conference table and almost absent-mindedly noted their presence. When she looked up, Ara got as far as, "We're from the g—" before Naki said, "Ara, please stop, already." He turned to Ms. Snow. "We don't work for the government, but on behalf of President Grainger, we are here to assist as best we can. We have a small group of people who have been assembled to help get the Gate prepared for operations and to help you assemble and train an operating staff."

Summer Snow stared at the two and said, "You mean to tell me that people who have never seen this thing are going to come in here and show me how to make it work? I've been trying to figure that out for years, and I don't think I'm stupid!"

Naki said, "Well, there is a little more to the story. These people have been working on the communications system, and it is now linked to the space fleet. The scientists and engineers in the fleet have the advantage of corporate memory as far as the Gate is concerned and can lead the Earth-based team through the operation and maintenance of the Gate. The fleet actually has a manual. Unfortunately, the transfer of information isn't going to happen very quickly, as there is a long gap between messages sent and received. However, there does seem to be plenty of time to work everything out."

"Hmm," said Summer, "plenty of time, huh? Well, I like the pi rule."

"Pi rule?" asked Ara.

"Yeah," said Summer with a sudden unexpected twinkle in her dark eyes. "Take the amount of time you think it will take, and multiply by pi, 3.14, and that's usually how long it will actually take."

"Why pi?

"Well," said Summer, "it is a universal constant, isn't it?"

"Oh, I love it," said Ara. "I'm definitely using that in the future."

Naki rolled his eyes.

Becoming more serious, Summer Snow went on. "Once we got word that there was going to be some effort put into the project, I had some construction done for housing within the compound. It should be enough to get us started. I'm going to be optimistic when I say that *when* we get ready to go, the housing and this office will be moved outside the security gate, just in case you were wondering. Anything within the perimeter of the infrastructure and not in the gatehouse itself will get fried when the Gate is functioning. I've got some photos from when it operated previously. Anyway, keeping everyone close by initially should make it easier to get the Gate up and running. By the way, when the president told me I would be contacted, I didn't expect you two. I thought you were in some kind of benevolent society." And, eyeing them up and down, she added, "And you're still wearing the same clothes."

"Yes," said Ara, "but they have been washed!"

Naki gave a disgusted look at him and responded with, "The president asked if some of our society members could provide logistical assistance as we have a broad reach. Ara and I agreed to help and asked if we could be assigned here. We are here for as long as necessary. We also have some different clothes, which we will change into when we have a chance."

"I don't seem to have a choice in the matter. So, OK, we'll make it work," said Summer. "You'll be shown to your quarters, and we'll have lunch in the dining hall at noon."

"Oh, and," said Naki, "I was instructed to make it clear that you are to remain in charge of the operation. At some point, a permanent technical staff will be stationed here to operate the Gate, and the intention is for them to report to you. No one wanted you to think you were being pushed aside. You have done an excellent job here keeping the Gate secure, and it is appreciated."

Four days later, on October 6, 2086, the Bickmeiers, Abel Fisher, and Megan Benoit arrived by transportation provided by the military. It was a long day: a truck ride from Poker Flats to Fairbanks and then an executive-jet ride to Sioux City, followed by a helicopter ride to the Gate compound. The parts of the Gate infrastructure they could see as they arrived were big, but not inspiring.

Most in the party had at one time or another been in the lower part of the United States except for Megan and Len, so most weren't too surprised by their new surroundings. Len, however, had been glued to the plane windows on the flight down and actually occupied the copilot's seat for a few hours. South Dakota looked nothing like Alaska. With him always wanting to go someplace, this was far beyond anything he had considered. He was certain he couldn't get more excited with the possibilities in front of him until he was introduced to Summer Snow. This woman was the most beautiful creature he had ever imagined. His knees went weak when she firmly gripped his hand, and he was capable of saying absolutely nothing.

Len's parents and grandparents watched this and each silently said to themselves, "Oh, boy."

Abel and Megan were oblivious to this interaction, as they had something else on their collective minds. It was understood that they would be sharing living quarters, and they had made it clear that they would like to unpack and freshen up before dinner. An hour and half later, they emerged from their room with nothing unpacked. Megan was smiling, and Abel looked beat.

Over the next few days, Summer showed the group around, providing as much detail as she could. As they got closer to the center of the complex, they saw how the aboveground cabling increased in height from the outside diameter of the complex while converging close to the center. The cables then came down from the thousand-foot towers into the gatehouse itself. Only one area was bridged, allowing a straight access to the gatehouse entrance. The gatehouse was five stories high, each twenty feet from floor to floor. The middle level was where the Gate itself resided, along with the main control room. This middle level had been designed with the Gate oriented so that exactly equal parts of the Gate were above and below grade. The floors above and below held the massive transformers and coils that made the Gate work. Each floor was close to two acres in area.

The actual Gate looked like a glass cylinder with sliding doors for an entrance. The interior of the Gate had a diameter of about 115 feet and was 15 feet tall. The doors would slide open before and after the actual transmission. Evenly spaced around the cylinder were variously sized electrical coils. The floor and ceiling of the cylinder looked like they were covered with electromagnets. This was far more impressive-looking than what the team had seen from outside. Throughout the tour, it was obvious that Summer was frustrated by her incomplete comprehension of the systems.

Kim Sue was impressed with the makeshift chapel that had been built. Maria was equally impressed with the kitchen and living facilities. They were simple but complete. Len was focused on Summer but tried to absorb some of what she was saying. Don absorbed every word. It wasn't clear what Karl thought, but he said it was "interesting." Megan and Abel were introduced to the computer systems. With his neural connection, he would use a specially designed program developed by Megan to virtually enter the computer software to do diagnostics. No one wanted to open anything up and operate anything for fear of breaking something. It all worked when it was shut down, so there was little reason to think it wouldn't work as long as this new team didn't damage it.

Once the group got started, transmissions from the space fleet were relayed to the Gate complex. With each transmission, the operating parameters became a little clearer. Everything was carefully documented.

Staff started to be added at the Gate. Slowly at first, but over the next several months as the team identified specific requirements, others were added to the core group. This is where Naki and Ara helped. By going to places where the skills existed, their very presence was usually enough to get people to say they would be part of the project. To these people, it became something of an awakening or a new calling that couldn't be ignored when they were asked.

While it was clear that Summer Snow was in charge, she gravitated toward the most senior person in the group from both an age and education standpoint. Karl found her very easy to work with. As a group, they decided to work on one workstation at a time in the main control room, receiving guidance from the space fleet as to where to start. Of course, with the huge time lag between question and answer, many questions went off before any responses returned from earlier questions. That meant they had to skip around and work one area until they became stymied. They would systematically study the control panels, review the plans to understand what each control was supposed to do or what they thought it was supposed to do, and then confirm their understanding with the scientists and engineers in the fleet.

As Summer already knew and Karl soon learned, the O&M manuals on-site were essentially useless. Initially it was thought that the O&M manuals from the space fleet would be the only thing needed to get the Earth Gate up and running. However, during the trip from Earth to EE, the scientists and engineers in the fleet had modernized some of the equipment, so the operating systems weren't 100 percent alike. It became Don's job to rewrite the O&M manuals as the puzzles were worked out with the space fleet. The manuals were reworked over and over again until they not only matched the intent of the manuals kept in the fleet but also went beyond to where people without an advanced degree could follow along. Protocols were carefully identified and taught to the eventual operators because no one wanted have people enter the Gate only to never appear again. As Ara astutely understated, "That would be rude."

Karl and Don decided they needed to keep Len away from Summer during work hours so he could stay focused. He ended up tasked with tracing piping and cables to make sure there were no breaks and to confirm that block diagrams were accurate. This meant he spent many hours out of doors, away from Summer, making sure the cable arrays were also intact. If they weren't, he reported this to Summer in the most awkward manner possible. Summer would then assign a repair crew from her staff.

In early December, Don met with Summer and Karl. He was visibly uncomfortable when he asked, "Do you know how much power this sucker needs to operate?"

"I guess not," said Karl. "They had this thing running before, so I guess I've been assuming that it wasn't an issue."

"Actually, I think it is," said Summer. "I've been so focused on the Gate itself, I sort of put the power needs in the back of my mind as something to worry about later. The Gate power is through a series of coils that pump up a DC power charge."

"Similar to the communications systems, is my guess," said Karl.

"I guess so," said Summer. "It produces a series of short-term charges that create what I call wormhole rings. Whatever is being teleported is reduced or sliced in one dimension, so the Gate sends pulses that are nearly two-dimensional. The receiving Gate basically adds the slices back together and fluffs up whatever it is receiving. Gates send and receive, but not at the same time. This is a long way around to say that the receiving activity requires sixty megawatts of AC electrical energy for conversion to DC."

"That's not so bad," said Karl. Then, looking at Summer, he added, "But sending requires more?"

"Yes," said Summer. "The Gate requires eleven hundred megawatts of steady power."

Karl said, "Hmmm. Interesting."

"Interesting?" said Don. "The only generators I've seen around here produce probably no more than a couple megawatts. Where does the power come from?"

Summer answered, "Actually, added together, we have about two and a half megawatts for on-site generating capacity, but that's just for site needs, not the Gate. When they were building the Gate, the government took over the construction of a new plant on Lake Oahe with the not-so-clever name Lake Oahe Power Station, or LOPS, as we used to call it. It is, or was, a twelve-hundred-megawatt nuclear station. It was built with its primary goal to service this facility. When the power wasn't needed here, I understand they just dumped it into the power grid. It's been shut down since the death flu struck. No need for the power and, of course, the entire crew died."

"I'm starting to understand the pi-factor rule," said Don.

That night around the dinner table, Karl explained the power situation and asked Naki and Ara if they could work their magic. The next day, Naki and Ara were absent, with no indication of where they had gone or how. Two weeks later, they returned just as suddenly as they had left. They had seemingly performed a miracle. LOPS would be operational when needed. Engineers and operators were being selectively pulled out of the US nuclear fleet. Because of their isolation, many ships' crews had remained unaffected during the pandemic. Some of these crews were getting a bit long in the tooth and wanted to get off the boats. They weren't allowed to retire, so an opportunity to get a land-based plant up and running was looking pretty good. President Grainger, with some urging from Gabe-Re-El, moved this along quickly. Still, it would take nearly a year to get the necessary people on-site and another two and half years to get the plant checked out and running. Even with the pi rule, there was plenty of time.

"Yup," said Ara, "times pi."

Chapter 32
Weddings

Ever since Kem-U-El and Ere-Mi-El had floated into his life a year and a half ago, Abel Fisher's life had been completely transformed. He had been happy, so he'd thought, operating his holdings, getting wealthy, never having to interact with any real people, and generally taking it easy. When he had first met Kem and Ere, all he wanted was to get one of their flying packs to see how it worked. These two guys flew around effortlessly. They had appreciated his fine wine and had somehow absconded with one of his barrels of merlot. These guys and their buddies were fascinating.

After their first visit, he'd felt different. He had washed, shaved off his beard, had his hair cut, and put on some clothes. He had even gone to the trouble of asking Megan if she was real or just a computer-generated image. Previously, he hadn't cared one way or the other.

Then these two had returned and convinced him to leave the comforts of his home and go to an isolated location in Alaska. He had even recruited Megan to come along, who not only was a real person but was also a technological genius with a last name! Then, to the amazement of both Abel and Megan, touching another person was not disgusting at all. It was magical. Megan couldn't get enough of Abel, and while Abel was initially completely exhausted from these intense encounters, he had built up body mass in the form of muscle he hadn't known he had. Megan kept finding new ways to test his stamina, but that, too, was building.

Megan had also transformed her physical appearance. Initially feeling embarrassed when she had first seen Abel shaved and clothed, she was now rounding out in the best of places and wearing clothes that showed off some of her new positive attributes. She paid close attention to what Summer Snow wore each day and even asked Maria and Kim Sue for some advice, which they were happy to give. Megan shocked herself with the realization that she was interacting with people on a regular basis and liked it. The Alaska trip had been a true, real adventure, and now she was in the middle of one of humanity's most imaginative creations, a wormhole gate. This new lust for life was exhilarating, and she wanted more—a lot more. These giant characters Naki and Ara seemed to stimulate her but at the same time allowed her to think with a calm inner self.

Unlike Megan, who was grabbing life with full force, poor Len was hopelessly in love, head over heels, with Summer Snow and didn't know what to do. He had only touched her once when she had gripped his hand when they'd all showed up at the site, but he wanted more. Len had had no opportunity to date before so was at a loss, and it looked to him like there wouldn't be any opportunities with Summer either. She was far more interested in spending time with his grandfather, learning as much as she could. Len was learning, too, and had actually solved a few problems in the controls hierarchy that no one else could, but that wasn't enough to get Summer to pay him any attention. The Abel/Megan duo's less than secretive love life only made things worse for him.

Len had assumed that asking his dad and granddad for any help with his breaking heart was a waste of time. Instead, he went to his mother and grandmother with a simple question: "How can I get Summer Snow's attention?"

Taking their advice, he started off easy with a question she would answer, even when he knew the answer, and thanking her for her help. He would compliment her on solutions as she added to the group's knowledge. He graduated to other compliments about her personal tastes.

Summer seemed oblivious but wasn't. She was confused, and Kim Sue and Maria suspected as much. Summer had no more idea of courting than Len did, and besides, she was in charge, and that could never be compromised.

After eighteen months, Kim Sue was tired of this nonsense, and one night while in bed with Karl, said, "Karl, honey, you know Len really likes Summer. You are with her all the time. Do you suppose you could mention that to her?"

"Interesting," said Karl. "Well, Len is a complete goof around Summer. It kind of reminds me of Don when he first saw Maria. I guess I could say something."

"Oh, and Karl," said Kim Sue, "try to be subtle."

"Me?" said Karl. "Of course."

The next day, a Saturday, when Karl and Summer were taking a brief break, Karl took Summer's hand and said in plain English, "You know, kid, Len would do anything you asked him to do. He is completely taken with you. How about giving him a break? You two are the same age, so you have something in common there. As a favor to me, could you at least indicate to him that he has a chance with you?"

Summer stared at Karl with her eyes wide open but said nothing. Just as suddenly, they were back at work. Karl thought he had blown it for certain. Maybe he had been too subtle.

No one worked on Sunday at the request of Kim Sue. She didn't insist on anyone going to chapel on Sunday, but no work. Naki and Ara approved. It also meant that the Saturday-evening meal was a bit more relaxed and wine and beer was served in generous quantities courtesy of Abel and his drone deliveries. This Saturday evening, Summer seemed to be preoccupied with something while consuming more wine that usual. Out of nowhere, she stood up, looked at poor Len, and in a less than a sweet tone of voice, said, "Come with me!" Everyone stopped what they were doing and looked at the two as they walked out into the evening sunset.

Len wondered what he had done to piss her off but followed along. They walked for some distance up over a rise and down to a little hollow. Confused Len said, "Summer, what's the problem?"

"Shut up, you asshole," said Summer as she grabbed his head with both hands, pulled his face down to hers, and planted a lip lock on Len that sucked all the air out of his lungs. It took Len a nanosecond to respond. And respond he did, and then so did Summer, and so on. An hour later, a rumpled couple reappeared holding hands. Len was smiling so hard, Don thought he was going to hurt himself.

The next day, Kim Sue was delighted to see everyone crowding her little chapel, including many from Summer's extended family. Kim Sue talked about the blessings she enjoyed being married to Karl all these years and how happy she was when Don had found Maria. She reminded everyone that marriage had once been something couples did when they were in love and wanted to raise a family. But time had passed, and this old-fashioned ritual seemed now to be a rare occurrence. Kim Sue concluded with a lament for the old traditions. Abel sat with Megan, holding hands. Summer sat with Len, though it appeared he was floating above the bench. Naki and Ara sat between the two couples.

When Kim Sue closed, Abel stood up and asked for everyone's attention. When he got it, he looked at Megan and said, "I will ask here so it will be difficult for you to say no. Will you marry me?" Megan jumped up and answered with a broad smile and kiss. This was a little surprising. Even though these two were already together in every way, asking someone to marry was unusual in this day and age. Certainly no one expected a marriage commitment between Abel and Megan. It was cause for a celebration, and all applauded.

When everyone finished congratulating the couple, Summer provided an even bigger surprise to everyone, especially Len, when she said to him, "If you ask me to marry you, I will. If you don't ask me, I'm taking my shotgun and shooting your sorry ass."

A shocked Len answered quickly, "I don't want any more holes in my butt, so will you marry me? Truly, I would be honored."

"You are such a smooth talker, Len. Yes, I will marry you," was the only answer Summer could give.

It took a few long moments for the surprised faces in the chapel to find their voices, but when they did, applause and congratulations erupted again. While applauding, Kim Sue said to Karl, "What on God's green Earth did you say to her?"

A stunned Karl didn't really answer; he couldn't. With a blank stare, he just quietly said, "Interesting."

Chapter 33

Epsilon Eridani b

The fleet was decelerating as it entered the Epsilon Eridani solar system. But while the ships were slowing down, the crews' excitement was accelerating. After twenty-eight years, they were finally here. Not quite to the planet, but somehow just entering the solar system made it feel like they were done.

As the ships approached the target planet, the scientists were getting a better idea of what might be expected on the planet's surface. The data they were gathering from long-range sensors and through telescope observations were both encouraging and discouraging. Admiral Sylva, like everyone under her command, was starting to feel the stress of the journey leaving until Richard came into the briefing session with a concerned look. The general positive tone of the conversations around the conference table stopped suddenly when Ada asked, "Richard, you don't look very happy. You're not going to ruin what I hoped would be great day are you?"

"Well, maybe. You want the good news or the bad news first?"

"Oh, great. Good news first."

Now with a slight smile, Richard said, "Before this mission even started the general belief was that EE b was Earth-like. At least close enough that mankind might be able to thrive here. Otherwise we wouldn't have headed this way. It still looks like the best planet in the solar system"

"But?" said his sister.

"In this case no 'but'. It seems the conditions on the surface are even better than we could have hoped for. The overall temperature on the planet's surface is slightly cooler than what we have on Earth. That's really good. The atmosphere seems to be nearly perfect. There are what appears to be a good covering of vegetation. There are seas, as we already knew, but naturally we don't know what might be below the waves. It's too early to predict weather patterns, but from what we can see from vegetation patterns, you know possibly trees blown over from high winds etc., severe storm damage isn't obvious."

"So," said Ada, "we have what appears to be the perfect planet. What's the bad news?"

"It seems there is a civilization already there. We need to get closer to get a better idea of what's there, but we can see structures and some kind of activity on the surface."

The ship's captain summarized what most were thinking when he simply said, "shit."

Ada sat for a minute thinking and then turned to Sherman and with a frosty tone asked, "Did you know about this? Was this one of your 'need to know' things?"

Sherman raised his eyebrows, shrugged, and said, "I understood there used to be a civilization on the planet," knowing full well that was true, but that wasn't exactly the full disclosure the Admiral was looking for. Gabe had, in fact, told him the planet was occupied.

The room became uncomfortably silent for a minute for what seemed like hours, as the Admiral looked at Sherman expecting more but nothing came. Finally, turning away from Sherman she said, "I guess we can't worry about this now. We'll need to play with the cards we've been dealt. Before we go into orbit, we need to prepare. What would we do, and I mean mankind, if all of a sudden a fleet of ships went into orbit around Earth?"

Dawn said, "I'm thinking the nations' leaders would get all freaky and activate the military."

Richard completed the thought with, "then when the big ships launched shuttles to survey the planet with the idea of making contact, Earth's military forces would be given the 'engage' signal and shuttles would be shot out of the sky. A typical 'shoot first and ask questions later' scenario."

"Right," said the captain, "Shoot! Ready! Aim!"

Ada thought for a moment before saying, "I suppose we shouldn't be paranoid. Not everyone is out to get us, not yet anyway. That being said, does anyone have any brilliant ideas? If not brilliant, any ideas at all? Give it some thought. In the mean time I don't see where we have much of a choice at the moment. We'll go into orbit around EE b. Maybe by the time we've done that, brilliance will shine upon us."

~##########~

The ships finally went to orbit around EE b and spread out around what was believed to be the equator. The earlier euphoria of the crews when they entered the solar system now turned into anxious weeks. With no one knowing what to expect from the planet's inhabitants, everyone was nervous; all, that is, except Sherman Hamer who had something of an idea of what to expect. And now with the ships no longer accelerating or decelerating everyone and everything adjusting to zero gravity only added to the anxiety level. Later the engineers would devise a scheme to negate the zero gravity, but that didn't help now.

No brilliant plan surfaced, so with some trepidation, Ada laid out her thoughts. A plan that might be something like a scenario laid out if giant ships started circling Earth. Transmissions to the planet's surface had already commenced and would continue with the hopes that some form of communication could be established. There was general consensus that any civilized beings on the plant's surface must have seen the fleet by now. If their leaders weren't concerned, they should at least be curious and should expect something. The transmissions yielded nothing.

When there was nothing coming from the surface, two shuttles from each ship were deployed to survey the planet from high altitudes. For over a month the shuttles gradually flew at lower altitudes. The fear of fighter aircraft of some kind that might intercept the shuttles and perhaps shoot them down never materialized. In fact there was no apparent recognition that the shuttles were even seen.

This was all very curious. It was obvious there was an intelligent species of some kind because of all structures on the planet. There wasn't a lot of movement on what might be roads, but

242

there was enough to make it obvious there was something happening down there.

The structures themselves were curious. There were some larger scale structures, buildings of some kind, that appeared abandoned and in disrepair. Others of a smaller size and scale looked somewhat sophisticated with a lot of activity around them. It appeared that the planet was evenly occupied with the exception of the snow covered polar regions. There seemed to be a number of species on the planet, though nothing like the diversity found on Earth. It was speculated that a large dog-sized species was the intellectually advanced species, but until they were actually met, no one would know for sure. The fact that the humans were being seemingly ignored made everyone wonder what that meant. There was still some speculation that perhaps the locals were waiting for the right moment to attack. If that were to happen, it would likely be a disaster as the only weapons on the ships were the small arms the Marines had. Nothing more. If anyone had ever considered the possibility of forcibly taking over a planet or defending the fleet, it never made it past the decision makers.

The Admiral decided she couldn't put it off forever so the next step was a landing party so the natives could actually see the Earthlings as they were; more or less, of course. The Admiral did expect the landing party to wear clothes.

Few could add much at this point, though choosing the landing party evoked a lively debate. No matter how the first encounter turned out, it would be historic, and nearly everyone wanted in. It was agreed that one officer representing each of the original six ships would go. Two people would disembark initially to interface with the native population. That would be the VAAS and *Russia*'s captain. This decision changed when the subject of communication came up and Sherman Hamer said, "I should go as translator."

All were puzzled, but the Admiral put everyone's thoughts into words when she said, "But you couldn't possibly know their language."

"I know many languages, so I stand the best change of providing an understanding," What he didn't say was that he actually could understand their language, or more correctly their form of communication, whatever it might be, and that he suspected it was nothing the designated landing party might understand.

"OK," said Ada after a pause. "I agree. There will be seven people on the mission besides the pilot, and three will disembark," and with no disagreements, it was settled.

It was time to get up close and personal.

Chapter 34
Second People

On January 23, 2095, Shuttlecraft #2 from the Starship *Russia* descended to the surface of planet EE b. It landed a quarter mile from what appeared to be a population center. Within an hour, there were perhaps a thousand beings holding a respectable distance from the ship. The shuttle crew noted that the beings looked a lot like Earth's ants, though much larger. They walked on their four rear appendages with their bodies aligned to a more upright position. Their front two appendages were apparently used in the same manner as human arms. They even had what looked like fingers. Most of the creatures appeared to be between three and four feet tall. The creatures were mostly dark gray and were wearing colorful clothing.

After the planned hour, Richard Sylva said with a big exhalation, "Ok, it is time for us to go forth." Richard, the *Russia* captain, and Sherman stood up as the shuttle door opened. As they descended the ramp, one creature started forward from the assembly. This apparent leader was soon joined by two more, apparently mimicking the number of humans standing in front of them.

Richard spoke in quiet unthreatening tones. "Greetings. I am Richard Sylva, vice admiral of academics and science from the interstellar space fleet sent from the planet Earth. We come in peace" Richard knew this was a waste of time. Even if these beings understood English, nothing he said would have made any sense, being so far out of context from anything they might understand. Still, he and the others waited for some kind of response. And they waited for what seemed an eternity though it was less than a minute.

Finally, Sherman said, "'Greetings, Earth beings. I am Spoosh, the governor of this province. What brings you to our planet?'" Then, turning to a stunned Richard, he said, "Sorry, that is the best I can do with the names and titles."

"But this Spoosh creature never said anything…" said a questioning Richard.

"They communicate with their eyes," said Sherman. "They have six. Two are used for communication. Their language is made up of subtle wave generation in the eye that forms words and the equivalent of our letters. They do it very quickly. It is as foreign to us as our voices would be to them. In fact, they can't hear anything you say, though they pick up the vibrations that your vocal cords create."

"I suppose you're not going to tell me how you know this and how you know their language," quizzed Richard.

"Probably not," was the answer.

After some pleasantries were exchanged, more serious questions were asked by the away team to see what the feelings might be toward the humans. There was no conclusion on this point the first time around. Richard did make it clear that he appreciated Spoosh coming forward and asked if he would be the spokesperson for his species in the future. Spoosh said he would let the humans know the next time they met.

Meetings went on for months. Spoosh was not the supreme leader, but he was authorized to be the ambassador for his people. The humans learned that there was one people under one planet-wide leadership. Through a difficult translation, it appeared as though Spoosh's people numbered in the many millions, with no group greater than a half million in any one community.

They called themselves the Second People. The Earth people were not shocking in appearance to the Second People, though the Second People were more than a little surprised to see them. The First People had populated the planet for thousands of years. They had looked much like Earthlings. They had been technically advanced to the degree that they had used various modes of transportation, including air flight. They had not, however, been advanced enough to venture outside EE b's gravity. The First People had thrived and their numbers had continued to grow, placing a strain on the planet's ecosystem. It all sounded uncomfortably familiar. The Second People didn't know why or how, but suddenly, within a five-year span, the First People had all died off.

The First People had treated the Second People well, but the intelligence level of the Second People had not been close to equal. However, the Second People had achieved a certain level of enlightenment well before this had all happened, so as the First People died, the Second People took on the task of disposing of the bodies by cremation. Then, without the First People around, the Second People had been forced to adapt and raise themselves to an even higher level of enlightenment. This was a steep learning curve.

Being smaller in size, the world seemed bigger to them than it had to the First People, but still, they knew they had to keep their numbers relatively small so they wouldn't overwhelm the ecosystem. They had learned how to use much of the technology left behind but often found little need for it. They had no major surface roads. Instead, all major transportation was done underground through tunnels. Many of the tunnels were built to such a tolerance that transportation pods were shuttled through them using compressed air and vacuum. This left the surface of the planet more pristine. The best of the First People's ruins had been kept as monuments to the planet's historical past. One could suppose that Earth's museums would be equivalent. Material from other ruins had been repurposed, and much of the planet's surface had been allowed to return to its natural state.

The Second People had a warm spot in each of their two hearts for the First People and so were sympathetic to the plight of the people from Earth. But they liked their planet and peaceful way of life just as it was, so they weren't about to turn their planet over to aliens. A hundred thousand aliens digging up their planet so more could come and perhaps take it over was not viewed favorably. On the other hand, they knew that the technologically advanced people from Earth could probably take what they wanted. If they could build ships that large to travel through space, the Second People were probably not in a position to stop them, though with few weapons on the ships, it wouldn't take much for the Second People to dominate. With both species thinking the other species could control the situation, all hoped for a peaceful and mutually acceptable resolution.

Many months of discussions ensued as both the Second People and the humans got to know each other better. It was slow going as only Sherman could translate, at least initially. During this time small groups of tourists were permitted to visit the rest of the planet. This helped the Second People to become more comfortable with the aliens and though no words were spoken, the Second People seemed somewhat eager to show the human aliens how their society functioned. With the size difference between the humans and the Second People it was sometimes awkward and often humorous when humans tried to enter some areas, but flexibility made it work. In many cases human children, being much smaller, got to play a major role being able to go where their parents could not. Initially, this made a lot of people nervous trusting their children's safety to the Second People, but soon a level of comfort was achieved. The young people took pride in their new roles. Something that made them feel very important.

Almost all of the major transportation needs were met with the extensive underground system. Likewise, most commercial and residential buildings were underground. Small looking homes on the planet's surface led to spacious underground dwellings connected with tunnels. There didn't seem to be anything resembling paint on surfaces, but with extensive use of various types of coverings, some cloth-like, interiors were bright and colorful. Interior lighting was fascinating. It seemed to come from the cloth-like coverings with no external power source visible.

There were, of course, paths between structures and farming areas on the planet's surface. These were more like paths. There were odd looking carts used to move things around, but as the humans soon learned, the Second People, like Earth ants, could carry huge loads with little apparent effort. Once this was realized, a level of anxiety was raised as the humans realized that without weapons the Second People could rip the humans apart with little effort. In the long run, this never became an issue.

While the human tourists on the planet's surface were learning about the Second People's civilization, Second People leaders were invited up to the starships. Shuttle rides were both exciting and scary. As the shuttles entered the starships' shuttle bays, the visitors had a difficult time grasping the size of these ships. Once on board, they were both fascinated and overwhelmed with what they saw.

It was determined that some humans might be able to learn how to communicate with the Second People. Since the Second People couldn't speak, it would be impossible for them to learn any of the Earth-based languages. The Second People had only one language, and if more people could learn it, the better. It was universally believed that there must be people capable of learning the language. After all, Sherman Hamer had learned it someplace!

Detailed testing of the hundred thousand people in the space fleet yielded twenty-nine who had the possible ability. Of them, only eight would learn. Five were Chinese, one was from India, one was English, and the last one was Native American. The one thing they had in common was a rare form of astigmatism. Saying they had volunteered was being kind. However, they were granted special privileges that took away some of the mental anguish and frequent headaches they would endure for over two years before they became proficient. And, to give credit where credit was due, the Second People selected for the training were unbelievably patient. Both the human translators and their Second people counterparts finally concluded this wasn't going to work in the long run and together they developed a new sign language that would work with the Second People's anatomy.

As they got to know each other better, it was learned that the Second People had two sexes. The males outnumbered females ten to one. The females were usually the ones in leadership positions and raised families while the males usually provided the labor and technical ability. The females laid eggs in nurseries, usually only one at a time. Law prohibited overpopulation. Spoosh was one of the rare males in a leadership position and had apparently won it because of his high level of intelligence. This also made him suitable in the supreme leader's eyes to be their ambassador to the humans. Spoosh turned out to be fair and compassionate.

Chapter 35
New Hope Island

While things were moving along at the negotiating table, the ships' general population was getting restless. Daily broadcasts throughout the fleet provided news relative to the negotiations in an attempt to keep people calm. A new feature to the news reports was weather reports. This actually did two things. It educated everyone on the planet's ecosystem, and as a bonus, the Second People could now better predict their own weather, with the ships substituting for the weather satellites that didn't exist. Of course, this helped the negotiations in the space fleet's favor.

Eventually, it was agreed that the humans could set up a colony on one of the planet's islands. It had been surveyed and found ideally located between the planet's north and south poles to accommodate the Gate. The terrain, weather, and soil conditions were all adequate for farming. It would work. It was named New Hope Island.

Any nonindigenous plants were to be approved by the Second People before being introduced. The Second People liked the honeybees and found no reason to exclude them from the planet even when told that the bees wouldn't abide by the rules and stay on the island. The chickens and dogs were allowed only on the island. The canaries had to stay on the ships. Some Second People were on the island, but they were relocated with no hard feelings. The humans could not build or settle beyond the limits of the island but would be allowed to visit other parts of the planet when escorted. The number of humans on the island wasn't to exceed seventy thousand, but it was understood that there would be people coming and going from the ships and from the humans' home planet of Earth once their Gate was built. In the short term far fewer than the maximum allowed would go to the planet's surface to build the Gate and support facilities.

The Second People weren't against technology and particularly liked being able to better predict weather. Weather satellites rose to the top of the list of what the humans could bring to the Second People. To this end, Admiral Sylva had satellites built and deployed around the planet. Some of the ships' crew members showed a remarkable affinity for meteorology, and a weather bureau was eventually set up to transmit weather information from the ships to both the colony and the Second People using maps and graphics rather than words.

Gradually the interaction between the two species became one of cooperation as both were realizing benefits. Trade was encouraged, though heavily controlled by the Second People. The humans would share technology, while the Second People would provide resources needed within the new colony. The Admiral was more than satisfied considering what could have been the outcome. As with any human enterprise, however, not everyone was satisfied. These people might have ruined everything if the admiral hadn't made certain they were isolated and sometimes locked away.

A lot had changed since the fleet had been launched. Certainly the end result of the trip was much different than first imagined. The newly defined mission of mixing the ships' crews with those left on Earth while maintaining an outpost on EE b was generating excitement. But even with this change in the mission, they still needed the Gate to be built and tested! The general feeling of "What are we waiting for?" would make things move quickly on New Hope Island.

And as for Schem? He started to realize that his mission might finally be coming to an end.

Chapter 36
The Open Gate

The first steps toward building the Gate on EE b started on June 1, 2095, Earth time. When negotiations with the locals were finally over, New Hope Island, approximately the size of the former state of Rhode Island, was turned over to the humans. They were allowed to work unimpeded within certain parameters sensitive to the environment. Since much of the construction would be underground, that set a positive tone for the Second People. Spoosh and a handful of subordinates were assigned full time to monitor the activities. Trust is a fragile thing, and the Second People weren't in the 100% trust category department just yet.

It was hard to hold back the people on the ships. They were fired up and ready to go, but work on New Hope Island had to be regulated and enthusiasm tempered. Certainly the agreed-upon population limit was far too many people to be deployed all at once. Everyone would be in each other's way. Only those with specific tasks would be transported down to the surface. Over the next few months it would include many of those who had grown up on the ships knowing nothing else and who had learned their skills playing games on the massive earthmoving machines' simulators. These individuals had a difficult time initially getting used to not having their views limited by ship's bulkheads, breathing fresh air, and weather changes. They quickly, and happily, adapted.

The first group to go down was a small contingent of civil engineers and surveyors to lay out the colony with the location of the Gate being the center of attention. This was the first priority. It would be exactly like the one on Earth with a circular area of about six miles in diameter. As work areas were laid out, the number of people on New Hope Island increased as construction got underway. A growing self-supporting community took shape rather quickly.

Most of the construction supplies on board the ships were earmarked for the Gate. It had been assumed that local materials would be used for dwellings and shops. Trees, or what might pass as trees, were few and not suitable as a building material. There was clay in the soils, so that became the main building material. This hadn't been planned for exactly, so before serious construction of any non-gate structures could start, the colony needed to dig into trade manuals and learn how to build kilns and then make bricks and mortar. Those newly trained in the fine art of masonry went down next.

One ship's engine was brought down and adapted as the colony's first source of electricity. A tunnel was carved into a hill for the engine and generating equipment just in case the thing decided to go critical. Operating engineers still didn't trust the engines.

Heavy construction equipment was brought down piece by piece. Operators anxious to get started came with the machines and set up camps just outside the work zones first in tents and then later in the masonry structures as they were built. Once started, operations went twenty-four hours a day, every day, except Sunday. People were ordered to find something else to do on Sunday, so ball fields of every sort started to appear. The big exception was maintenance of the big machines. Sunday was heavy-maintenance day.

The Earth month of June recognized on EE b had no relationship with the time of year on EE b. Still, the human population stayed with Earth time. It was confusing at first, especially when coupled with the ships' duty scheduling and now with the EE b solar cycles of 6.85 Earth years. While a little confusing, it had no effect on the actual work, and construction progressed rapidly. The day/night cycles were close to Earth's at twenty-eight and a half hours. One clever soul proposed a twenty-four-hour clock slowed down so that seconds, minutes, and hours were stretched to match the longer day cycle, providing some degree of familiarity on New Hope. The Admiral rejected the idea after she considered synchronizing with the ships' operations. She reasoned, an hour is an hour, period.

Boring machines were used to lay in most of the underground portion of the antennae array. The big excavators dug the six-mile power tunnel and massive hole in the center for the underground portion of the gate-operations rooms and transmitter itself. Aboveground work had to wait until the below-grade level came up to the surface. Once the belowground activity was nearly completed, the aboveground poles and towers needed for the Gate cables were brought down from the ships in sections and assembled in place. Guy wires were everywhere.

A second tunnel was carved into another hill face to accommodate the two engines needed for the Gate's power. Starship *South America* was determined to be in the worst shape, so it was chosen as the first ship stripped of anything necessary for the ground project. Since the one spare engine was already in use for general power, *South America* gave up two propulsion engines. They were handled with kid gloves and, as was the case with the first engine, shuttle pilots were strictly volunteers for these moves. The operating engineers and pilots were complete nervous wrecks during the transfer, and after each successful move, they were found in the newly built pub, belting down drinks.

Nearly everyone worked together at a fever pitch. After all, this was the hoped-for culmination of a twenty-eight-year mission! Unfortunately, nearly everyone meant that there were some who didn't. A few thought they were special and wanted only to set themselves up for a more leisurely life and not contribute to the cause—maybe do a little treasure hunting. Then there were other special people who wouldn't follow the standard rules of society. The admiral agreed they were special and gave them special accommodations back on the ships in the brig. Some people never change no matter where they are.

Spoosh and the other Second People who were on New Hope Island were overwhelmed and fascinated with the orchestration of the huge, yellow excavation machines transforming the island. Was this what it was like when the First People had ruled the planet? Maybe allowing the Earthlings to do this wasn't such a great idea!

Just about one year from the start, the scientists and engineers who would operate the Gate declared that it was ready. The Gate was complete. The Admiral declared a holiday, and a message was transmitted to Earth recommending an activation date of December 15, 2096, Earth time. She did this with the ships' systems, but also had Sherman use his device as well. It would have been silly not to use it.

The request was for real beefsteaks and bottles of scotch to be the test items transmitted to EE b. If successful, one day later live chickens would make the return trip. Each subsequent transmission would come closer to transporting people. Once operating, the Gate provided the added bonus of no longer having to rely on the ships' communications arrays that required a six-month turnaround. Written messages were sent with each transmission. It also meant that the clandestine system became less important.

On December 15, just as scheduled, the Gate on EE b was turned on. Pallets of coolers filled with steaks appeared, along with a pallet load of twelve-year-old scotch. Both the steaks and scotch required significant quality control "testing" for the rest of the day. The message capsule that was part of the shipment confirmed that Earth's Gate would be in receiving mode the following day.

Each transmission over the next couple of weeks got closer to actually transporting people. All were anxious for this to happen, but for some reason no one wanted to be first. The people most enthusiastic for this final test suddenly had other important "responsibilities" that needed their attention. A somewhat amused admiral half expected this and ended up making deals with some she had placed in the brig. So instead of ranking dignitaries making the first human trip through the Gate, former special guests of the brig would make the trip. There was some disappointment when the less than first class citizens came through the Gate, but no one dwelled on their apparent past transgressions. They were now celebrities.

On Earth, dignitaries were invited to come to the Gate reception area to celebrate. Many wondered why it had taken so long to do what was now so obvious—that is, pull together teams of intelligent, dedicated, people to put things back on track. After all, these strange guys from some unknown benevolent order seemed to be able to do it with ease. Not said was that if these strangers hadn't stepped in, the space fleet would have been stranded.

Gabe and his team were there when the first person came through the Gate from New Hope Island. All of his team that is, except for Schem, who would remain on EE b for a little longer. All the Bickmeiers were there, as well as John Carpenter, Abel Fisher, and his new bride, Megan. President Grainger and Colonel Sheffield were there, along with many newly identified world leaders. As predicted by Ara, a few that had done little or nothing to make this all happen were not reluctant to take credit for this effort.

News of the event was followed worldwide over the remaining broadcast systems. Combined with the help of many very large people who usually dressed in white, the wave of despair that had followed the death flu was being replaced with the seeds of optimism.

No celebration would be complete without food and drink so a celebratory brunch of sorts was opened at both Gates when people were successfully transported. It was larger at the Earth Gate, though not at the Gate itself. All the non-Gate structures had been removed before activation to keep them from being roasted during transmitting. Summer's office, now outside the Gate was transformed this day into celebration central. With the food and drink, there was plenty of congratulatory backslapping to go around.

After a few glasses of wine and a large bite to eat, Gabe confided his thoughts to his team. In a quiet corner he had each of his team members raise their glasses in a toast, saying, "It looks like everything is back on course. Here's to a bright future." They then quietly left the party, put on their antigravity packs, and lifted off for Augustine Island into an evening sky.

Perhaps by chance, Abel had been outside with Kim Sue, talking to her as his emotional counselor, trying as best he could to understand how his life had changed over the past decade. They were somewhat in the shadows and stopped talking as they watched the little scene with Gabe and his team. Kim Sue and Abel were the first ones in their group to see the antigravity packs in use, and for whatever reason, they never spoke about the "flying" to each other or anyone else. As the team lifted off, Abel said, "You know, when I first saw that, all I wanted was to get hold of one of those packs and reverse engineer it to see how it worked. I kind of forgot about it until Kem reminded of a deal we had made. I told him thanks, but it was OK. Kem just smiled and shook my hand like he already knew what I was thinking. Who do you think they are?"

Kim Sue said, "I don't know for certain, but I have a pretty good idea. I'm also pretty sure they have been here before and will be again at some time in the future when we mortals screw things up again. I'd be willing to bet, those guys knew you and I were here. And they left the way they did for our benefit. I'm glad we got to see this." Then they hugged each other as two people subconsciously understanding that they were sharing a new faith.

Kim Sue and Abel had been the first to see these very large people fly, and they were the last; at least this time around.

Epilogue

Transmissions between the Gates went on nearly every day, with one day for receiving and the next sending. People were transported between the two worlds, and over time, everyone who wanted to return to Earth could. Among them were Ada Sylva and her entire family as they were relieved of duty and replaced with much younger people. Ada was now eighty-six years old, and while she was as healthy and youthful looking as someone twenty years younger, she was mentally exhausted and wanted to go home. The reunion with her brother, Karl, who was now eighty-four, was emotional, bringing everyone to tears. Ada and her husband went to Alaska with the Bickmeiers and never left.

Ada and Jesus's children, Richard and Dawn, were placed as the Operations Director and the Science Director of the new UNSC. At first they were excited to be writing the next chapter in the UNSC's history, but excitement soon faded when they realized the UNSC seemed to have lost any sense of direction. Conditions on Earth had improved so much since the fleet had first left Earth's orbit that leaving for a better life on another planet was no longer a must. Without the incentive of saving mankind, some new initiative was needed for the fleet.

The twins did reopen the offices and brought some additional people on board using funds that had been languishing in various accounts for some time. They recruited new, but much smaller, crews for the still-functioning Starships *United States, British Commonwealth, China,* and *Russia*. The ships would stay in orbit around EE b with only the smallest of crews to keep systems functioning. It was less than exciting duty.

There were thoughts of building new engines on New Hope Island to refit *South America*. The fear of destroying the Gates when transferring nuclear material put an end to it.

Eventually a mission of discovery for the fleet was developed and after considerable effort by the UNSC Directors, it gained some traction. But it took such a long time that the twins retired soon after it got underway.

None of the Second People ventured to Earth, but a few did join the new UNSC mission when it eventually launched. Spoosh remained on New Hope Island with his family as the ambassador between the two worlds. Communications steadily improved between the humans and Second People once the new sign language was developed and eventually the use of written words.

The human population on New Hope Island never exceeded seventy thousand, as agreed. The resident population was usually much less. Since the original intent of potentially relieving the population pressure on Earth was no longer an issue, New Hope Island became a trading post and would become the relay communications station to the interstellar space fleet when it was finally deployed on it's new mission. People were allowed to travel with escorts and trade all over EE b to the benefit of both species.

Len Bickmeier and his bride, Summer Snow, stayed at the Earth Gate and, as promised, Summer remained in charge of the operation. Len, who had at one time hoped to see a little more of one world got to see two when he visited New Hope Island on EE b. Len and Summer would have one child they named Dakota.

Abel and Megan never returned to their homes. Abel ran his FarmVille operation while they traveled the world, giving speeches about living to the fullest. A birth defect wouldn't allow Megan to have any children. Abel did visit Homer, Alaska, and rode in Karl's 1914 Model T Ford.

Sergeants Falkner and Roberts were finally permitted to retire when they both reached the age of seventy-two. They combined their resources and bought a cabin next to a lake and as far away as possible from any real road.

Wars in Africa ended as most of the African nations united to become the Union of African Nations under a charismatic leader. No one knew where she had come from. Some believed she was a Nubian Princess, but it was rumored that she was the last of a small benevolent order based in Africa. The rumor was that their compound and all within had been destroyed by some natural disaster. Everyone had been asleep at the time except for this one woman, who had a strange yet familiar-sounding name. She was a tall, dark skinned beauty that had an uncanny ability to persuade people in positive ways.

Fighting in the Middle East also deescalated between about 2086 and 2096. But soon after that, regional skirmishes started once again. Some people are so thin skinned and rigid in their thinking they can't consider any belief other their own as acceptable. And if it isn't acceptable, it turns to fighting and nothing can bring them peace.

Nine months after the Gates became functional and people started to return to Earth, a kind of baby boom started. The comparatively few people of childbearing age started to find each other. Many felt drawn to traditional weddings and started to have children at a rate that would stabilize Earth's population. However, the new awareness of what could happen meant that both government controls and a general sense of doing the right thing resulted in one billion people being the maximum number allowed. It was a universal doctrine accepted by virtually everyone under the new world order.

Gabe, Kem, Ara, Naki, and Ere returned to Augustine Island after taking a holiday and seeing what they wanted to see around Earth. In due time, Schem returned to Earth through the Gate and joined his companions in a weeklong celebration of food and drink. He had made many friends on the space fleet, but they were not his kind, and he had missed his companions.

Part of the weeklong celebration was to prepare to reenter stasis. Schem had been out of it for nearly thirty years, and it was now showing. The rest had been out for nearly twelve years. It was time to go back under. Ara was supposed to have been the first to come out of stasis the next time, whenever it was needed, but given his occasional tendency to try to be funny, Ere was tagged as the next one up.

A corrected course of behavior was now established as humankind was helped along to a brighter future…again!

Some Significant Dates

1962: *Silent Spring* is published

2052: 10 billion people inhabit Earth, Gulf Stream ocean current stops

2057: Starship Construction Starts

2067: Starships Launched towards Epsilon Eridani 10.5 light years from Earth

2071: Death Flu strikes

2075: 1 billion people left on Earth, mini ice age starts

2085: Order members awake, Earth population is 800 million

2086: Earth wormhole Gate recommissioning begins

2095: Starship fleet reaches Epsilon Eridani

2096: Epsilon Eridani wormhole Gate connects with Earth

More by Richard Cutler

Carbon Neutral (Course Correction Series #2)

After a successful space mission on a fleet of Star Ships, Earth's best and brightest minds return to find their planet ravaged by a viral catastrophe. Without leadership or direction, the loosely reorganized United Nations Stellar Commission (UNSC) sits in a state of stagnation.

The newly appointed commissioners of the UNSC must decide whether or not to risk the four functional Star Ships that remain in the hope of discovering another inhabitable planet. What they don't realize is that there are other forces at work, gathering power on Earth and, possibly, in the skies.

When the travelers encounter a powerful being who cannot recall his past, they discover that helping each other might open just the right doors for everyone. Working as a team, they make a discovery that could change the future of mankind—if they can make it out alive.

Altered Horizon (Course Correction Series #3)

In the distant future, humanity has mastered space travel, conquered immense interstellar distances with wormholes gates, and discovered new worlds, all while secretly guided by an ancient Order. But after early successes, ongoing problems on Earth have kept the Star Ship Fleet in a holding pattern awaiting further instructions.

Then, in 2147, the United Nations Stellar Commission decides to launch a series of new and exciting missions with the primary goal of setting up a colony and wormhole gate on one of the planets orbiting Alpha Centauri. Led by a mixture of experienced and not-so-experienced space Admirals, the Star Ship Fleet embarks on the mission with high expectations that a true colony for mankind can finally be established.

But the new mission exposes an old and shocking secret—a botched attempt by the Order and the world's leaders at colonizing another planet years before that left behind humans with no knowledge of Earth. When it becomes clear that the Order has failed to fix the mistakes of the past, it's up to the best and brightest of humanity to make the right decisions and steer all the species of the galaxy towards a new and better horizon.